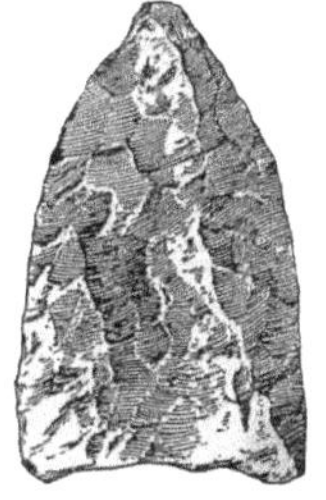

She found the body at 6:30 on Friday morning, March 4. He was sprawled on the floor near his desk, face down, a dried pool of blood around his head. Someone had hit him with the dark brown ceramic statue, the one with the chimpanzee imitating Rodin's The Thinker. It lay beside him, spattered with blood and hair. At that moment, for some mad reason, all she could think of was that it had been his favorite knickknack. He'd kept it on the mantle of his rolltop desk, beside the box of thin Nalgene gloves. He'd stare at the chimp, then let out a series of hoots, as if expecting an answer from the inscrutable face staring back at him.

His desk and file cabinets had been ransacked. It smelled of alcohol and formalin. She saw the slick yellowish liquid pooled on the linoleum tile. She checked the chemical fridge and -20 Centigrade freezer. They'd been opened and emptied, the glass jars smashed, the tissue tubes crushed.

Suddenly, she realized she was treading on the DNA of an Aleut from Adak, or a Sioux from the Great Plains, or a Siberian Yupik from Russia—bits of their genomic code extracted from snips of hair or swabs of saliva. Someone had also taken a hammer to the table-top sequencer.

NATIVE BLOOD

Also by Leonard Krishtalka

The Body on the Bed

Dinosaur Plots

The Harry Przewalski Mystery Series:

The Bone Field

Death Spoke

The Camel Driver

Native Blood

NATIVE BLOOD

LEONARD KRISHTALKA

Anamcara Press LLC

Published in 2024 by Anamcara Press LLC
Author © 2024 by Leonard Krishtalka
Book design by Maureen Carroll
Caslon Pro and Octin Vintage, Lucinda Sans Unicode.

Printed in the United States of America.

Book Description: Hard-Boiled Detective Series Uncovers Bones, Bodies and Murder. Paleontologist turned private investigator, Harry Przewalski, excavates the dirty underbelly of people's lives, unearthing sexual betrayals, treachery, fraud and murder buried beneath the science of petrified shards, skin and bones. Ultimately, he must face a brutal killing in his own past, when he fled to a desert war and came back with a gun and a license to detect.

ANAMCARA PRESS LLC
P.O. Box 442072, Lawrence, KS 66044
https://anamcara-press.com/

Ordering Information:
Quantity sales. Special discounts are available on quantity purchases by corporations, associations, and others. For details, contact the publisher at the address above.
Orders by U.S. trade bookstores and wholesalers. Please contact Ingram Distribution.

Publisher's Cataloging-in-Publication data
Krishtalka, Leonard, Author
Native Blood/ Leonard Krishtalka

ISBN-13: 978-1-960462-19-0 eBook
ISBN-13: 978-1-960462-18-3 hardback
ISBN-13: 978-1-960462-17-6 paperback

[1. FIC027260 FICTION / Romance / Action & Adventure.
2. FIC022010 FICTION / Mystery & Detective / Hard-Boiled..
3. FIC022090 FICTION / Mystery & Detective / Private Investigators]

Library of Congress Control Number: 2023939681

To Aagje Kroos Ashe and, in memory, Helena Kroos

1

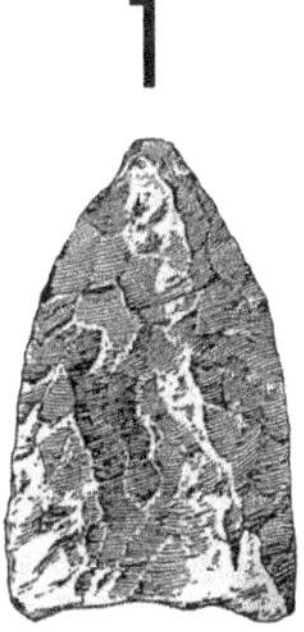

December Tryst

The motel room was clean enough. A plastic coffee maker on the dresser. Brown and green packages of a weak grind. A basket on the bathroom counter with miniature soaps and lotions. Bath and face towels, no longer quite white, waiting for the next bit of skin. The lives of previous guests preserved in the crevices.

Her blood didn't stop them. He pulled back the coverlet and spread a bath towel under her to keep from staining the sheets. She kissed his mouth, opening his lips with her tongue, inviting his hands down to caress her. They made love in a desperate, fevered silence.

Before they left, he scooped up the bloodied towel, folded it twice over the deep red stain, and put it in his messenger bag.

By seven in the morning, he was back in the neon-lit outskirts of town. The sun was below the horizon but had begun teasing the sky with errant strands of light. He eased his car through the night's fresh dusting of snow into the alley behind the strip mall. He got out and looked around. No one to see his breath condense in the frozen air. Or see him pull the towel out of the bag. Or toss it into the dumpster.

Only then did he notice the sign:

RECYCLING: CARDBOARD BOXES ONLY

2

February Tryst

I'm being blackmailed."

"What do you mean?"

"Blackmailed! You know what that means. He knows about us."

"Who?"

"Lasher, that's who. Herbert fucking Lasher."

"What? That's impossible."

"He knows."

"I don't believe it! We've been careful."

"Yeah, well, he knows—about me, not you. He said he knows I'm fucking someone … and it isn't my husband. Those were his exact words. He asked me who it was."

"Bastard. He's just baiting you. How the hell could he know?"

"Got me. The way he said it. He ... he seemed so sure ... y'know ... that fucking leer of his."

"What did you say?"

"What do you think I said? I told him he was crazy. I told him he was way out of line. That my personal life was none of his business. That certainly who I'm fucking was none of his business."

"Good."

"Then he said he could make it my husband's business."

"Really? Did he threaten to tell him?"

"No, not directly. He just leered at me. Just said he could make it his business."

"Son of a bitch. What does he want? What the hell could he want from you?"

"Guess."

Pause

"No, not sex. Tell me it's not sex he wants from you."

"You got it."

"I'll kill him. I swear, I'll kill him."

"Good. Do it. I wish someone would. Y'know what the fucker did?"

"What?"

"He called me. Told me to come to his office. Said he had something important to show me. I went over there. His door was open. He told me to shut it. Stupid me, I did. He was sitting behind his desk. A bunch of books were lying around, open. There was something playing on his laptop. Music, voices. I asked him what he was watching. He said to come around and have a look. It was a fucking porno flick ... some blonde going down on a priest ... on a bench in the middle of a park."

"Christ!"

"Yeah, it gets better. He's sitting there in his leather chair, rocking. His fly is open, his bone is out. He's slowly stroking himself, wearing those plastic lab gloves."

"Jesus Christ!"

"He tells me to pretend he's the priest."

"What did you do?"

"What the fuck do you think I did? I ran out. I didn't think. I should have grabbed my phone, taken a picture. Even better, a video. I'd have evidence. But I just ran. To the bathroom. Threw up."

"Christ."

"Then he called again, the fucker. Said it was my choice. Him or …"

"I'll kill him."

"Someone should. I should have grabbed that fucking monkey statue he has on his desk and smashed his head in. You know he's been screwing students forever—grades for blow jobs."

"I know. So does Warden."

"What happened?"

"A grad student a couple of years ago. She reported him. He denied it. Said she made it up. Said she was retaliating for his giving her a C. They believed him."

Silence.

"Listen, does the fucker hunt?"

"What?"

"Does he hunt, y'know, deer, ducks, geese, whatever you guys like to shoot at?"

"I don't know. Why?"

"Hunting accident. You mistake his round wrinkled head for some fucking Mallard. Like Dick Cheney did. Then you finish him off between the legs. No, that would be hard to explain."

Laughter.

"Well, I could invite him out. With me and the bird guys. When they go collect. Lasher likes to shoot birds … photos. He's got that big camera in his office."

"Where do the bird guys go?"

"Rivers usually. The Neosho. Or the Republican."

"What do they collect with?"

"Shotguns."

"Really? With bullets? Christ, there'd be nothing left of the fucking bird!"

"No, not bullets. Shot. Small pellets."

"Would those kill him?"

"Damn right it would kill him. That close behind him, a shotgun would blow his head apart. Think of a watermelon exploding."

"Yum. I like that thought. So, you're at the river with the rest of 'em. Hunkering down in the grass. Everyone's got a shotgun. Not Lasher. He's got that fucking camera around his neck. He wants a good shot. He'll get one all right. A bunch of birds gets scared up. BLAM BLAM BLAM BLAM. Everyone aims at the birds. Not you. You aim at Lasher! Head shot. No, back-of-the-head shot. Oooops!"

"Could work. So could deer hunting. Tromp around in the woods. Sound shootin' they call it. Hear a noise? See movement? See Lasher? BLAM. Accident."

"Oooops."

Laughter.

"Maybe it's easier that I kill him. It's me the bastard wants to fuck, not you. I could do it."

"How?"

"I dunno. Poison. In that fucking tea he drinks in that office. He gets it from Mexico, packages of loose tea. I find out his schedule. Get in there when he's in class. Dose of something in the package. Something hard to detect. Prussic acid, y'know, hydrogen cyanide. He's dead in two minutes."

Pause.

"Or colchicine."

"What?"

"Colchicine. Geneticists used it for chromosome studies. It stops the chromosomes from separating during mitosis, y'know, during cell division, so they're all lined up in the nucleus, easy to see under the microscope."

"How the hell do you know that? You were an art major."

"Yeah, well, I worked as a tech in a genetics lab when I was a grad student. Took care of the mice ... watched them get injected. Heart cells just quit dividing. Then the ol' pump just quits. Takes a while. Probably painful. It hit me then that it would be a great way to kill someone. Don't know if a coroner would pick that up, y'know, those 23 chromosomes lined up, not moving, like little coffins. Would be a fitting way to die for a genetic anthropologist."

Silence.

"Or I could shoot him. In his office. Behind that fucking desk. I call him up. Tell him I'm coming over for hot sex. Get ready, get your pants down. I walk in there. I got gloves, gun, silencer. First bullet between the legs. Give him a second to realize he's no longer got it. Finish him off between the eyes."

"You're serious?"

"I dunno. Gets more fucking serious more I think about it."

"You have a gun?"

"There's one in the house. Belongs to you know who. Big fucking pistol. In the nightstand beside the bed. His side. He takes it out sometimes. Pets it. Likes to release the clip and jam it back in again, like he's screwing the fucking pistol. That's about all he screws. Brought it back from Iraq way back when. Says it's not registered. He calls it 'TK—Turban Killer.'"

"Turban Killer? You married a guy who calls his gun Turban Killer?"

"Yeah, fuck it all. I didn't know before I married him. Doesn't matter now. TK was his nickname in the army. In Iraq he'd wear a turban under his helmet. Anyway, he's not the problem. Lasher is."

"Okay, here's an idea. Make him the shooter."

"Who?"

"Turban Killer! Your husband! Tell him what Lasher said. Tell him what he did in his office. The porno flick. Asking you to go down on him. Be graphic. You told me he's violent. Provoke him. Make him furious. Tell him to take that Turban Killer out of the drawer. Tell him if he doesn't do it, you will."

"That could work. Listen, a few weeks ago I looked up an old grad student classmate. I told her about Lasher. About that time in his office. And his blackmailing me about our affair."

"What! You told her about us!

"Yeah, I trust her. She lives in Abilene. She knows Lasher. We took the same classes from him. Her name's Ruby, Ruby Pettecek. I'd bet the fuckin' farm that he propositioned her too. She was married to Hans Knopfler, y'know, the art history guy ... the Fulbright business, the one—"

"Oh, that guy. Yeah, I know."

"I thought she could help. With the blackmail. Maybe figure out how the hell Lasher could know I was sleeping with someone who wasn't my husband."

"Did you tell her who I was?"

"No ... relax."

"Okay. What did she say?"

"She said she might have an idea about how Lasher knew."

"Oh yeah, what idea?"

"She didn't say. She said she'd talk to Lasher about it when she was in town at the protest march at KU."

On the road back to Lawrence he noticed a gray minivan in his rear-view mirror. It followed him into town, then turned south toward Clinton Lake.

3

Killed by an Ape

She found the body at 6:30 on Friday morning, March 4. He was sprawled on the floor near his desk, face down, a dried pool of blood around his head. Someone had hit him with the dark brown ceramic statue, the one with the chimpanzee imitating Rodin's *The Thinker*. It lay beside him, spattered with blood and hair. At that moment, for some mad reason, all she could think of was that it had been his favorite knickknack. He'd kept it on the mantle of his rolltop desk, beside the box of thin Nalgene gloves. He'd stare at the chimp, then let out a series of hoots, as if expecting an answer from the inscrutable face staring back at him.

Lasher's desk and file cabinets had been ransacked. Manila folders, printouts, and papers lay scattered by his chair. His MacBook was gone. Also, the terabyte drive backup. The gray, thin cord from the power supply dangled over the edge of the desk.

The room smelled of alcohol and formalin. She saw the slick yellowish liquid pooled on the linoleum tile, littered with broken glass and tubes—Christ, the frozen extracts! She checked the chemical fridge and -20 Centigrade freezer. They'd been opened and emptied, the glass jars smashed, the tissue tubes crushed.

Suddenly, she realized she was treading on the DNA of an

Aleut from Adak, or a Sioux from the Great Plains, or a Siberian Yupik from Russia—bits of their genomic code extracted from snips of hair or swabs of saliva. Someone had also taken a hammer to the table-top sequencer, the four centrifuge machines, the racks of pipettes, and the weigh scale.

She tiptoed over to the phone on Lasher's desk. It had a red sticker emblazoned with the number of the campus police.

"Dr. Lasher. He's … he's on the floor. There's blood. What? I'm in Spooner Hall. The room number? I don't know the goddamn room number. It's in the basement ... the lab. I think he's dead. Everything's been ... What? My name? Jennifer Finch ... a grad student ... a lab assistant. Yeah, I'll stay here. No, I won't touch anything."

A few minutes later she heard the sirens on Jayhawk Boulevard. Two blue uniforms came in: a tall brunette with long hair, a short, burly man with a buzz cut. The brunette grabbed a pair of gloves from the box on the Lasher's desk, went over to his body, placed two fingertips against his carotid artery, and eyed the blood and hair on the ceramic ape. She turned to short and burly and told him to radio someone.

The brunette looked at Finch. "You the one called this in?"

"Yeah," Finch nodded. A swath of magenta-dyed hair hung down over the right side of her head. It hid half her face. The left side was shaved down to the skin. Cyberpunk, the salon had called it. She'd added three silver clicker hoops through her left ear and a couple of copper labrets through her lower lip.

"What's in there?" The policewoman pointed to an open doorway.

Finch led the brunette across the wet floor into a stark, gray, cinder-block room. Three rows of white, -80 Centigrade chest freezers hummed in unison, a dull, bass monotone. Everything looked in order. The freezer lids were still down. The thick electric cables were still hooked to the large, black breaker box on the wall. The lever on the box was still set to ON.

Then Finch saw them. Plastic racks with thousands of small, clear cryogenic tubes lay heaped on the floor between the freezers. The policewoman bent down, picked up one of the tubes, held it out to Finch, and raised her eyebrows.

"Frozen tissues ... blood ... saliva. From indigenous people."

Finch quickly checked the digital gauge on the freezers marked "USA-ALASKA." Perfect. Still at -76 C." She opened the lid. Empty. Three other freezers labeled "RUSSIA" and four marked "CANADA" had also been emptied.

"Christ," she yelled, "the tissues will be shit!" She waved frantically to the policewoman. "We gotta get these tubes back in the freezers!"

The brunette shook her head. "Don't touch anything," she ordered .

"Piss on that," Finch muttered and grabbed one of the racks. The tubes were warm to the touch. She slammed the rack down on the floor. "Never mind. They're already shit. There goes my fucking dissertation."

The brunette shrugged. She walked back into Lasher's office. The closet door behind his desk was open. Propane lanterns. Tents. Sleeping bags. Air mattress. Air pump. Field boots. Case of beer, half empty. Bottle of Canadian rye, two-thirds down. A stack of DVDs. Porno flicks. A pair of black, high-top rubber waders under the bottom shelf. A white piece of terrycloth protruded from the top of the right wader.

The policewoman pulled it out. A rolled-up towel marked "Ramada Inn." It had a large, rusted blotch in the middle. She knew dried blood when she saw it.

Then they noticed the three large red letters spray painted on the opposite wall: "IRN."

"Fuck," Finch swore. "Lasher was afraid they would do this."

4

March Tryst

Did you kill him?"

"Who?"

"Lasher, that's who! Do you know anyone else who got killed?"

"All right, cool it. No, I didn't kill him. The bird guys and I were going to take Lasher hunting this weekend. Like we planned. But we got lucky. The chancellor's kid got to him first ... during that IRN protest. Go figure. Lasher won't be blackmailing you any longer."

"Or exposing himself. Except to the fucking worms in the coffin. Serves the bastard right. But I don't think the kid killed him."

"What? The cops say he did. They say he and his girlfriend waited for Lasher in the lab after the IRN smashed it up. They killed him, then ran."

"Yeah, I know what the cops are saying. I also know Nalren. He's in one of my classes."

"Really?"

"Yeah, my indigenous art class. He's quiet. Studious. Sensitive. Smart. Too smart to do something that stupid. He was also in Lasher's biological anthropology class."

"You mean the one that caused the uproar with the IRN?"

"Right. Lasher insisted on calling it 'Native Blood: Genomic History of Indigenous Americans.'"

Pause.

"I was sure your husband did it. Except Lasher wasn't shot. Just whacked over the head."

"Fuck no, George didn't kill him. He went off to work on Thursday morning, as usual."

"Yeah, but he could have been there later, packing his gun. What does he call it again?"

"TK—Turban Killer."

"Right, Christ, Turban Killer. Did you tell him about Lasher? What he'd done to you in his office? Y'know, asked you to ..."

"I did. He was furious. Swore he'd kill him. He went to the bedroom and got the gun, started playing with the clip, ejecting it, slamming it back in, over and over. But, like I said, he went off to work. He wasn't anywhere near campus."

"How can you be sure?"

"I guess I can't. But when I got home that night he was there, in his recliner, in front of the tube. You'd think he would have acted weird, y'know, like he'd just killed someone. But he didn't."

"Doesn't mean anything. But you don't think he did it?"

"No."

"Or the kid, Nalren?"

"No."

Pause

"Okay, I gotta ask. What about you?"

"Me?"

"Well ... you'd talked about it ... killing him. You were there ... at the protest march. You stayed late. You called me. Remember? Did you go into Spooner, into his lab ... and ... well ... do it?"

"No, I didn't. Yeah, I know, we'd talked about it. It would have been fucking delicious. But I didn't kill him. I didn't go into the building."

"Had to ask."

"Right. What about you? Where were you then?"

"Uh ... you won't believe this. I was actually in the building ... in Spooner."

"Really? Last Thursday evening? What the hell for?"

"I had to go see Page. He'd called me."

"You mean the guy, that archeologist, the one who rails against the whole indigenous thing?"

"Yeah, him."

"Doesn't he have that distinguished prof lecture next week?"

"Yeah."

"What a fucking coincidence—no, an opportunity—you being in Spooner. Tell me you killed Lasher."

"No, I didn't. I went up to Page's office on the second floor. Lasher's is in the basement."

"Did you see anyone?"

"Yeah, Montanares. Walked by her office next to Page's. Her door was open. You'll never guess who else was up there."

"Who?"

"The weirdo. You know, the one who crawled under the table in the courtroom."

"Yeah, fuck, what's her name? She sued Lasher and half the university a year or so ago. He was chair of the department. She accused him of discrimination, not recommending her for a raise, giving her shit committee work. Kovitch, Miriam Kovitch."

"Right. Kovitch. She was there in her office at the end of the hall—it's more like a closet."

"Did you tell the cops all this?"

"Uh uh. And I'm not about to. None of them saw me. Page wasn't in his office. Montanares' door was partly closed. Kovitch had her head on the desk, mumbling something. Probably drunk. There was a bottle of wine by her head."

"Did you hear anything?"

"No, not really. Funny thing, though, when I was going up the stairs to Page's office, I heard the front door open and close. It creaks."

"Maybe somebody came into Spooner behind you?"

"Maybe, I don't know. I didn't see anyone."

"Or it could've been somebody leaving."

"Yeah, maybe one of the IRN bunch from Lasher's lab. Anyway, if it's not you, or your husband, or me, or Nalren, who the hell killed Lasher?"

"Who the fuck knows? But now you're telling me that Page and

Montanares and Kovitch were there. Maybe it's got nothing to do with the IRN."

"Yeah, could have been any one of them. They all hated Lasher."

Later, on US 40 East into Lawrence he spotted the gray minivan behind him. A Dodge, it looked like. Maybe a Caravan. At the light at the K-10 intersection it took the ramp south toward Clinton Lake. He caught a quick glimpse of the driver. Someone wearing a baseball cap.

5

Tribes, Blood, Genes, Roots

"Last time you were here, Mr. Przewalski, I threw you out of this office." Margaret Warden, Chancellor of the University of Kansas, raised a corner of her mouth in a bemused look. "When was it, last June?"

Harry grinned. The Fulbright murder. He'd asked Warden straight out then whether the rumor was true, whether she and Joyce Fulbright, the Dean of the College, had been an amorous item. Warden had unceremoniously shown him the door.

"Yeah, I deserved it, Chancellor. I pushed you a bit hard ... a bit dirty. You pushed back."

"I did. I promise not to throw you out this time. And, please, skip the 'Chancellor.' Formality is not for us, certainly not now. 'Margaret' is good. And, if I may, 'Harry'"?

"Sure."

Warden had evolved. A year ago, she was outfitted in a KU blue jumpsuit to camouflage her serious poundage. Now she was svelte: white blouse, tan slacks, flat, blue shoes. She'd also ditched the mustard-dyed hair for her natural, honey-brown wave, long enough to brush the nape of her neck. But her face hadn't softened. It was still all business, all metal, a pistol with the safety on, the industrial armor required to run a university with 28,000 students and 6,000 faculty and staff.

The office also hadn't changed. It smelled musty, it looked musty: the dark teak desk, the matching credenza, floor-to-ceiling bookshelves stuffed with novels and tomes of English criticism; two brown leather couches and three sofa chairs surrounding a massive limestone coffee table. It was a foot thick, carved in the shape of Kansas, and engraved with the KU chant, "Rock Chalk Jayhawk." A tall window at the back of the office looked out over the north expanse of the campus: a grove of trees, a pond, a crisscross of cement walkways, and a grassy knoll rising in the distance to a couple of red brick, prison-like buildings.

"Last time I made the mistake of sitting there." Harry pointed to the sofa chair with a large red-and-blue Jayhawk, the KU mascot, embroidered on the cushion. "The bird kept pecking into my backside. Likely punishment for rudeness."

Warden laughed. "Between you and me, Harry, I hate this kitsch—the limestone slab, the ever-present Jayhawk. But I'm stuck with it … this office and its accoutrements. They are a chancellor's inheritance. And burden. Obeisance to this heirloom is *de rigueur*."

Harry leaned forward. "When you called me last Friday you said your son had been arrested for murder. Now it's Tuesday. Tell me what I don't know."

A wince of pain creased her face. "Yes ... Nalren ... that's his name. For killing a professor, Herbert Lasher, an anthropologist."

Harry raised his eyebrows. "That's two for two, counting Fulbright."

"Right ... Joyce ... the Fulbright business. For which, by the way, I never thanked you, properly. You must think anthropology is some kind of homicidal discipline."

"Well, primal, anyway. Tribes. Blood. Genes. Roots. Age-old motives for murder. Or genocide." Harry pointed at her wall of books. "Not like literary theory."

"Really?" Warden grinned. "Clearly, you've never been to a meeting of the Modern Language Association. Blood is spilled over Austen. Or Derrida and deconstructionist philosophy. Or the Oxford comma. Anyway, Professor Lasher was actually in the geography department. We had to move him there last fall to keep the peace in anthropology. It's of no matter now. He's dead. He was a biological anthropologist. It seems to be what got him killed. He studied the genetics of indigenous people."

Harry nodded. "Let me guess. The peopling of the Americas 13,000 years ago. Likely earlier. Like I said, tribes, blood, genes, roots."

Warden tipped her head in grudging respect. "I'm impressed, Harry. How do you come by this esoterica?"

Harry shrugged. "I used to dig up the past. Paleontology. That life is done." He thought of Nicole, his fiancée, a social worker, at the farmhouse north of Pittsburgh, dismembered, stuffed into a 50-gallon drum. Mazeroski, the cop, had tackled him, cuffed him, and tossed him into the back of the police cruiser to keep him from killing the psychopath who was being led away.

"Are you okay, Harry?" Warden was leaning toward him over the limestone slab, her lips pursed, her eyes squinting at him in concern. "You seemed to have left us for a moment."

He nodded. "Yeah, I'm fine. Tell me more about Lasher."

Warden took a sip of whatever was in the red, ceramic go-mug with a blue, stenciled Jayhawk decal. It was two-thirty. Harry thought he'd caught a whiff of peat. A bit early for Scotch.

"As I said, his studies might have gotten him killed. A group called IRN, Indigenous Rights Network, organized a protest march in front of Spooner Hall."

"When was that?"

"Last Thursday afternoon. Spooner is where Lasher had his office and labs. Nalren took part in the march. Also his girlfriend, Winona. Lasher was killed that evening."

"What were they protesting?"

"His research. The IRN is opposed to it. They accused Lasher of obtaining his genetic samples illegally, under false pretenses."

"You mean the samples from the Native Americans? Blood, hair, saliva? For DNA sequencing?"

"Yes."

"Is it true? Did he get the samples illegally?"

"Not according to Lasher's records. He had acquired signed statements of informed consent. But the IRN says he misled the participants. One of his field assistants, a graduate student, filed a complaint with the university last year about one of Lasher's research trips ... to Alaska. She claimed he had bribed a tribal elder to get the people to agree to provide the samples. She lost the case."

"Her word against his?"

"No, not quite," Warden declared. "Two other grad students came forward and confirmed the accusation. They'd also been on the trip. But the university committee ruled for Lasher—the informed consent documents. Then he turned around and sued the three graduate students for slander. His lawyer attacked them, one in particular. So did Lasher, during his testimony on the stand. It was vicious. The defendants ended up settling out of court. They had to pay Lasher a substantial amount."

Motives for murder are like weeds, Harry thought. They sprout adjacent to the dead. "Anyone else in the department have it in for Lasher?"

Warden frowned, almost in despair. "Miriam Kovitch. She's had her differences with him. When he was chair of the department, she accused him of gender discrimination—not getting the annual raises she thought she deserved. She sued the university and lost. I can't say more. There's an ongoing case. She's ... she's a difficult individual. Bitter."

"Oh yeah? Bitter enough for murder?"

6

Egotistical Scumbag

"What!" Warden exclaimed, a bewildered look on her face. "No. She's ... well ... now that you said it ... maybe."

Another weed, Harry thought. "Was she at the protest march?"

"I don't know. You'll have to ask the police."

Harry sat back. Motive. Opportunity. "Okay. What about the three students Lasher sued?"

He caught the sudden sag in her steeled face. She got up, went over to the window, and stared outside, seemingly wishing she could wander through the grove of trees beyond the pond. After a long moment she turned to face Harry.

"I can tell you that one of them was not at the protest march or in Spooner. He committed suicide a month before Lasher's murder. Max Dennison. Max was what we term a 'non-traditional' student. He'd come back to the university, to graduate school, for a second career. His wife happens to be a faculty member in Anthropology, Elena Montanares. I met with her."

She sighed, walked back to the couch, and sat down. "Harry, there are times I despise being chancellor. That was one of them. She blamed Lasher, she blamed the university. The university is me. She blamed me for Max's suicide. For leading an institution that nurtures scoundrels. I'm being polite. She called him a 'scumbag.'"

"Was he?"

"Of course, he was. An egotistical scumbag, to boot. No one deserves to die, but few in the university mourn him. It's likely that the suicide helped trigger the IRN demonstration, certainly over whether Lasher had obtained the genetic material legally or ethically. But there was a deeper issue, a sociocultural one. The IRN claimed that Lasher's research was violating indigenous heritage. 'Genetic appropriation' is the current term—denying native peoples their own sense of history and identity, their own tradition, their own origin stories."

Harry shook his head. "Yeah, well, three hundred years ago the Enlightenment did that to everyone. It tossed out everyone's origin stories, everyone's scriptures, everyone's gods."

Warden pursed her lips. "True, to some extent. But the science can't erase the historical persona."

Harry nodded. "No, nor should it. I gather the protest got out of hand."

"Yes. My son said it turned ... well ... violent, once they were inside the building."

"Any police around?"

"Sure." Warden's voice turned indignant. "We're used to protests on campus. Pro-life. Pro-choice. Anti-war. They're peaceful. It's not the 60s or 70s. We even get those hardbitten fundamentalists from Topeka ... the Westboro Baptist Church ... the Phelps clan ... the ones that protest at military funerals. They show up here with their signs—'God Hates Fags,' 'Fags Go To Hell'—at the annual drag queen show on Jayhawk Boulevard, in front of the student union. Just across the street from Spooner."

A steam whistle blew a deep bass note across the campus. Classes letting out. Harry thought of the tugboats hooting on the Monongahela River as they chugged past his office on West Carson Street in Pittsburgh. "Tell me about the violence."

Warden shook her head. "The plan, according to Nalren, was for a few of them to enter Spooner quietly, as if they were going to class, then occupy Lasher's laboratory—a peaceful sit-down protest to stop the research. That part worked. The campus police didn't notice. But, once inside, the protest got out of control, as these things usually do. All it takes is a couple of agitators. Some of the IRN began vandalizing the place. They smashed the instruments and glassware. They opened the freezers. They dumped out the tubes with the samples. Also, the jars in the refrigerators with—"Warden scratched her head. "I forget the term. Some sample."

"DNA extracts?" Harry prompted.

"Yes, that's it."

"What about your son?"

"He says he tried to stop the trashing of the laboratory, but couldn't. The vandals—everyone—then left. He and Winona stayed behind to apologize to Lasher for the destruction. He wanted to explain that the protest was supposed to have been non-violent. Lasher is on his doctoral committee."

"Honorable," Harry said, "but in this business, if crime doesn't pay, neither does honesty."

Warden glared at him. "My son is not a criminal. He wanted to do the right thing."

"Where was Lasher?"

"On a flight back from Montreal. He'd been to a conference at McGill University. Nalren told the police that Lasher showed up at Spooner around seven-thirty. When he walked in and saw the destruction, he became enraged, ran over to the closest freezer, slipped on the wet floor, hit his head on the tile, and was knocked out. Nalren panicked. He and Winona fled. A lab tech—she's a grad student—found Lasher about six-thirty the next morning ... last Friday. She called the police. They have the details."

"What do they have on Nalren?"

Warden raised her hands in disgust. "I don't know. Maybe his fingerprints on what they say is the murder weapon. A ceramic statue of an ape imitating Rodin's *The Thinker*. It was in Lasher's office, on his desk. Apparently, his kitsch."

"Motive?"

"The police say he was carrying out the IRN agenda. He's typecast. He's Native American ... Athabaskan ... from Canada. He, Winona, and the grad student that committed suicide were best friends."

"Tell me about Nalren."

Warden leaned over the coffee table and began tracing her forefinger along the grooves in the limestone that spelled "KU," as if divining a story from a distant time and foreign place.

"In Athabascan, his name, 'Nalren,' means 'he is thawed out.' He was forcibly taken as a child ... then orphaned ..." She stopped, reached for the go-mug, and downed whatever was left. "The details don't matter. Ghastly business. We ..." she hesitated, "I ... I adopted him. I was a dean at the university in Fairbanks. Later, we—Nalren and I—moved to Anchorage. I'd become chancellor of the campus there. My husband ... I left him in Fairbanks. Divorced. Usual soap opera. Familiar score. Music and lyrics below the waist. Affair with a graduate student. Tawdry business."

Abruptly, she straightened up, sat back, and squinted at Harry. "Anyway, Nalren's not a murderer. I believe him. That's why I called you."

Harry nodded. "Sensitive question. I imagine he knows his history, his being orphaned ... the 'ghastly business.' Has his resentment thawed out?"

Warden stared past Harry to a forlorn windswept tundra, a frozen expanse of blinding white, children standing in the snow in front of a four-story red brick building, and, in the distance, a long string of barbed wire.

After a long silence, she said, matter-of-factly, "I don't know. Memory is a terrible burden, Harry, virulent, viral, with no antidote. But forgetting is a terrible sin."

7

White Guy History

"Well, stone the fucking crows, not you again!"

Harry had forgotten how easily Detective Pat Duggan could pass for Josef Stalin: black, bushy eyebrows; faint brow ridges; deep-set eyes; a bulbous nose; a broad forehead; a thick, drooping mustache; and coal-black hair that angled out of his head like a thousand steel spikes.

"Christ, Przewalski, last time you sat in that chair—what was it, a year ago?—you were wearing enough bandages to wrap a cadaver. Hell, you looked like a cadaver. That pickup truck had sideswiped you."

Duggan ran his right hand through his spikes. "So, I don't need to ask what brings you back from Pittsburgh. Lemme guess. Normally, I'd say it'd be that little lady out in Abilene ... the one at the truck stop. What's her name ... Ruby. But I got a hunch this ain't normal, y'know, you stopping in to see a Lawrence police detective for old times' sake. Nah, don't think so, not while passing through to a hot date out west. Y'know, Przewalski, that's one of the tough questions I had to pass on the police exam before I got my shield."

Harry grinned at him. "Gotta hand it to you. Your brain hasn't lost a step." He motioned at the Pittsburgh Steelers calendar on the wall. It was an aerial shot of Three Rivers Stadium on the north side of the Ohio River. Duggan was from Kittanning, a former steel town a few winding miles up the Allegheny River from Pittsburgh. With the smelters gone cold, its economic life was being crushed between the Paleozoic accordion folds of the Appalachian Mountains.

"They tore it down," Harry said, pointing at the picture. "Three Rivers. Built two new stadiums in the same spot. Heinz Field for the Steelers, PNC Park for the Pirates. They share a parking lot."

"Yeah, I know," Duggan cracked. "I keep up. It's called the Internet. I pay good money to read the *Pittsburgh Post-Gazette* online. Costs less than having the paper sent here. Lets me live there without the fucking traffic on the Fort Pitt Bridge. Or getting mugged in the Hill District. What do they call that? Vicarious?"

"Yeah, vicarious," Harry said. "You know that's just hifalutin for 'secondhand.'"

Duggan shrugged, as if he was apologizing for showing off his vocabulary. He was sporting a green checked shirt and a blue tie plastered with yellow bicycles. There was a faint blotch on one of the bicycle wheels.

"Goddamn yogurt the wife makes me eat," Duggan grunted, brushing the blotch. He loosened the tie, unbuttoned the collar, and scratched his neck. "Okay, Przewalski, enough of the small talk. Why're you here? Hope it's not about the kid we got downstairs for bopping that professor last week?"

Harry grinned at Duggan. "Afraid it is. I just had a talk with the chancellor, Margaret Warden, up there at the university. That's her son you're holding. She's hired me to get you to let him go."

Duggan let out a guffaw. "Boyle will like this one. You remember Boyle ... Stella Boyle? The assistant D.A? She hasn't forgotten you or that prof, Porter. She had him all set up for the Fulbright murder. You made her look bad. Could be why she's still an assistant D.A. She was pissed. She wanted to charge you with reckless endangerment. Y'know, that mess of metal and glass and car grilles that you caused on New Hampshire Street."

Harry raised his eyebrows. "What stopped her?"

Duggan leaned back in his chair, put his feet up on the desk, and let a self-satisfied grin spread across his face from underneath his mustache.

"Me, Przewalski, that's what stopped her. Hell, I also had Porter pegged for it. But, gotta admit, you did good. Even saved us a trial. What do they say in cycling? *Chapeau*?" Duggan raised his hand to his head and pretended to doff his hat. "Well, *chapeau* to you."

Harry's eyes widened. "Didn't know you were into the peloton."

"Yeah, well, doctor told me I had to exercise. I went down to Sunflower Bike Shop on Mass Street, talked to Dan Hughes there, the owner. He remembered the road bike you borrowed. I remembered your bandaged face. So, I got me a gravel bike. Even learned the lingo. It's a one-by. That means—"

"I know what it means. Single chainring up front, big gear spread in the back on the cassette."

Duggan flashed an embarrassed smile, proud of his newfound expertise. "Cost more than a few grand. But the wife says a coronary is more expensive. Kansas has a million miles of gravel, Przewalski. No reason to ride road and chance getting whacked by one of those pickup trucks with the big side mirrors—like you did. I also got enemies. Every goddamn thug I've ever arrested."

Duggan slid his feet off the desk and sat up. Harry decided not to tell him that the sole on his left shoe was developing a partial sinkhole.

"About Warden's son, Nalren. What do you guys have on him?"

Duggan's bushy eyebrows danced up his forehead. "What do we got? We got a murderer. And we got a murder confession—without the words. The kid waited around for the prof ... Lasher. He says, to apologize. Apologize, my ass. He waited to bop him on the head with a ceramic ape. Kinda fitting, don't you think? Using an ape to kill an anthropologist who studies our evolution from the apes?"

Harry grimaced. "Okay, Duggan, stick to the detective business. Lasher's work had nothing to do with apes. He studies DNA of indigenous—"

"Yeah, I know what he studied. I read up on it ... when they got here ... Indians, Inuit, natives down there in the Amazon, Chile. Kinda interesting how the hell they made it all the way down there back when, down to the tip of South America ... Tierra del Fuego."

Duggan paused, then folded his arms on his chest, suddenly indignant. "Y'know, our history books told us Magellan discovered it, as if he got there first. But they didn't tell us about the real guys getting there at least 13,000 years earlier. Same with Columbus. The wife—she teaches high school—she says that's because our history is white guy history. This archeological stuff? That's brown guy history. Anyway, fat lot of good it did Lasher. It got him dead."

"How do you figure it?"

Duggan shrugged. "Easy. Lasher kept that ape statue on his desk. When he walked in, Nalren picked it up and whacked him hard over the head. Hard enough to kill him. And he didn't bother to apologize."

"According to Warden, the kid and his girlfriend were there when Lasher came in. He slipped on the gunk on the floor, fell, hit his head, and was out. They panicked and ran. You don't have any evidence that they killed him."

Duggan tugged at his mustache. "Happens, in fact, that we do."

"What?"

"Get serious, Przcwalski, what do you think this is? Free evidence day at the county building?"

"Was worth a shot. You got a motive?"

"Sure, like I said, what Lasher studied. The kid didn't like that. He's part of that group ... the IRN ... the protesters. Warden likely told you about that. They didn't like Lasher messing with native blood. And he's a native."

"Anything else?"

"We're working on it. You're gonna hear the street talk at the university. Lasher was a letch. We found a stash of porno flicks in the closet in his office. Word is, he preyed on anyone in skirts. Or pants. As long as they had two X chromosomes. Students mostly. Sex for grades. We think he hit up the kid's girlfriend, Winona. She was in his class. There's motive number two."

Harry wanted a cigarette. He fished out the blue pack of Zig-Zag papers, then remembered the layers of duct tape wound around the pouch of Drum tobacco. It was working. "Screw the smoke."

Duggan yanked open a desk drawer, produced an open pack of Pall Mall, red, unfiltered, and put a cigarette between his lips.

"That doc also told me to quit the cigs. So, I did. I just let 'em dangle, pretend to take a drag."

Harry laughed. "Yeah, you can pretend you're Bogart in a cop movie."

Duggan lifted his hands in mock defense. "Okay, smart ass, don't knock it. It's worked for me. I'm addicted to it ... the vicarious smoke." He chuckled and handed Harry a Pall Mall. "Try it."

Harry held it between his fingers—factory-made, perfect, industrial, million after million. Not like his hand-rolled, one by one, each misshapen, idiosyncratic, each an act of creation.

"Y'know, Przewalski," Duggan said, picking a piece of tobacco from his lip, "half the life we lead, half the stuff we look at and dream about, they're vicarious. Smoking. Fancy cars in showrooms. Travel mags. The spreads in the deli case that'll kill ya."

He pointed the Pall Mall at Harry. "The only things that are real are the drunks, the vagrants, the crooks, the wife-beaters, the kid molesters, corrupt politicians. Also. dead bodies, like our anthropologist." He dropped the cigarette on the desk. "Also cancer. It ain't vicarious. Give that shit up."

"I'm working on it. Slowly." Harry got up and went over to the window. Duggan's office was on the second floor of the Douglas County Courthouse on Massachusetts Street between 11th and 12th. The window looked out onto South Park. The first yellow buds had begun to sprout on the forsythias, but the grass was still a dead, desiccated brown. He cranked the window open, lit the Pall Mall, took a long drag, and blew the smoke toward the large gazebo in the middle of the park. Its silver dome rose incongruously into a scattering of bare trees. He remembered watching two vagrants crawl into its midnight shadows the last time he'd stood at this window, smoking a Drum.

He turned to Duggan. "You have fingerprints?"

Duggan grinned. "Boyle will spank me for this. It don't matter. Yeah, we have fingerprints. Fresh ones. The kid blew it. Lasher kept a box of those disposable vinyl gloves on his desk. He used them in the lab. Anyway, the kid could have put on a pair while he and the girlfriend waited for Lasher to show up. I guess they didn't."

"Like I said, that's not how Nalren tells it. Lasher walks in, starts over to the freezers, slips—"

"Yeah," Duggan interrupted, shaking his head, "we know what Warden's kid is saying. Y'know that chimp statue? It didn't fly off Lasher's desk by itself, rub against his noggin, and get a good dose of his blood and hair. Someone helped, Przewalski. And that someone is your client's son."

Harry stubbed out the Pall Mall, cranked the window shut, pulled the chair back from Duggan's desk, and stretched his legs out. "Seems pretty thin. Can't believe Boyle will press charges. She'd have to be pretty desperate. Even an ambulance chaser could win this one. Lots of people fingered that ceramic. Nalren's prints could be from anytime he'd been in that office. After the kids leave, someone else waltzes into the lab. Lasher is on the floor, out cold. They put on those gloves, pick up the ape, and make sure Lasher stays cold. Could be anyone."

"No one else was seen going in."

"Big deal. Boyle won't chance a career on negative evidence."

Duggan shrugged. "Anyway, the outside door to Spooner is locked at six. Who could get in?"

"Anyone waiting to slip in when someone else hits the crash bar and leaves. Or anyone with a key. I bet grad students and profs from years ago still have one."

"Anyone? C'mon Przewalski. I don't make a living on hypotheticals. Neither do you. Got somebody in mind?"

"Sure. Lasher had enemies. There's the IRN people. There's the anthropologist, Montanares, whose husband was a grad student and committed suicide. There's the other two grad students Lasher screwed over in court. There's the prof, Kovitch, who sued him and the university. Then there's academia, Duggan. Remember the Fulbright business? Everything is personal. Murder is personal."

Duggan pursed his bushy eyebrows. "Yeah, smart ass, I remember. I live in this town, just down the hill from those guys. I gotta deal with their shit that doesn't stink. Give me a steelworker any day."

Harry chuckled. "No pity here. I'm guessing you have a list of the protesters. I'm also guessing you have an army checking their backgrounds. Care to share that list with me?"

"Dream on, Przewalski. This is a one-gift visit. The fingerprints were it." Duggan leaned back, rubbed his mustache, then grinned at Harry.

"On second thought, I'm feeling generous. One more gift. Your lady friend from Abilene ... Ms. Pettecek ... the waitress at the truck stop diner. She was here last Thursday, marching with the bunch of 'em."

8

So You're Here to Get Me Off

Harry took the elevator outside Duggan's office to the basement of the county courthouse: A long, gray hallway, a low-hanging bank of naked fluorescent lights, a row of cells along the left side. They had solid doors with a view window and an off-white plastic facing. A booking desk stood in the middle of the hallway, beat-up, brown, flanked by two wooden chairs.

An officer was slouched on the chair facing the cell doors. He seemed to be studying them, as if the dense scatter of black streak marks on the plastic facings were pieces of abstract art. Harry wondered if he was a fan of Jackson Pollock. The officer looked like he belonged on the gridiron, an offensive guard on a football team: burly, 5-11, with a blond brush-cut and a lineman's neck that bulged over the collar of his gray shirt. The black name tag read, 'B. Landesman.'

Harry handed him the form Duggan had given him to visit Nalren. Landesman wrote Harry's name into a visitor log, pausing three times to check the spelling.

"You his lawyer?" It was half bark, half question.

"No," Harry said.

"Good. You don't look like one."

"I'll take that as a compliment."

Landesman chuckled and walked Harry over to cell four. He checked the view window, unhooked a jumble of keys from his belt, unlocked the door, waved Harry in, and locked it behind him.

Nalren, in blue jeans and a thick, gray flannel shirt, was propped up on his cot reading a journal. Harry made out the title: *Plains Anthropologist*. It had a glossy cover with a large drawing of a projectile point. Nalren looked up, swung his legs off the cot, and leapt to his feet. He was slightly shorter than Harry's 6-1 and thickset, with a broad, regal face, a square chin, black hair that hung to below the ears, and dark, deep-set eyes that squinted guardedly at the world.

"Who are you?" He spoke slowly, articulating the beginning and end of every word. His voice was closer to baritone than tenor.

Harry handed him his card. "Your mother tell you she'd hired me?"

Nalren studied the name on the card and inspected Harry, the eyes still guarded. "No, she didn't. But I remember you. The Porter case. More than a year ago. Fulbright's murder. It was the talk of the town. And the department. The newspaper articles are still up on the notice board in Spooner."

Harry nodded. "Better that than my obit."

Nalren gave him a nervous smile, then motioned to the chair on the other side of a metal table. The cell was spartan: dirty cinderblock walls, a cot, table, two chairs, a sink, a shelf, a small mirror, and a commode. There was a stack of journals on the table, a coffee cup, a ballpoint pen, a Sharpie, and an open MacBook. On the screen, a strikingly attractive woman was winking out at them with a devilish smile and ice-blue eyes. She had short blond hair parted on the side, a long, serpentine nose, prominent cheek bones, angular jaws, and a tattoo of a large, triangular projectile point on her neck. It looked to Harry like a Clovis point, the signature killing tool of archeological peoples in America 13,000 years ago.

Must be Winona, Harry thought. Behind her face, a grove of tall prairie grasses framed a white clapboard church, narrow, simple, unadorned except for the plain sign nailed above the door: "U.S. Center Chapel." Harry remembered stopping there on a bike ride from Fort Riley, where he'd done infantry training before being shipped off to Iraq. The church, he'd thought, was fitting for a god with a soft spot for prayers from the geographical center of the 48 states.

"So," Nalren said, "I'm curious. I've studied the anatomy of Przewalski's horse. Are you Russian? Related to the general, Nikolay Przhevalski?"

Harry shook his head. "Not that I know of—to him, or to the horse."

A slight smile. "So, you're here to get me off."

"Only if you and Winona didn't whack Lasher over the head with that porcelain chimp. Your fingerprints are on it."

Nalren glanced at Winona on the laptop screen and sighed. "No, neither of us hit him. Like I told the police, Lasher came in, saw the mess, and ran over to the freezer at the end of the lab. The floor was slick with the chemicals from the smashed jars. He slipped, fell, and hit his head on the floor. He was unconscious. But not dead."

"How do you know?"

"I felt his carotid artery." As if to demonstrate, Nalren placed a forefinger on the side of his neck. "He had a pulse . And we could see that he was breathing."

"Any blood on the floor from Lasher hitting his head?"

"No. I looked. He was just conked out."

"So, how did your fingerprints end up on the chimp."

"Crap!" Nalren exclaimed. "I've explained that a hundred times. I picked it up when I was in Lasher's office about a week ago. I was meeting with him about my dissertation research. He's on my committee ... uh ... was, I guess. That chimp always sat there on his rolltop desk. Lasher would bark at it and laugh. It was an ornament, a conversation piece. I bet lots of people handled it. So did I. There's gotta be other fingerprints on it."

"If there are, the police aren't saying. And they think you were the last one there when Lasher was bopped."

"Damn it," Nalren swore, "I wasn't. The murderer was the last one there. We took off when we saw that Lasher was out cold."

Harry sat back, began to reach for his pack of Drum tobacco, then stopped. It was either addiction or dementia, thinking he could smoke in the cell block. He voted for addiction.

"Right. When did Lasher get there, to the lab?"

"Around six-thirty, seven."

"You and Winona must have been waiting for quite a while."

"Yeah, about an hour or more." Nalren shrugged. "I felt guilty. About the protesters smashing all the jars, tubes and lab equipment. Emptying the tissues from the ultracold freezers. It was supposed be peaceful ... a sit-in. I tried to stop them, but couldn't."

"What about the protesters? Could one or two have hidden out in the lab or in the building while you and Winona were waiting?"

Nalren leaned back and scratched the back of his head. "Not in the lab. We walked around his office and the cryogenic room with the ultracolds. Didn't see anyone."

"What about outside Lasher's office and lab in Spooner?"

"Yeah, sure, it's possible. Why? You think one of them killed Lasher after we left?"

"Maybe. Murder has lots of alleys. One might lead somewhere." Harry shifted in his chair. "So, during those hours in Lasher's lab you and Winona could have put the tissue tubes back into the ultracolds—saved the genomic samples."

Nalren got up, shoved his hands into his jeans, hunched his shoulders, and paced slowly to the cell door and back. "Interesting that you say that. We started putting the tubes back in the racks and into the freezers. Then we stopped."

"Why?"

Nalren stopped pacing and looked squarely at Harry. "I don't know how much my mother or the police told you. There's history here, nasty history. Lasher got most of those samples—the blood, the saliva, the hair—through fraud, trickery. Without proper consent. He didn't give a damn. He only cared about his research, his career. People on his expeditions knew all about it. They witnessed him deceiving the very indigenous people he was studying. He duped them into giving up their genetic heritage."

Nalren pulled the chair back from the table, sat down, and folded his arms across his chest. "So, we took it back. Allowing frozen tissues to thaw is as peaceful a protest as one can make."

9

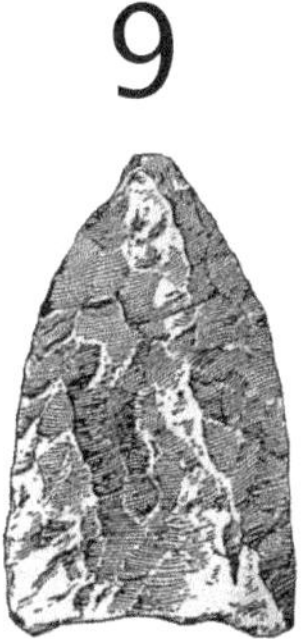

The Twelve Mile Creek Projectile Point

Harry pushed his chair back and stretched his legs out under the table. "Did Winona agree? Deliberately waste the samples?"

"Absolutely," Nalren said, adamant. "We're both philosophy minors. But you don't need to read Plato or Hume to know what's right here. It's immoral to profit from the abuse of victims."

"True," Harry said. "Tough choice, though. The DNA sequences might have been critical to telling the indigenous story."

Nalren leaned forward. "I don't care. It's like the Nazi medical experiments at Auschwitz. How the knowledge was obtained was evil. So, the knowledge itself is evil. It's means and ends. Who cares about the results, even if they're breakthrough. They belong in the graves with the victims."

Harry shrugged. "Okay, but Lasher didn't torture or kill anyone getting those samples. He didn't deserve to get whacked for that."

"No, he didn't," Nalren said. "But he did steal our genes for his research. You know, genes are all that we have left. Everything else has already been taken from us. Our lands. Our lives. Our livelihoods. Our language."

He turned to the laptop, hit a few keys, turned it around to face Harry. "Also., our parents. Our childhoods."

A photo filled the screen in shades of black and white: a long, dark brick building; four floors of windows; a flat roof; L-shaped wings at each end; steps to a landing and two tall doors; a barren, snow-frozen prairie; a distant wire fence. It looked to Harry like an old penitentiary. Except for the line of children arrayed in front, bundled in boots, hats, and coats, staring at the camera under a low, overcast sky.

Warden had mentioned a ghastly business. This looked like it, Harry thought. "Elementary school?"

Nalren twisted his mouth in dismay. "You can call it that."

"I'm guessing this is personal," Harry said, gently.

"You guessed right." His face darkened as if an apparition had ghosted out of the photo. He motioned to the screen. "I'm one of those kids."

"Another guess," Harry ventured. "Alaska?"

Nalren shook his head. "No. Canada ... Saskatchewan. My Indian Residential School." Abruptly, he turned the laptop around, closed it, and looked at Harry. The reel had stopped projecting in his mind.

"Anyway, I gotta get out of here. There's a bond hearing tomorrow morning. We have to convince a judge that I'm not a flight risk. It ought to carry some weight that the chancellor of KU is my mother." Nalren didn't hide the sarcasm.

Harry heard a cell door slam down the hallway outside. "It should. For what it's worth, I know you didn't kill him. Otherwise, I wouldn't be here. What about the grad students who went on the expeditions?"

"Not a chance," Nalren declared. "Expose Lasher to the university? Sure. But kill him? No. Doesn't make sense."

"Yeah, well, cemeteries are full of murders that don't make sense. They filed the complaint with KU against Lasher. Then he sued them, made fools of them in court. I understand one of them committed suicide."

Nalren pursed his lips. "Max. Max Dennison. He ... he was older, in his fifties. Good guy. A 'non-traditional student.' That's what the department called him. But they treated him like shit. So much for touting lifelong learning."

"Tell me about it."

"Not much to say. He retired early. Stocks, real estate. Decided to get a degree in archeology. His wife is in the department."

"Yeah, I know, your mother told me. Elena Montanares."

"Right. She's on my committee. She's also a genetic anthropologist, like Lasher. But she works on Andean natives. She's Chilean. His area was Northern Hemisphere people: Native Americans, Inuit, Aleut, circumpolar people. Anyway, Max didn't pass his orals—his doctoral candidacy exam."

"When was that?"

"Near the end of the fall semester. After he got back from the expedition in August. After they'd filed the complaint with KU. When he failed, his committee didn't give him a chance to repeat."

Harry remembered his doctoral qualifying exam. Four Pitt faculty members facing him across an oak library table in the Carnegie Museum. A fifth, the external committee member, a paleontologist from Yale, was on speaker phone. He'd said, "describe the evolution of birds from dinosaurs," then added, "and, yes, do it *en français*—I see that it's listed as your foreign language." Harry froze, blanking on the French word for "feathers" in describing *Archaeopteryx*, the missing link between dinosaurs and birds from the Jurassic of Bavaria. That evening, Nicole had laughed, leaned over, and whispered in his ear, "tonight you may tickle me with a '*plume*.'"

"Is that standard here for doctoral orals?" Harry asked. "No second chance?"

"No. Usually, you get a few months to brush up on readings, then a repeat exam. But not Max. The committee told him he didn't have the aptitude for the doctoral program. He thought that Lasher had engineered it. Max said that Lasher had told him the same thing during the expedition that summer—not to even bother with the oral exam; that he couldn't hack it. Anyway, that was the end of his graduate studies. Max was devastated."

Outside, a bright floodlight suddenly flashed on, illuminating the cell window. Snow flurries floated into and out of the bluish beam.

"When did he commit suicide?"

Nalren shook his head. "It's ironic you ask me that in this building. The slander trial was in a courtroom a few floors up." Nalren pointed to the ceiling. "During testimony, Lasher accused Max of lodging the KU complaint with the other students just to get back at him. He repeated what Max's committee had said, verbatim: 'He doesn't have the aptitude for a doctoral degree in anthropology.' The next day it was in the papers, the *University Daily Kansan* and the *Lawrence Journal-World*, in their accounts of the trial. Max was humiliated. That evening he swallowed a bottle of sleeping pills."

Harry grimaced. "His wife, Montanares. Was she at the IRN protest?"

Nalren blinked hard, glared at Harry, then let his voice drift off. "Yes, she was there."

"Did she go into the lab with the rest of you?"

"I don't think so. At least I didn't see her. Her office is up on the second floor. If you want to know about Max you should talk to her."

"I plan to. About the samples in Lasher's lab. They're all gone. What does that do to your doctoral research?"

Nalren knit his brow. "Not a problem. Not my dissertation. I don't do genomics of native people. And actually not all the samples are gone. The IRN just dumped Lasher's freezers—the stuff from Alaska, Russia, and Canada. They didn't touch the tissues in the freezers from Central and South America. Lasher had one student. Jennifer Finch. She's also the lab tech. Her work on the Aleutian Islands is certainly screwed up. But she wasn't that far along. She can change her dissertation topic."

"And you?"

"Like I said, not genomics. The first people in the Americas—their blood, their genes—they're gone to wherever they go." He pointed to the journal with the projectile point on the cover. "Archeology is what's left of them ... in the ground ... what the earth chooses to reveal to us."

Harry nodded. It was how he'd felt about paleontology, waiting for the badlands to erode the petrified bits of jaws and teeth and skeletons of ancient beasts. Then he'd reach down and pluck them out of deep time.

"Anyway," Nalren said," this is what I'm working on." He tossed him the copy of the *Plains Anthropologist* with the drawing of the stone spear point on the cover. The lead article was "Before Clovis: The Twelve Mile Creek Site and the Peopling of the Americas."

"It's a double mystery," Nalren continued. "Twelve Mile Creek is a Pleistocene bison-kill site in western Kansas. Around 13,000 years old. It was excavated in 1895. Could also be '96. Even '97. That projectile point on the cover is from that site. It looks like a Clovis point. It was found lying under the right shoulder blade of one of the adult bison—allegedly."

Harry nodded. "I know about it. A KU paleontologist at the time found it. Handel T. Martin. He was excavating the site."

Nalren raised his eyebrows. "I should have guessed that you'd know about Martin. A fellow bonehunter. I read about you after the Fulbright case. Anyway, Martin mounted that bison skeleton in the Natural History Museum. Dyche Hall, across from Spooner. It's still on display. At the back of the third floor."

"I'll stop in there. But if that's a Clovis projectile point, Martin dug it up 37 years before the official Clovis discovery in New Mexico in 1932."

"Right." Nalren acknowledged. "But archeologists didn't accept the Twelve Mile Creek find at the time. That's the first mystery. Then it disappeared."

"What happened to it?"

"That's the second mystery," Nalren said, a glint in his eye. "Anyway, Lasher was interested in that spear point. There's a former archeology graduate from KU who worked on Twelve Mile Creek years ago. She has a research file on it. She wanted to show it to Lasher. She's in Abilene."

Harry pushed his chair back. "Lemme guess. Pettecek. Dr. Ruby Pettecek."

Nalren's eyes widened in surprise. "Right. You know her?"

Harry stood up and shoved his hands into the back pockets of his jeans. "Yeah, I know her."

10

Feed 'em to the Horses

There are places on Earth, Harry thought, that would never know cold. And places that would never know heat. But there wasn't a place that would never know wind, that ever-present demon howling down from the sky, skittering the leaves through the forest, bending the prairie grasses to the ground, swirling the snows on the tundra, dune-shaping the sands in the desert, rolling the tumbleweeds across the plains.

Strong winds were gusting from the south, buffeting the Toyota 4Runner on I-70 as Harry headed west toward Abilene. He'd taken it over a Lincoln Navigator that Hertz had offered him at the Kansas City airport. It was red metallic, not the black one they'd given him a year and a half ago.

Harry fished his mobile phone out of his jacket and slid it into one of the cup holders in the console. After Margaret Warden had called him in Pittsburgh, he'd conceded defeat to the digital world. He'd gone out and armed himself and his father with a couple of iPhones. Nicholas Przewalski had cursed the contraption. Then Harry showed him how he could text him instantly about Emilia. During the past weeks, his mother had slipped deeper into her netherworld—real to her, dementia to him and his father. He'd visited her in the nursing home before heading to the airport. Clouds had settled over the blue in her eyes, her mind marooned in a distant space. He couldn't tell if she knew him. She didn't gesture. She didn't speak. She didn't squeeze his hand. Mourning didn't have to wait for death, he thought. Without cognition, life had already left. When God wants to destroy someone, Nicolas had cursed, he first takes their mind away. It was an old Polish proverb.

On the other side of Topeka, a violent dusk had bruised the sky purple. The windows were down. The scent of the hard red winter wheat rode in on the wind, as if spring were lurking on the other side of the Flint Hills. The scatter of fields ran brown and barren. Short yellow stalks spiked up through the earth, mute remnants of last fall's corn crop that once had rustled in the wind. Amid the burnt umber landscape bits of painted pasture appeared, magically color-washed a deep hue of violet blue. Probably henbit. It reminded Harry of Rouffignac, their room in the hotel on the cobbled square, Ruby breathing beside him, her breasts rising and falling in the violet blue shadows of the neon light.

Harry punched in the only number he had for Ruby, a landline. He'd last called her nine months ago from the house on Mississippi Street in Lawrence, after the police had left, after the blood of Fulbright's murderer had dried. Twice he'd started to call her from Pittsburgh, then stopped, staying in his foxhole, emotionally safe. It was long past time, he knew, to crawl out.

"Hi, Ruby."

There was a long, hard silence before she answered. "Ah, detective." Her voice was cool, almost perfunctory. "It's been a while. Been wondering … whether you'd become a stranger or a memory."

Harry grimaced. "Don't ask. Probably both. I know I should've called."

"Yeah, well, that's yesterday's history. So, what's the occasion? How's the detection business in Pittsburgh? I see that crazy camel driver case at the Carnegie made the papers. You were famous there for a few minutes."

"Not what I was looking for."

"When you find out," Ruby said, a touch more acidic, "tell me what you're looking for. More important, how's your father, Nicholas? Still doing the bike shop thing?"

"Yeah, he's fine."

"And your mother?"

Beyond the highway the land had disappeared into a flat blackness. Like his mother's mind, Harry thought.

"She's no longer the person you met. Good you saw her when you did."

"Damn. Sorry to hear that. She's a special lady. When you visit her today or tomorrow, give her a hug for me."

Harry hesitated, then told her. "Listen Ruby, I'm not in Pittsburgh. I'm here ... in Kansas … headed your way ... on I-70. Just passed the turnoff to Alma. Should be on your porch in a bit over an hour. But I won't blame you if you tell me to buzz off, turn around, and head back to wherever I came from."

Another long silence, except for a metronomic click, click, click, as if Ruby were tapping the receiver with her fingernail. Finally, she said, "Okay, if you're waiting for the wrath of a woman scorned, forget it. And Przewalski, you're named for a horse. So, you might read up on that Egyptian king, Busiris. When a stranger would set foot on his territory without warning, he'd sacrifice them to the gods—feed 'em to the horses."

Harry spotted the exit sign for the interstate service area just east of Junction City. He pulled in beside two semis in the darkest corner of the parking lot and cut the motor.

"Ruby, this is as close to diary as I'll ever get. There is only a sliver of the world that's important. In Pittsburgh it's my father. And Emilia. She's become a memory; he's become a stranger. There's a lady at the Carnegie I don't want to hurt—we know enough not to want to know too much. And there's you, churning inside my head ever since I walked into your truck stop diner in Abilene last year. You must know that. I'm ... I'm not good at this ... at being domesticated."

Harry heard her pour something into a glass, put the bottle down, and gulp it. He bet it was Scotch. It's how she drank it. He pictured her licking her lips.

"So, Harry, when you didn't call, I wondered where the fuck you got lost all these months. You once told me 'the future's what's ahead, not behind.' Kind of ironic coming from a paleontologist. I get the feeling you're running from 'what's behind.'"

Harry looked at the digital numbers on the dashboard: 8:30. A glimmer of light still grasped the horizon. He punched the ignition and turned on the headlights. He'd never told her about Nicole, her body parts in a 50-gallon drum, and wouldn't now.

"Yeah, you're right. You probably know about the Lasher murder. About Warden's son being arrested. She called me in Pittsburgh, asked me to come back out and get him. I said, 'sure.'" Harry paused. "It was just an excuse ... the chance to see you."

He heard her take another gulp.

"An hour you say?" Ruby rasped. "Tell you what, detective. Keep driving. I'll use the hour to decide whether to turn the porch light on or feed you to the fucking horses. I'm drinking Scotch. It'll inoculate me against a sentimental pardon."

Harry laughed. "Okay, I'll take those odds. Listen, I'm gonna ask you about Lasher. You knew him. You also know the kid, Nalren."

"Funny you should ask, detective. Might have a story to tell you. That's if I let you on my goddamn porch. You're not the only shamus in town."

"What do you mean?"

"I'm helping some people out. Lasher was blackmailing them—well, at least one of them. Lasher was a bastard. He deserved to get bopped. The word 'lascivious'—it was coined for him. Anyway, they coulda done it. The kid certainly didn't."

Harry straightened up in his truck seat. "Who are 'they'?"

"Don't know whether I can say, just yet. Maybe. We'll see. Shit. Wait, somebody's hitting the fucking doorbell. Hang on."

He heard her plunk the receiver down on the table. He imagined her walking past the stairs to the front door, pulling the curtain aside, turning the big brass knob—

He heard voices. Loud but muffled. Then the first gunshot. Then the second.

11

March Tryst Two

Someone is following me."

"Oh yeah? Is it a woman? That's every man's dream, isn't it."

"I'm not kidding. The last few times we were here. I think someone followed me back to Lawrence. In a gray minivan. A Dodge, I think."

"Okay, where did you see it?"

"On the outskirts, on West 6th Street. Each time it turned south on K-10 toward Clinton Lake."

"You're sure you're not being paranoid? Could just be a coincidence. There are probably lots of gray minivans in Lawrence. For a while, every fucking family had one. Dodge made a fortune, y'know, with their Caravan."

"Yeah, I know. Still, hell of a coincidence."

"C'mon, it's not a coincidence until you know it was the same gray minivan. Did you get a look at the license?"

"No, how could I? It was behind me. Anyway, I didn't see a front license plate."

"What about other distinguishing marks? Dents? Missing fender? Broken headlight? Y'know, the kinda crap clues you get in lousy detective novels and movies."

"No, I didn't notice anything like that. Nothing distinctive."

"What about the driver ... the guy? I assume it was a guy you think was tailing you."

"I couldn't tell. I only got a quick look. Could be a guy. Could be a woman."

"Great! That narrows the odds."

"Yeah, well, it could have been either. Anyway, he or she was wearing a ball cap. And a hoodie."

"Any insignia on the cap? KU Jayhawk? Nike? Maybe one of those crazy nutjobs wearing a MAGA hat?"

"No, couldn't tell."

"Okay, if you're really being followed, who would it be? And why?"

"C'mon, that's obvious, isn't it? Who? Your husband or my wife. Why? You and me ... here."

"Un uh. My husband drives a big, honking, black F-150, not some gray, matronly minivan. It's not him. Anyway, I'd know if he suspected anything. We usually meet up here on Mondays or Saturdays. Those days he's too wrapped up watching football or KU basketball to care where I am, or if I'm even around."

Pause.

"What does your Betsy drive?"

"A Prius."

"There you go. It's not her or my husband."

"The minivan could be a rental to throw us off."

"Really? When was the last time you saw an old gray Dodge minivan on a Hertz or Avis lot?"

"No, not them. I was thinking of those rent-a-junker places in KC or Topeka."

"Yeah, it's possible. Farfetched, but possible."

"Or maybe one of them hired a detective to follow us."

"Nah, my husband is too cheap to do that."

"Betsy isn't."

"Maybe not, but I can't see a private eye running around in a gray minivan. Listen, I teach this stuff in my art history class. Think of the pulp novels, the noir movies. *Lady in the Lake*, a '46 Ford de Luxe. *Bullitt*, a '68 Ford Mustang. *Chinatown*, a '35 Ford Phaeton. *Dirty Harry,* a '68 Ford Galaxie 500. Christ, I'd believe you were being followed by a minivan if, at least, it was a fucking Ford minivan not a Dodge, y'know, like a Ford Windstar."

"Very funny. If I ever find out who it is I'll give them the *Vogue* issue on cars for gumshoes. But, I gotta say, I'm impressed. I didn't know about you and cars."

"Yeah, it was my father. He started on me when I was two years old. He got me a big blue toy dump truck. Not plastic. Metal. And one of those big green John Deere toy tractors. I still have them. Then came the cars—the 'wheels,' as he called them. Iron die-cast replicas of the classics. My friends were playing house with their dolls and here I was racing muscle cars up and down our long hallway. At one of my birthday parties, someone gave me a blonde Barbie all dolled out in pink. My father tossed it in the trash right after everyone left."

"What about that red VW beetle sitting on your desk? The one with the doors that open and close."

"Yeah, he gave me that, too. Y'know, I use all these cars in my contemporary art history class—how modernism evolved through the twentieth century. Cars were art on the street, parked or in motion—the curves, the colors, the fins, the grilles. It was the surrealism of allure, the abstract expressionism of sex in metal."

Pause.

"Listen, that friend of yours from Abilene, the one who was gonna find out how Lasher knew about us."

"Not us—me. What about her?"

"Did she get back to you?"

"No, uh uh. Forget it. It doesn't matter anymore. The fucker is dead."

"It might matter. He might have left something about it ... on his computer ... in one of his goddamn files."

"Yeah, I guess so."

"Christ! Call her ... what's her name."

"Ruby."

"Grab your cell and call her."

"Okay, okay."

Silence.

"Fuck, it's busy."

"Keep trying."

Pause

"Shit, still busy. I'll try again later. All she's got is a landline. Phone's probably off the hook."

12

Head Shot

Harry skidded to a stop behind the yellow police tape strung across the street. Three cruisers and an ambulance were parked in front of Ruby's house, their beater-bars slapping blues and reds across the wraparound porch. He'd called 9-1-1 from the road 45 minutes earlier and told them about a shooting in Abilene at a house on 5th Street, a Victorian job with three floors and a big porch just east of Eisenhower Park. No, he didn't know the address.

At the ambulance, two medics were shoving a stretcher into the back. Harry ducked under the yellow police tape and dashed over. All he could see was the sheet covering the body, that silent, sudden, symbol of death. At the last moment, before the medics shut the double doors, he caught a glimpse of blood and bandages. The sheet hadn't been pulled over her face.

He stood in the middle of the road and watched the ambulance wail down 5th Street and turn left at the next corner. The siren sliced through his head, a long shriek receding in the night. For an instant he was back in the desert war, his body in a trench, the air horn warning of incoming missiles.

The front door was open. Harry flashed his PI license to a couple of uniforms, jostled past them into the entryway, and stopped.

A technician, wearing gray latex gloves and white Tyvek booties and cap, was crouched beside the door, dusting the handle, then moved to the door frame. She squinted up at him, shook her head, and barked.

"OUT! NOW!"

Harry spotted Bob Blevins on his knees at the back of the entryway. He dug something out of the wood paneling, held it up to his eyes, then dropped it into a plastic evidence bag. Likely a squashed bullet.

He called over to Blevins. "Tell me she's still alive, Sheriff."

Blevins stood up, turned around, glowered at Harry, and walked over to him. "I wondered how long it would take you to get here, Przewalski. Yeah, she's alive. Barely. One slug missed. One didn't. Small caliber, 22 short, round nose, not hollow point. Probably from a mini revolver. Went clear through part of her head."

Harry grimaced. "Which part?"

"Don't know. Medics said it might've missed the vital regions."

"Did they say which vital regions? Brain stem? Temporal lobe?"

"No, we didn't have time for a goddamn anatomy lesson, Przewalski," Blevins growled.

"So, she was still breathing? Conscious?"

"Breathing, yeah. Conscious, no."

"Where'd they take her?"

"Memorial Hospital. About ten blocks away." Blevins pointed to the porch. "You're not supposed to be in here. Contamination."

Harry nodded. "Get me a pair of gloves and booties."

"Horse shit," Blevins snarled. "You know better, Przewalski. It's a crime scene. And it ain't yours. So scram. Go sit yourself down outside."

Harry heard the steady stream of monotone beeps coming from the hallway. "You can hang up that phone, Blevins. I'm the last person she talked to today."

"Yeah, smart ass, we know that. Actually, you were the second-to-last person. The shooter was the last person." He waved at the door. "Get outta here. And get your story ready. We wanna hear it."

On the porch, Harry parked himself in the lounge chair with the pink cushion. It was leaking stuffing along one seam. He remembered sitting here last June in the wet evening heat after they'd made love. He'd left Ruby sleeping upstairs on the white wrought-iron bed, come down to the porch, rolled a cigarette, and watched the moon smear yellow across the sky through heavy clumps of clouds.

Harry dug into his jacket pocket and pulled out the Zig-Zag papers and the pack of Drum. It was wrapped in a silver strait jacket of duct tape. A week ago, he'd decided on this cheap, blunt alternative to nicotine patches, nicotine nasal spray, nicotine chewing gum, and therapists. Ruby, he thought, would have made a wisecrack about it. He ripped off the tape, took out a Zig-Zag, rolled a cigarette, and lit it. Cheap and blunt had worked for a few days. The smoke curled up through the red-and-blue light of the police cruisers, the rhythmic beat of a Mark Rothko color field hitting the air.

Blevins stooped as he shuffled out the door. He peeled off his gloves and booties, walked over to one of cruisers, grabbed the radio, said something, got an answer, came back, and sat down beside Harry.

"She's still alive. I've asked for regular updates. They put her in a coma and opened her skull. Gives the brain room to swell."

Harry raised his eyebrows at him. "Can that hospital handle it?"

"I dunno, Przewalski," Blevins rasped. "I'm a cop, not a medical honcho. I want her to live as much as you do. Maybe more." He blinked at Harry, almost as a challenge. "She ever tell you I look out for her? At the truck stop diner? Around here? Truckers can be trouble. 'Specially for women like Ruby—smart, easy on the eyes. Sometimes we … we do dinner or drinks." Blevins looked away, then fiddled with the hearing aid in his right ear. Harry noticed a crimson blotch appear on his throat.

"Anyway," Blevins declared, "if Memorial can't handle it, we got helicopters and planes. They'll life-flight her to Denver or KC. We're not hicks here in Kansas, Przewalski."

"I know that," Harry said. He took a last drag on the cigarette, then buried the butt in the flowerpot beside the chair.

The police technician stepped out onto the porch and took off her gloves, booties, and cap. A thick, black, braided ponytail hung to below her shoulders. "I'm done," she announced to Blevins. "Not much in there. Clearest prints are on the phone. But—"

"Any on the doorbell?" Harry interrupted.

She narrowed her eyes at him, then checked with Blevins. He nodded.

"No. It's clean."

Blevins grunted. "Thanks, Tamara. Take one of the cruisers."

The radio crackled as she got in, turned off the beater, and eased down 5th Street.

"She's damn good," Blevins said. "Lucky to have her. Got her from Wichita seven months ago. Goddamn bigoted precinct. Don't like Blacks. 'Specially not Black women techs. Treated her like shit. Hit on her. Gave her crap work. She put in for a transfer. I grabbed her up. First time at the diner, she and Ruby hit it off. She was also an anthropology major. At KU. Go figure. Anyway, they hang out together."

Harry stood up. "Listen, I need to take a look around the place. There's a folder—"

"Forget it," Blevins snapped. "You're not lookin' anywhere. Not until we're done in there. And not until you tell me why we have a murder in this town every time you show up."

Harry shoved his hands into the front pockets of his jeans. "Attempted murder."

"Yeah, okay. We knew you called 9-1-1. Your cell phone. You can forget privacy. Congratulations. Why the hell are you here?"

"It's business. The guy who was murdered at KU, a couple of weeks ago. The archeologist. You know about that."

"Yeah, I know about that. What's his name ... Lasher. Duggan's fingered that kid for it. So?"

"It's the chancellor's kid. She called me and asked me to look into it—to get her son off."

Blevins raised his eyebrows. "So, you're gettin' mileage from the Fulbright business. How does Ruby come into this?"

"I don't know yet. There was a protest march in front of the building where Lasher got whacked. Duggan told me Ruby was there. I figured she knew Lasher from her time at KU in archeology. Turns out she's also helping the chancellor's kid in his research project, a projectile point found at a dig in 1895. He told me she's looked into it, has a folder of information for him. Just checking an angle."

Harry slipped a Zig-Zag paper from the blue packet, rolled

another Drum and leaned against the porch. He looked at Blevins and shrugged. "I said it was business. But it was also personal. I … I wanted to see her."

"Personal, huh?" Blevins frowned at him. "She told me you went missing after the Fulbright thing. Off the map. Never called her. She got looped one evening. Her birthday. We were out drinking. She let it slip. I could see it hurt."

Harry lit the cigarette. The pain in his face pulsed red and blue in the lights of Blevins' cruiser. "I know."

13

Rosebud

Harry drove the 4Runner from Ruby's house to the Holiday Inn on Old Highway 40 near North Buckeye Street. It shared a parking lot with the Abilene Truck Stop & Diner, a long, low building with aluminum siding and a bunch of gas pumps. The motel lobby smelled of chlorine from the indoor pool. The rug looked as if it were sprouting mold, speckling the pattern of yellow sunflowers. Motels, like species, were the epitome of stasis. It was likely that nothing had changed since last June, since Joyce Fulbright, Dean of the KU College of Liberal Arts and Sciences, had turned up dead in her room, strangled in her bed at five in the morning.

Harry got a room, showered, tried to sleep, but couldn't. He switched on the TV and flipped channels until he hit a black-and-white shot of Joseph Cotten talking to a character called Susan Alexander. *Citizen Kane*. Rosebud.

After nine minutes of noir smoke and Bernard Herrmann's dark fugues, Harry drifted off. He dreamt of pulling a red sled through the snow between rows of granite gravestones. Ruby was lying on the wooden slats. They were in the cemetery north of Strong City, where he'd first kissed her last year. He turned to kiss her again, then shrank back in horror when he saw the white sheet covering her body and face. He tried to pull it back, but it was stiff, unyielding, as if it was welded to the sled. Suddenly, an ambulance careened into the cemetery, its lights flashing, its siren blaring, gunning after him between the rows of graves. He tried to hold up his hands and yell at the driver, but his arms wouldn't move and the sounds stuck in his throat. He woke with a start, his body tensed, his mouth open, his throat dry. A blond newscaster was on the TV. The red numerals on the digital clock read 7:13, Wed., March 9.

He got up, stood in the shower long enough to drown the dream, called the police station, reached Tamara, and arranged to meet her at the diner next door. Outside, an inch of sticky snow had fallen overnight. He thought of Rosebud and shivered. Dreams, he believed, were the realm of demons, the mind lured across the border of the night into a cinematic madness, the reels of memory gone haywire, unspooling through a malevolent editing machine.

14

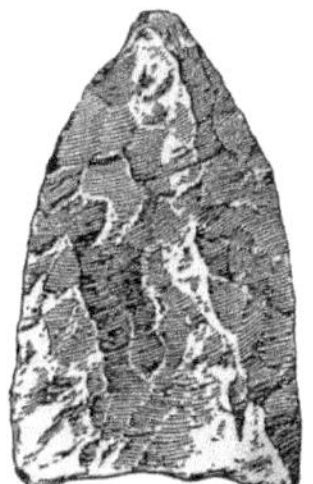

Two Rules About Eggs

Harry crossed the parking lot to the diner. For a disoriented second he looked for Ruby behind the counter. A year ago, on a sweltering evening in June, he'd walked in and noticed her—the hay-colored hair, the pink shirt, the pink clasp holding her ponytail. A trucker had reached across the counter to make a pass at her. She'd calmly pulled out a meat cleaver, smacked his hand away with the flat part of the blade, and told him: "I'm a Kansas farm girl raised along the Nebraska border not to take shit from anyone. Especially not you. Stick that hand out again, and it'll never touch a woman, a book, or whatever you got between your legs."

Tamara wasn't on any of the counter stools. Just truckers hunched over their plates, staring blankly at the food and the long miles ahead. About half the booths were occupied, mostly by families. Kids bounced up and down on the red Naugahyde. He spotted her in a booth at the far end of the diner.

"Okay, here's the update," she announced as he sat down opposite her, "Ruby's still in an induced coma. And they've life-flighted her to KC, to the KU Med Center."

"Good to know," he said. "I called the hospital this morning. All they told me was 'condition unchanged.'" He didn't tell Tamara that it had made him think of his mother, Emilia, in the care facility in Pittsburgh, condition unchanged, her mind silenced.

Tamara was in uniform: gray shirt, two pockets, black tie, and a black name tag that read "T. Halliday." A gray, peaked cap lay on the table. Her hair was woven into short box braids, pulled back and pinned up into a bun, the portrait of a severe, no-nonsense professional. The high nose, thin lips, and squarish chin helped. Only the eyes, large and round, hinted of a droll mirth. Harry imagined her braids released, hanging to her shoulders, a beaded persona waiting to be parted.

She shoved her police cap to the side of the table, folded her hands in front of her, and flashed him a quick smile. Game-show teeth, short nails, no wedding band, no evidence of there ever having been one. Harry guessed she was in her forties.

"Blevins tell you why I'm here?" Harry asked.

Tamara nodded. "He did, this morning. The Lasher murder."

"Right." He paused, then added, "also Ruby."

"That sorta didn't work out, did it." Her eyes told him it wasn't meant as a gibe, just a philosophical shrug on the contingencies of history.

"No, it didn't," he said, quietly. "Blevins told me that you and she hang out."

"Yeah, we talk, Ruby and me. We talk a lot." She raised her hands in feigned indignation. "Hey, it's Abilene. Two women. Educated. Smart. Solo. Not planning to get hitched. So we hang out."

A waitress wearing a blue smock and KC Chiefs cap came over, poured two cups of coffee, put the pot on the table, and plunked down a single menu in front of Harry. Her name tag was pinned on the cap over the Indian-head logo: Gloria. She looked at Tamara, somewhat mockingly.

"Yeah, I know what you want. The usual: fried potatoes, scrambled eggs, grits." Gloria turned to Harry and eyed him with the suspicious curiosity evoked by strangers. He smiled at her, asked for a double order of bacon, a big bowl of fruit, and some plain yogurt, and handed her the menu.

"Okay, mister, you get two out of three," Gloria stated. "No yogurt. Ain't on the menu." She shoved the order pad and pencil into her smock and left.

"Gloria is all right," Tamara said. "Just ornery in the morning." She paused, then grinned at him. "So, no eggs?"

Harry took a gulp of coffee and shook his head.

"Y'know, she talked about you. Ruby." Tamara continued.

"Cussed me out, no doubt."

"Yeah, some. But not about this ... about the first time you walked in here."

Harry gave her a quizzical look. "Tell me."

"You told her you had two rules about eggs: 'Don't eat 'em, don't fertilize 'em.' Gotta say, that's savvy. She thought so. It hit her where it counts." Tamara tapped her temple with her forefinger. "Anyway, I sure eat 'em. But I don't let anyone fertilize 'em." She pinned him with her eyes, a posted warning.

"Got it," Harry said. "About Ruby. Any idea who shot her? Some pissed off trucker she sent packing? A wannabe boyfriend?"

Tamara scowled. "No. None that that she ever said. And none that I got any gist of. But we're gonna ask around." She pointed toward the counter and the kitchen. "Everyone here. Her friends, the few she's got. Don't think there's any family. She never talked about 'em."

"No," Harry said. "Her mother's dead. Maybe her father too. Her older brother never came home from Vietnam, one of the last over there. Her hometown is North Branch, a couple of miles south of the Nebraska border."

"We'll check it out."

"Blevins said you and she were both at KU. Anthro majors."

"Yeah," Tamara said. "For me, add chemistry and philosophy to anthro. Triple major." She raised the left side of her mouth into a frown. "Fat lot of good that did me. Except maybe the chemistry." She fingered her police badge. "Anyway, Ruby was a couple of years ahead of me at KU. But we had the same profs, the same assholes."

"Lasher?"

"Didn't I just say, 'the same assholes'?"

15

Slime Trail

Gloria appeared with their food. She plunked the plates down, gave them a few seconds to register a complaint, and left. Harry looked at the pile of bacon and the few chunks of canned pineapple and tangerines swimming in syrup. The math was clear: farms around Abilene raised more pigs than fruit. He grabbed a strip of bacon and crunched it down.

"So," Harry said, "I keep hearing 'Lasher' and 'asshole' in the same sentence—from the chancellor, from her kid, Nalren, now from you."

Tamara raised her eyebrows. "Believe it. As they say, 'nothing with God is coincidence.' The Baptists drummed that into me. I don't cuss much. Ruby does enough for both of us. 'Asshole' is my limit—at least out loud. Lasher was an unreserved, arrogant asshole. I would bet it got him killed."

"I won't bet against it. You ever do field work with him?"

She speared a chunk of fried potato with her fork and jabbed it at Harry. "You have to be kidding. Go to Alaska with Lasher? For what? To get saliva, hair, and blood from the Aleuts? I knew his reputation. We all did. Students talk. Word gets around."

"Tell me more," Harry said.

She chuckled. "We had two nicknames for him. 'Herbert the pervert.' 'Lasher the flasher.' Kind of tells you everything. Word was he'd unzip and pull it out for anyone with two X chromosomes. In private, of course—deniability. So, no, no field work with Lasher. I stuck to archeological digs ... y'know ... pits, flint flakes, animal bones, hearths, pot sherds. Dead crap, as Ruby would say."

"What about his classes? Any incidents with women?"

Tamara downed a forkful of scrambled eggs, grabbed a napkin from the dispenser, and wiped her mouth.

"There was the usual talk. Grades for sex. I took his seminar in genetic anthropology. He approached me once. I convinced him he didn't want to mess with Black. Listen, it was bad enough that he took samples from us—oral swabs. He said it was for his comparative DNA database, y'know, to see how much our gene frequencies differed from those of the Aleuts and other native peoples. Course, he never asked our permission back then. It still pisses me off."

Harry finished off the bacon and fruit, put the bowl on the plate, and shoved them aside. "The sex for grades—did any of the women report him?"

Her eyes widened in astonishment. "Wait, you're a detective. And Ruby said you'd been to grad school. Pitt, right? Paleontology?"

"Yeah, back in the Pleistocene."

Her eyes narrowed from mirth to disapproval. "This isn't a joke. You know the score. Academia is a sanctuary for lechers—educated lechers. We women tried to steer clear of them. Still do. But you can't if he's your major advisor. Y'know, these students just want to get their degree and get out. So, no, they didn't report him. And the few who did, they paid for it."

Harry sat back and downed the rest of the coffee. It tasted like sheet metal. "Yeah. Like the guy in anthropology at KU, Max Dennison. He paid for it with his life. He was one of three students who—"

"I know," Tamara interrupted. "We read about it. He committed suicide after Lasher humiliated him in court. What a damn tragedy. But, still, I give the students credit, especially the women. At least they reported him. They've begun to wake up since my days there. They aren't standing for shit anymore." She smiled, wryly, and added, "Okay, add 'shit' to 'asshole.'"

Harry grinned, picked up the pot of coffee, waited for Tamara's okay, and refilled their cups. "This Dennison, he was married to a faculty member in the anthro department."

"You're well informed. Elena Montanares. We took classes from her, Ruby and me." She raised a quizzical eyebrow at Harry. "Wait, let me guess. You got her on your radar for offing Lasher?"

Harry looked at her, noncommittal. "Revenge is good at filling coffins."

"Don't we know it. She's a tough woman, Montanares. I wouldn't put it past her. Y'know what they say: 'Women do most delight in revenge.' That's one of the lines English 101 was good for. I can't remember who wrote it. Anyway, if a guy makes a pass at me, that's the first line they hear."

That was her second caution sign on the road to romance, Harry thought. The first was about fertilizing eggs. "Well, when it comes to revenge, men get the same fever in the blood. Oldest motive for murder."

Tamara shook her head and held up the palm of her hand. "Uh uh—the second oldest motive. Envy came first. Cain and Abel. The Baptists beat that into me too."

Harry silently graced his parents. They'd kept religion on the other side of the door. It had entered their home, but only through Emilia's art history, her folios of ecclesiastical paintings. She'd once showed him various renderings of the *Adoration of the Magi*. They were much more opulent than the simple, humble telling in the New Testament. Forget historical accuracy, she'd said. Art has always rewritten history to suit the version preferred by the artist or the patron. The *Adoration* had to embroider the narrative with the awe, grandeur, and reverence that would befit such a momentous religious event.

"One more thing," Harry said. "It's a long shot. According to Nalren, Ruby had been working with him on an archeological controversy, the Twelve Mile Creek projectile point. And Lasher was interested in it."

"Yeah," Tamara said, "she's met with Nalren a couple of times. She did a paper on the find as a grad student."

Harry nodded. "He mentioned Ruby had a file on it. Have you seen it?"

"Well, more than 'seen,'" Tamara stated. "Like I said, it's Abilene. It doesn't take much for two aging archeologists to pass time. Ruby and I looked at what Nalren uncovered. He thinks it could be a fraud. Maybe so. The evidence is tantalizing, but it's circumstantial."

"You know where Ruby keeps it? That file on Twelve Mile Creek?"

"Yeah, in her study ... on the second—" Tamara stopped, then grimaced, apologetically. "Sorry, no need for the geography lesson. You've been up there."

Harry felt the sudden ache of intimacy. He remembered Ruby's small alcove off the bedroom, the window that looked out on the back alley, the cupboard stashed with wine and candles, and the white, wrought-iron bed that groaned when they'd made love.

"What's the chance I can run up there to get the file?" Harry asked. "It's for the kid, Nalren."

"Really?" Tamara smirked. "For the kid? Get serious, Przewalski. Did I put enough Polish into that pronunciation?"

Harry grinned. "Seriously, Nalren told me that Ruby wanted to talk to Lasher about it ... Twelve Mile Creek ... the new material in the file."

"Yeah, she did." Tamara knitted her face into a look of skepticism. "But Lasher wasn't murdered over an archeological site. Sounds like you're getting desperate."

Harry shrugged. "Maybe. You know how it is. It's a trail, a slug's trail—short and slimy. Gotta follow it out."

"Be my guest." Tamara quipped. "In any case, Ruby took the file with her to KU last Thursday ... when she went to the IRN demonstration. She was going to show it to him, talk to him about the Twelve Mile Creek point."

"Did she get to see him? That's the day he got whacked."

Tamara shrugged. "Yeah, I know. Got me. She never said. I called her that night. She'd just gotten back from Lawrence. I asked her if she wanted a drink, to wind down. She begged off, said it was late, that Lasher had been a 'fucking asshole'—that's a quote. She sounded a bit strung out."

Tamara looked at her watch and reached for her police cap. "She was also going to meet up with some woman she knew at KU. Something about Lasher and an affair and sexual blackmail."

Harry leaned forward. "Oh yeah? What woman?"

"No idea. Ruby is still wired into that place. Not me. Ask her when ... uh ... when she comes to." Tamara paused, put her hands together into a prayer sign, then added, "We goddamn hope she comes to."

Tamara stood up, put a protective hand over the braided bun at the back of her head, slipped on the police cap, fished a twenty out of her wallet, and threw it on the table.

"That's the end of this interrogation. Call me when you find something. And careful on that slime trail. Easy to slip."

16

Road Cut

Harry walked across the parking lot from the diner to the 4Runner. Gray clouds hung thick and amorphous in a low, motionless sky. The snow was melting into small pools, victim of a light drizzle. He drove through town to Ruby's house on 5th Street, then circled down the back alley. There was a police cruiser by the curb, yellow tape across the front door, and more tape across the back porch. From the alley he'd spotted a white Tyvek suit moving across Ruby's bedroom window on the second floor. There was no chance to get upstairs and grab the Twelve Mile Creek file.

He headed back to Old Highway 40 and turned east toward Lawrence. The interstate would be faster. But he chose to avoid the onslaught of billboards. The scriptural ones advertised the route to heaven, the commercial ones to the next burger joint, as if both were tourist destinations.

There were no billboards on old U.S. 40. It was a narrow two-lane job, no shoulder, the tarmac cracked and patched in an artistic splatter of black tar that only road engineers would understand. A railroad track flanked the highway on the right, parallel enough to make Euclid proud. Beyond the tracks, over a low bank, the Smoky Hill River wound east in a series of lazy, S-shaped meanders. The older farms embodied the agrarian reality of rural Kansas, the barns larger than the homes.

On a rise at the outskirts of Chapman, a tall road cut interrupted the view of the even terrain. Harry slowed the 4Runner and eyed the thick, hard ledge of rust-brown rock exposed along the top. It was the wrong color for the Cottonwood Limestone, the dense gray blocks that had built the Douglas County Courthouse, where Duggan was likely sitting in his office, and Nalren lying on his cot in jail. Unless he'd been freed on bail at the court hearing yesterday.

A sign by the road cut read "Creswell Limestone, Permian Period." In the annals of deep time, Harry mused, the Permian lived in infamy. It ended in the Great Dying, a mass extinction 250 million years ago, when much of life on Earth vanished—ninety-five percent of plants and animals in the oceans, seventy percent on land. The event was cataclysmic, Nature callous, cruel, unmerciful, unsparing. Yet the explanation is cool, professional, text-book sober: it was just a change in the weather, a chain reaction that started in what is now Siberia. Massive volcanic eruptions. Tons of lava, CO2, and methane. A global hothouse. Air and water poisoned. Life gasping, choking, suffocating.

Harry hit the gas pedal and pushed the 4Runner to forty-five. Death, he thought, was the defining mark of history, whether geologic or human, whether the quieting was manifold or one simple murder.

17

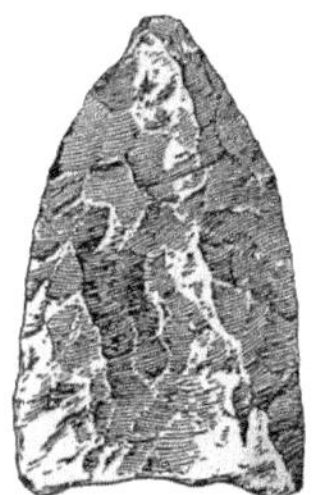

Seven Hundred & Fifty-one Bodies

Old U.S. 40 ended abruptly at a T intersection near Junction City, its tarmac and traffic devoured by Interstate 70. Five miles on, Harry passed the exit sign for Fort Riley. He'd done basic training there, seeking refuge in a desert war after Nicole's murder, adrift in a madness, unmoored from sense or purpose. He'd walked away from his life, from the ancient bone fields of Wyoming, from his graduate studies in paleontology at the Carnegie Museum. In the end, after eighteen months in the army, in the heat and the sand and the black stench of burning oil, he realized he'd just traded one madness for another. There had been no solace in the soldiering. But it had given him distance, a dose of fatalism, and a gun—a Beretta M9 semiautomatic.

Harry pulled off into the service area east of Topeka. He noticed a gray minivan switch lanes, roll in behind him, and park at one of the slots at the far end. A guy got out and dashed over to the bathrooms. A ball cap with some kind of insignia. Beneath it, hair shaved close along the sides and back. Black hoodie, black jeans.

Maybe not a guy. Maybe a woman. Couldn't tell. Either way, a full bladder.

Harry grabbed his cell phone and called Nalren to find out how the bond hearing had turned out. Eight rings, no answer, no voice mail. Harry punched in the number of Margaret Warden's mobile. She'd know whether her son was out on bail or still reading archeology journals in the slammer while awaiting trial.

"Harry. I'm between meetings." Warden was breathing heavily. He could hear street noise in the background, the belching of a diesel bus, and the quick click click click of Warden's heels on the sidewalk. He pictured her hurrying along Jayhawk Boulevard.

"Okay, what happened at the bond hearing?"

"Well," Warden panted, "I don't know what you said to Detective Duggan, but it worked. He must have spoken to the district attorney. She dropped the charges. She seemed angry ... what's her name ... Stella something."

"Boyle."

"That's it—Boyle," Warden said. "Anyway, Nalren was released from jail immediately. Boyle insisted that they were still investigating. She called Nalren 'a person of interest' and warned him not to leave the Lawrence area."

True to character, Harry thought, a bottle redhead trying to be Rita Hayworth in a noir film. "Yeah, well, that's courtroom speak for 'I don't have a case.'"

"I imagined as much," Warden stated. "But, Harry, this doesn't alter our contract. Except now the university is your client, not me. It's in the university's best interest for you to proceed with your investigation and find the perpetrator—Professor Lasher's murderer—as quickly as possible. I hope you will agree."

It only took him a few seconds. He didn't care about Lasher or who'd whacked him. But he cared about Ruby. And about who had put a bullet in her skull. Earlier he'd called the hospital 30 miles down the road in Kansas City. She was still in an induced coma.

"Yeah, I'll do it," Harry said. "But the university might not like what I dig up. There's a smell coming from its anthropology department. And it's not Tom Ford's Fucking Fabulous."

"Ah, never tried that one," Warden quipped, unperturbed. "Not at two hundred dollars an ounce. Listen, Harry, the whole university smells. Some of it smells of knowledge—the library; some of it of learning—the classrooms; and some of it of sweat and money—athletics. But the most pervasive smell is of intellectual dishonesty. I'll wager you that's the odor you'll detect behind Lasher's murder."

Harry grinned. "Okay. Is Nalren around? I tried to call him. He's probably out celebrating."

The clicking of Warden's heels on the concrete stopped. "No," she said, her voice suddenly disconsolate. "He's neither here nor celebrating. Surely. you've seen the news."

"No." He hadn't turned on the radio in the 4Runner. And last night at the Holiday Inn in Abilene he'd quickly flipped through a couple of channels before landing on Rosebud. "What happened?"

"It's horrific ... unspeakable. One of the Indian Residence Schools. They've found what they think are 751 bodies buried on the grounds. Mostly children. The graves are unmarked. They were detected with ground-penetrating radar."

Harry grimaced. "Is it Nalren's school?" He remembered the stark, black-and-white photograph on his MacBook: the gray, low-hanging sky; the long, bleak brick building with the L-shaped wings; the children in their hats, coats, and boots facing the camera, somber, unsmiling.

"Yes," Warden said. "It's Nalren's school. In Saskatchewan. He's gone up there. He flew to Regina yesterday. Some of his schoolmates might be in those graves. I told him I'd handle Boyle's directive not to leave the area."

"She won't be a problem," Harry said. "How old was Nalren when he left that school?"

He heard Warden sigh. "That's not a subject for now. The short answer is nine. He's reticent to talk about his time there ... just bits and pieces."

The archeology of memory, Harry thought, excavating shards—broken, sharp-edged, stained with evil.

"Have him call me when he returns."

"I will," she said, sounding impatient. "I have to go, Harry."

"One more thing. Professor Montanares. Can you text me her number?"

He heard Warden tapping on her mobile.

"Elena works mostly from home, ever since Max ... her husband

..." Warden let the sentence drift off. "Check your messages. I just sent you her home address and phone number." Then she added, "I'm a grammarian. I refuse to use 'text' as a verb," and hung up.

18

March Tryst Three

"Wow, another nooner, two days in a row!"

"Yeah, listen—"

"Y'know what else they call this? S. A. L. T. And that's not Strategic Arms Limitation Talks. It's Sex At Lunch Time. Also known as scrunching. Get it? Screwing and lunching."

"Yeah, I get it. Listen, I've got something serious to tell you."

"Uh oh. Coming from a guy, that's the six-word overture to being dumped."

"I'm serious."

"So am I. And the dumping usually comes after screwing. It's called scrumping."

"No, no, no. Let me tell you."

"Okay, but it better be good."

"It isn't. I know who's been following me."

"Oh yeah? You mean the character in that crappo Dodge minivan?"

"Yeah, him. Or her."

"What do you mean, 'him or her'?"

"I mean ... I can't tell. Listen, I went out to my Jeep in the lot beside Spooner. Out of nowhere there's a rap on the window. Someone on the passenger side ... black hoodie, sunglasses, a KC Royals ball cap. First I thought it was a guy. Then I wasn't sure. He made a yapping motion with his hand. I rolled down the window."

"You what? You rolled down the window! Because some guy made a yapping motion! Are you crazy? He could've had a gun! He could've robbed you. Or hijacked your Jeep. Or, hell, just shot you!"

"Yeah, yeah, yeah, I know. It was none of that. It's the guy who's been following me. Y'know, the guy in the Dodge Caravan. He wanted to give me a message."

"A message? Why is this guy accosting you in the parking lot to give you a message? What message?"

"That if I don't pay the hundred thousand I owe them, they'll break my arms."

Silence.

"I'm trying to stay calm. To whom do you owe a hundred thousand dollars? See, I was calm enough to get the fucking prepositional grammar right. But I'm gonna scream now. I SAID 'TO WHOM DO YOU OWE'— INSTEAD OF 'WHO DO YOU OWE A HUNDRED FUCKING THOUSAND DOLLARS TO?'"

"It's a loan shark place in KC."

"And why do you owe a hundred thousand dollars to a loan shark place in KC?"

"They're part of a gambling outfit. I've ... I've got ... uh ... a problem."

"No kidding. You gonna tell me what it is?"

"Yeah, it's gambling. I've never told you. Or anyone else. It's ... uh ... compulsive. Horses. Sports betting. Casinos. Slot machines."

Pause

"Christ. How long have you had this ... this gambling thing? And why the fuck didn't you tell me before? Isn't what we're doing here ... these motels ... enough gambling for you? It's our own fucking casino. We're gambling with our marriages, our jobs at the university, hell, our lives!"

"Yeah, but it's not the same. Listen, a while ago I actually went to see a psychiatrist about it ... my gambling. She told me it's an addiction. She gave me some literature to read. It's pathological. It's compulsive. Three million Americans are compulsive gamblers. I'm one of them."

"Okay, did she tell you what causes it?"

"Well, it's not the psych version of cracking nuclear fusion. It's problems. Deep-set problems. According to her, they can cause compulsive behavior."

"You have deep-set problems? I haven't seen any."

"Well, I'm good at hiding them. You name it, I got it. Worry. Anxiety. Pressure of the job, managing that academic asylum. Living with Betsy."

Pause.

"I should have noticed. I guess it's no wonder that I didn't. Christ, the only time I see you is here, at this dump, in bed. Maybe this is the only place you don't have problems."

"Pretty close."

"Did the shrink say how you can beat the gambling thing?"

"Yeah, lots of private sessions. Or GA, Gamblers Anonymous. Like AA."

"Does Betsy know about any of this? The gambling?"

"No. And that's one of the problems."

"What do you mean?"

"Money. For gambling. It's like drugs—you always need more, want more. I took out a second mortgage on the house. Betsy doesn't know. It's gone. They just let me run up the tab."

"A hundred-thousand-dollar tab?"

"Yeah, they said they knew I was good for it. That I could always get more. They're full of advice. Dip into the museum's endowment funds. Or sell off a few specimens from the museum collection. No one will miss them. Those pre-Columbian pots from Costa Rica ... they must be worth a fortune. Or a couple of leopard or tiger skins. Or a rhino horn. Or some elephant ivory."

"Don't even think about that. You'll end up making license plates in Leavenworth. And you'll still be into these bastards for a hundred grand. How about negotiating time payments?"

"I can try, but they charge interest. More than credit cards."

"Did this guy ... this he-or-she guy ... did he give you a deadline?"

"They want half by Friday."

"Fifty grand?"

"Yeah, fifty grand."

"By Friday? That's two fucking days from now! You have that kind of cash on hand?"

"No. Like I said, I already got a second mortgage."

Pause.

"Shit. I got some savings. I also got TIAA retirement, but there's a big penalty if you dip into that. What'll they do if you can't pay it Friday?"

"I told you. The guy said they'd break my arms ... for starters."

"What do you mean, 'for starters'?"

"You don't want to know."

"Dammit, of course I want to know."

"Well, after the arms, they'll break my legs. Then, y'know, what's between my legs. I don't have to spell it out. He was pretty graphic. Then ... then they'd come after you."

"ME! WHY ME?"

"The creep knows all about us. He threatened to tell Betsy if I don't pay up. Your George too. Or go after them for the hundred grand. He knows where we live, where we work, who we're married to, where we meet—this motel. Shit, he could be outside right now in that fucking minivan. Anyway, he's been following us everywhere."

"Y'know, now, considering, I'd be much happier if you would've dumped me."

"Very funny."

"It wasn't a joke. This he-she guy isn't a joke."

"No, he isn't. I had a crazy idea about him. Remember I told you about going over to Spooner to see Page last Thursday night, when Lasher was killed?"

"Yeah, I do."

"Remember I said I thought I heard a noise behind me when I was going up the stairs to Page's office?"

"Yeah."

"What if it was that fucking creep following me?"

19

Stonehenge

Elena Montanares lived in the country, south and east of Lawrence. Harry punched her address into the 4Runner's GPS and followed the rise and fall of the rural roads over the undulating terrain. In the pastures, the tall wisps of prairie grasses leaned toward the east, as if they'd been made to grow a-kilter by the west winds.

On the right side of the road, Harry passed a long stretch of barbed wire fence strung between wooden posts. Perched on top of each post was a large sandstone boulder, held there with baling wire. Whoever ranched here, Harry thought, this was their variation on Stonehenge. It wasn't circular or oval, or for threading the sun's first rays of winter solstice. It was the rancher's long running homage to the land, the thousands of rocks cleared from the fields, and the fence posts hewn, sawed, and augured into the ground. The rancher had wrapped his piece of earth with the labor of his hands. And he'd done so long before Christo wrapped the edges of landscapes and buildings in industrial fabrics and called it environmental art.

Lasher's killer, Harry thought, had gotten lucky. Timing. Opportunity. Just had to finish him off after Nalren had fled from the lab at 7:30 that night. A quick, hard blow to the skull with the ceramic ape while Lasher was lying unconscious on the floor in a pool of formalin and Native American DNA extract. No shortage of people with motive enough for murder: the IRN protesters—any one of them could have remained hidden in the lab. Or the graduate students who had joined Max Dennison, Montanares' husband, in reporting Lasher to KU for scientific misconduct, without success. And who was the woman Tamara had mentioned—sexual blackmail that somehow involved Ruby and Lasher? But it was Montanares who had the visceral vendetta for murder. Max had downed a bottle of pills after Lasher had humiliated him in court, testifying that Max had failed his graduate oral exam because he lacked the brains to get a degree in anthropology.

The Stonehenge fence ended abruptly at a double-wide gravel driveway. The rusted mailbox said 'Montanares/Dennison' in red cursive letters. A beat-up white RV trailer sat on one side of the driveway behind a beat-up green GMC half-ton pickup. A Tesla Model S sat parked beside the truck, gleaming red in the low rays of late afternoon sun. The front vanity plate spelled 'ANTHRO' in gold block letters. Beyond the driveway, in a grove of old cottonwoods, loomed a large, old clapboard house. Hitchcock could have filmed *Psycho* here, Harry thought: two stories and a tower, listing to the east, boards rotten, bits of cloth flapping in the broken window panes, porch sagging almost to the ground. All that was missing was the mummified skeleton of Norman Bates' mother in her rocking chair at the bedroom window. Harry had expected a grand house on manicured grounds that would befit Max's successful career in real estate.

Harry rapped on the metal door of the trailer.

"Enter." It was a brusque command.

Instinctively he stooped when he stepped in, then straightened up without hitting the ceiling. Elena Montanares looked up at him from her laptop, slid out from behind the small Formica table, and thrust out her right hand. No rings, long fingers, strong grip. She was wearing black: black slacks, black loafers, and a black turtleneck, the sleeves pulled up to above her elbows. It was warm in the trailer.

Harry guessed she was five-nine and in her late fifties, but she looked younger, her black hair pinned loosely behind her head, her skin a raw umber ochred earth, her forehead broad with faint worry lines. She looked at him, unsmiling, lips pursed. Her eyes would normally have been welcoming, large, round, chocolate brown. But now they bored into him, a current alternating between outrage and mourning.

"I'm Harry Przewalski. Thank you for seeing me on such short notice."

Montanares motioned him to the table, opened a small refrigerator, took out two cans of Jumex Guava Nectar, and handed him one. "It would be polite for me to say that it is nice to meet you, Mr. Przewalski—and it is. We in the anthropology department remember the Fulbright affair. Now you're here to find Lasher's killer."

"Right." Harry flipped open the pop-top and took a guzzle of guava. "I'm hoping you can help me."

Montanares frowned. "It would also be polite to say that I will. But, if you'll excuse my frankness, I really don't care about that."

"Okay, were you ..."

Montanares raised her palm. "I can anticipate what you came to ask. Was I there when Lasher was killed? Yes. In my office on the second floor of Spooner Hall."

Harry nodded. "Anyone see you?"

"No, not that I know. Now you're going to ask whether I killed Lasher. Let me answer it this way. The person who did may well have beaten me to the act. Did I think of killing him? Of course. And, whether or not you find the killer, I have already celebrated their good deed in having rid this place of an evil person, an evil presence." She spoke with a slight accent—every "r" sounding like a burr grinder.

She sat back, reached behind her head and tightened the clip holding her hair. "Do you still have questions for me, Mr. Przewalski? Interesting name, by the way. Did you know that there was a Przewalski's horse at the Topeka Zoo? He died in the '50s. His name was Rolf. If you'd like, I'll introduce you to him. His skeleton is in the osteology collection in Spooner, a few rooms from where Lasher was killed."

20

Archaic Real Estate

Harry smiled. "Thanks. I'll take you up on that. I've only met my namesake twice. First time was in a zoology textbook. The other time was at the back of a cave near Rouffignac, France—a painting on a ceiling trying to pass for prehistoric art."

Montanares twitched her eyebrows. Dark arcs danced up her forehead. "Hmmm, that's much like you, isn't it? A paleontologist trying to pass as a private eye. The Fulbright business made me look you up. Pittsburgh. Carnegie Museum. Eocene mammals. PhD candidate in vertebrate paleontology."

Harry shifted in his chair, jarred by her digging up his past. If he could, he'd bury it deep enough never to be excavated. "Yeah, well, it's like your osteology collection. Dead horse, old bones, a past life. Tell me about Max."

Montanares shook her head, picked up the can of guava, popped it open, took a sip, then started rotating it with her fingers. "Well, what's there to say? He died. He's paid the debt of nature, as they say. Life is a loan, not a gift. In this case, it was Lasher, the bastard, who called in Max's loan. But, he got his payback."

"You find solace in that?"

She leaned back, her face pensive. "My counselor asked me the same question. When I heard about his murder, there was a moment of euphoria, a sense of vengeful justice—a violent justice. But that quickly became hollow."

She quit fingering the can and pushed it away. "I'll tell you, time heals nothing. It just hardens the skin, thickens it, stiffens it. Like rigor mortis." She brushed her fingers over her left forearm. "So, no ... no solace."

Harry thought about Donald, the psychopath who had raped, murdered, and dismembered Nicole. He was locked away in a Pennsylvania insane asylum. No solace there either.

"Tell me, why did Max quit an established real estate business for archeology?"

Montanares grinned. "He said he wanted to do it before it was too late. Before he had to give in to hearing aids, false teeth, knee replacements, and incontinence. Of course, he'd made enough money that he could. He was good at real estate. He'd joke that archeology was basically about real estate—archaic real estate. He had a quick mind, sharper than many of my colleagues in the department. And Max had also accompanied me on my work in Peru and Chile. He was great in the field. So, I encouraged him to go to grad school."

Harry waved at the shabby insides of the trailer and the tumbledown house outside. "Okay, what explains this?"

Montanares frowned. "We had a great house in north Lawrence—new, modern, avant-garde. Max bought this place—that old hovel out there, this trailer, the junk heap in the back—as an investment, to develop something he'd wanted to do for years. It's twenty acres. He was going to turn this into a green community, build a mix of houses and lofts, each different, modern architecture, solar, with native plants, a park, and a playground. Oh, and charging stations for electric vehicles." She motioned to the window. "You saw the Tesla."

Harry nodded. "Couldn't miss it."

"Well, then he died ... killed himself ... in our bed." Her brown eyes clouded over into a turbulent sky turned black. "I stood there, rooted to the spot, motionless, like him. But the earth took no heed and continued its slow spin. Somehow, I expected it not to."

She looked away for a moment and shook her head. "Sorry. Anyway, there's nothing like suicide to mutilate one's home. The space is forever disfigured. I couldn't bear to be there. So it's for sale. And I moved out here. The trailer will do fine until that pile of clapboards out there falls down and I put something up." She stood and stared out window. "Damn thing is stubborn. Look at the damn thing. It wants to fall down. But just won't."

Harry hesitated. "Any reason you don't just knock it down?"

She laughed. "Yeah, Max was going to bring in a front-end loader. He said it would be a mercy killing. One good nudge and it would tumble to the ground. Like a pile of pick-up sticks. But I got him to hold off. Now ... now it doesn't matter anymore."

"What stopped you?"

Her breath began to fog the trailer window. "I don't know. Maybe it was being sentimental. Maybe it's the archeologist in me. We venerate the pieces of the past. We don't tear them down. It doesn't matter how much time has gnawed at their innards."

She pulled down the sleeve of her turtleneck, wiped the window and nodded at the old house. "We dig them up for their lessons, for their moral aesthetics."

Harry nodded. "There's a piece of Polish lore about houses that refuse to fall down and die. It's the stories they tell that keep them up—the voices from the past, the births, the deaths, the laughter, the music, the intimacies."

Montanares turned to him. "Yes. The creak of the floorboards when they danced ... the groan of the bed when they made love."

Harry saw a slight blush creep up her neck.

She turned back to the window. "I'll let it fall down when it's ready."

21

Stone Flakes

Harry pulled out the Drum and Zig-Zag papers from his jacket pocket. The guava and the conversation had made him desperate for a smoke.

"Do you mind?" He lifted his eyebrows at Montanares.

She smiled, cranked open the window, and held out her hand. "Roll me one, please. It's been a long time ... since my student days in Santiago. I'm out of practice. Domingo tobacco was the best. I don't think you can get it here. But after a while it killed your taste buds."

Harry rolled two cigarettes. Montanares lit hers, inhaled deeply, and immediately started coughing. She shot him a rueful grin, picked up the can, and drank some of the guava.

"I smoked till I met Max twenty years ago. He made me quit. But it still tastes good. You never lose it, that craving. It lurks in the background, more pleasurable in memory than in reality. Much like sin. Even the worst of sin."

She licked her lips, took another drag, and slowly let the smoke filter out of her mouth. "I'll tell you, there was a priest in our Santiago parish who confessed to abusing the altar boys. He knew it was sin. He said he'd feel its abomination after the act. But then, later, the memory of the pleasure kept luring him back to sin again."

She put an ashtray on the table, flicked off the ashes, and looked up at Harry. "In a sense, we are all seduced into being serial sinners. Take Lasher. I know it is a sin to celebrate his death, even silently. Yet every time I remember that he is no longer breathing, the satisfaction of it warms the bile in the gut."

Montanares downed the rest of the guava, crumpled the can, and smiled at Harry. "I don't know why I'm telling you all this. Maybe it's living out here. I don't get much company. Maybe it's because you'll be headed back to Pittsburgh once this opera is sung. There won't be anyone to make me face my words."

Harry reached for the ashtray to put out his smoke. "Does Miriam Kovitch have an aria here? Warden told me about her falling out with Lasher when he was chair."

She wrinkled her forehead. "Yeah, she's ... what can I say ... a sad soprano. She's a social anthropologist."

"Is her office in Spooner?"

Montanares nodded. "If you can call it that. More like a closet. Down the hall from me."

"Was she there that night?"

"I didn't see her. Maybe. There might have been a light down by her door. I told the police all this."

"Okay, anyone else who had it in for Lasher?"

"Well, while we're counting, you might as well toss in the archeologists in the department. Lasher derided their work. He would tell them that it was all in the genes—only the DNA could reveal which people first populated the Americas and where they came from. Not some crappy old pieces of worked stone."

"Like the Twelve Mile Creek projectile point? Nalren Warden's research?"

Montanares nodded. "I should have figured you'd know about that. I'm on his dissertation committee. Anyway, the genomic evidence appears to be overwhelming—peoples from Alaska to Tiera del Fuego came out of East Asia. Same conclusion from skull anatomy. The Clovis people got here at least 13,000 years ago. Most of the literature agrees that they probably hugged the unglaciated edges of land along the Bering Straits, tracking the animal herds.

They might have traveled by boat, following the ancient coastlines of the Americas as far south as modern-day Peru."

She paused, then her mouth curled into a sarcastic grin. "But you can't believe everything you read. I know. I wrote some of it."

Harry chuckled. "What do the archeologists say?"

"Hah," Montanares smirked. "They're, what shall I say, wriggling uncomfortably. As hard as they try, there's no good ancestral Clovis-like stone culture in Asia to fit this canon. So they feel their science has been shown up by us, the genomic anthropologists, that archeology is no longer relevant to the story. Lasher goaded them—in faculty meetings, in his lectures and seminars, on student committees. He even told the new provost to save money by restructuring the anthropology department—no archeologists. 'Dump the stone flakes,' he said. That's what he called them: 'stone flakes.'" She shrugged. "What can I say. Typical academic tribalism. Vicious. Infantile. Anthropology departments are among the worst."

Harry raised his eyebrows. "Vicious enough to kill?"

"No—" She stopped, pursed her lips, then raised her arms in skeptical disgust. "Well, who the hell knows? Look at your Fulbright business. Who would have thought that would have led to ... to murder."

She leaned back and drummed her fingers on the table. "Okay, you need to talk to Sam Page. When you do, ask him about his real first name."

"What is it?"

"I'll let him tell you, and how he got it. He's an Old-World archeologist, an expert on the Solutrean people, a culture that flourished in France and Spain around 17,000 years ago. He's an outlier. He thinks they came across the North Atlantic to America. He's also old guard. He has no patience for—how shall I put it—the nativist thing. He's vocal about it. He calls it performative theater, victimhood, identity politics. Lasher called him a racist stone flake. Which is ironic. Page is Black. But I guess it worked."

"How so?" Harry asked.

"Well, they had a fight at a faculty meeting. Almost came to blows. Rumor has it that Page attacked Lasher in his office last semester."

"Anything to do with that Twelve Mile Creek find?"

Her eyes opened wide, then she burst out laughing. “Really? Murdered over a 13,000-year-old archeological projectile point?”

Harry shrugged. “Like I told Nalren, check out our cemeteries—lots of people killed for less. Page apparently has a temper. So did Lasher. Page confronts him in his lab after the IRN protest, after everyone has left. Things get heated, out of hand. Where’s Page’s office?”

“In Spooner Hall. Two floors up from Lasher’s lab. He ... uh ... was there that evening.”

“You mean Page?”

“Yes.”

“How do you know?”

Montanares put her hands behind her head and smiled. “Remember, I was there too. My office is next to his. So, there you go, no shortage of suspects.”

22

They Came From Somewhere

Harry headed back to Lawrence on the local gravel roads. A gray metallic sky hung low to the horizon, threatening rain. Behind him, a dense cloud of dust trailed the 4Runner. Lasher, he thought, had gone out of his way to assemble enemies: Montanares, Kovitch, two grad students, and some woman Lasher might have been blackmailing. Sam Page just got added to the list. How many of them were in Spooner Hall the evening Lasher got whacked? Hell, even Ruby might have been in the building. She'd gone to the protest to meet with Lasher about the Twelve Mile Creek projectile point. Could she have whacked him? Harry pictured her, the raw grit behind the sultry face. Yeah, she could have, given good reason.

Harry slowed to a stop at a deserted intersection. At the corner, an iron fence bordered a small cemetery. He pulled over onto the shoulder, rolled a cigarette, got out of the truck, crossed the gravel road, and walked through the gate. Low, gray granite headstones jutted up from the earth through the straw-yellow grass. They were badly weathered, the names and dates as eroded as the souls beneath. A few of the gravestones bore faint Hebrew letters and a Star of David. A rusted sign on an iron post said the cemetery dated to 1858. German and Polish Jews had emigrated to Chicago, then travelled west to Kansas to a long knoll above a bend in the Kaw River a couple of miles north of here and helped found a new town, Eudora.

Near the southeast corner of the cemetery Harry spotted the piece of ground where the emigrants had brought the first coffin, taken the first shovel to sod, and held the first funeral. The small, tablet-shaped stone, half sunken in the ground, was still decipherable: "Isaac Cohn, born 1857, died September 5, 1858, one year old." Nearby were the graves of his mother, Sarah, and his father, Asher.

The first spatter of rain hit the ground as Harry got back in the 4Runner. It would settle the dust on the gravel route back to Lawrence. He thought of his mother, Emilia, in the nursing home in Pittsburgh, his father, Nicholas, visiting her, holding her hand, talking to a blank stare. Then he thought of the piece of ground waiting for her in the Homewood Cemetery.

By the time he pulled in to the lot beside Spooner Hall on Jayhawk Boulevard it was raining hard. The water sheened on the red-tiled roof before spilling into the brass gutters along the edge. Sam Page's office was on the second floor. Harry took the stairs two at a time but quit halfway up, breathing hard. It was time to duct-tape the pack of Drum, again.

Page's office was dark behind the single pane of glass. Tacked to the door was a large poster with a charred clay background and a drawing of two long, slender projectile points arranged vertically, side by side. One was labeled Clovis, the other Solutrean. Harry couldn't tell them apart. Then again, he wasn't an archeologist. Science was a cabalistic art, he thought—deciphering the culture of a people from stone spear points hafted more than 13,000 years ago. Or, as he had once done, deciphering the lives of extinct mammals that had died 50 million years ago from their petrified bits of jaws and teeth.

The poster announced:

Dr. Sam Page
Department of Anthropology
The Distinguished Professor Lecture
They Came From Somewhere:
The Peopling of the Americas
Alderson Auditorium, Kansas Memorial Union
Thursday, March 10, 3:30 pm

Someone had drawn a thick black line through the date with a magic marker, then scribbled below it "Wednesday, March 9." That was today. Harry checked his watch. Three-forty. He wondered whether Elena Montanares would be there. Odd that she hadn't mentioned Page's lecture.

He hurried down the stairs and crossed Jayhawk Boulevard, avoiding the puddles in front of the Memorial Union. He didn't see Montanares's red Tesla in the Spooner parking lot. Or her beat-up green pickup. She'd likely heard it all before. Or, after Max, whether the first Americans had come across the Pacific or Atlantic ocean had ceased to have meaning.

23

The Death Of Theory

Alderson Auditorium was standing-room only. It looked as if it had been recently refurbished and rebranded in KU colors: new blue rug, new crimson-cushioned seats, a huge screen, and a seven-foot Jayhawk stenciled on the back wall, staring back at the crowd. Only the doors were original: oak, double-wide, framed windows; antique brass knobs and hinges; deep scratches beneath the coats of varnish beating back time. One of the hinges groaned as Harry eased into the room.

Margaret Warden was at the podium, wrapping up her introduction of Sam Page.

"As all of you know, this Distinguished Professor lecture was originally scheduled for tomorrow, Thursday. But, also as you all know, tomorrow is the start of March Madness: KU is in the Big Dance, a number one seed. We will shimmy with six different partners and waltz them off the floor, one by one, until the Crimson and Blue are the last men standing."

The crowd roared. Harry watched Warden paint a big smile across her face while flaunting her crimson scarf and blue shirt with the Jayhawk patch over her left breast. She motioned to Page sitting in the front row.

"Dr. Page has graciously agreed to move his Distinguished Professor lecture from tomorrow to today so that we and the rest of Jayhawk Nation are not kept from the first game."

Theatrical satire, Harry thought, the kind that only an English professor turned chancellor could script, stage, and perform—athletics waltzing academics off the floor.

Page got up and sashayed up to the podium. That got him a standing ovation before he even started the lecture. He was tall and lanky, with a receding fuzz of white hair, and a sandpaper beard that looked as if he'd dipped his chin in a bowl of salt and pepper. His silver, wire-rimmed glasses accentuated his ebony skin. Harry pegged him at about 6'6". His tan suede jacket looked expensive and made to measure. He wore it unbuttoned. Page opened a folder on the podium, glanced at it, then held up his hand to the audience, acknowledging their applause.

"Thank you. Thank you very much. And thank you, Chancellor Warden, for your very kind introduction. However, there is one item you did not mention. I assure you it was not through oversight. It just isn't on my vitae. At Tennessee I was on the basketball team. A bench warmer. Coach put me in only when we were ahead by twenty points."

The crowd laughed. Page had the kind of deep, stentorian voice that, Harry thought, could reverberate across the auditorium without a microphone. If he hailed from Tennessee, he'd lost any vestige of a twang. His enunciation was surgical, his rhythm unrushed, as if he enjoyed loitering around each word.

"I am humbled by the turnout for this presentation. I did not get to play for a packed house in Tennessee. But now, here, I will. It helps when you tell enough students in enough classes that attendance at this lecture will get them extra credit."

Page held up the palm of his hand to quiet the laughter.

"We are here in the arena of ideas. So, ladies and gentlemen—people of all gender identities—it is time to be serious. Deadly serious. I mean that literally. The lesson of anthropology is the death of theory. That may shock you. Good. Let me put it more bluntly. From the very outset of anthropology in the late 1700s, anthropological theory was bullshit. Horrific racist bullshit as it turns out."

Harry heard a few gasps from the audience.

Page held up a hardcover book with green covers and orange lettering. "Listen to Immanuel Kant, the Enlightenment's heralded philosopher, and one of the fathers of anthropology. Listen to what he wrote in 1798 in this tome, *Anthropology From A Pragmatic Point Of View*."

He put on a pair of black reading glasses, turned to a marked page in the book, and boomed out Kant's words as if each sentence were a proclamation.

> Humanity exists in its greatest perfection in the white race
> The yellow [race] have a smaller amount of Talent.
> The Negroes stand far lower, and
> the lowest are the [Native] American peoples.

More gasps. Not surprising, Harry thought, having to square Kant, the moral philosopher, with Kant, the amoral racialist.

Page closed the book, took off his glasses, and slowly surveyed the room.

A man in the back row leaned over and murmured something to the woman beside him. He had short dark hair, a balding patch on the crown, and was wearing a tan corduroy sport jacket. Harry guessed they were faculty.

Page's voice rose. "So much then for anthropological theory. Picture a common illustration at the time of anthropology's tree of life. 'Caucasians, the white race', are at the top of the tree. On a lower branch sit the 'Mongolians, the yellow race', below them the 'Malayans, the brown race', and below them the 'Ethiopians, the black race'. On the lowest branch sit the 'Americans, the red race'. What determined their place on the tree? Their increasingly diminished mental, behavioral, and cultural development. At the base of the tree sits an ape, the chimpanzee. You might be quick to blame Charles Darwin for this. Don't. His *Descent of Man* wasn't published until 1871, three quarters of a century later. And to Darwin, all of life—and all *Homo sapiens*—were equally descended."

Darwin lost that battle, Harry thought, before the ink was dry on the page. Eugenics pushed the race ideas, politicians legislated them.

The auditorium had turned deadly quiet. Page looked out at the crowd, seemingly reveling in their uneasy stillness.

"From the outset, then, anthropology, the study of humankind, was nothing less than a full-blown theory of race and racial superiority. A person's skin color was the measure of their intellectual capacity. This became the paradigm, the canon of humanity's natural order. And this racial virus became our cultural pandemic. It spread and infected generation after generation through religion, science, art, literature, history, classroom education, newspapers, magazines, theater, film, television, world's fairs, zoos, and museums. It suffused society and our consciousness. It became systemic."

Page paused and looked over at Warden. She nodded, almost imperceptibly.

"Was Kant alone in this?" Page thundered, waving his hand at the audience. "No. Take Carolus Linnaeus, the father of taxonomy. Half a century earlier, in 1758, he classified all known species of plants and animals, including *Homo sapiens*. He called it *A General System Of Nature*. Here are his 'human varieties':

> Europaeus--white; gentle, wise, inventive, governed by laws.
> Asiaticus--tawny; haughty, covetous, governed by opinions.
> Africanus--black; crafty, sly, lazy, negligent, governed by caprice.
> Americanus--red; obstinate, governed by rites.

Page held up the book. "It was a taxonomy that Kant bought, embellished, and sold as the theory of anthropology. Again, then, so much for theory."

The man in the back row leaned over again, whispered something to the woman, got up, and strode out. As the doors closed, Harry noticed a slight figure slide out of an adjoining alcove into the hallway: ball cap, black hoodie.

Looked like the same guy who had gotten out of the gray minivan at the I-70 Topeka rest stop earlier that morning.

It also looked as if he was tailing the guy in the corduroy jacket.

24

Ball Cap & Hoodie

Harry slipped out of the auditorium and, nonchalantly, joined a group of students exiting the building. He hit the sidewalk just in time to see the guy in the corduroy jacket disappear through a set of double doors into the Natural History Museum up the street. Ball Cap lingered a bit, then punched the blue square handicap switch plate, waited for the doors to swing open, and went inside. He was scrawny and short, about five-six, maybe seven. Harry followed him into the museum.

A sign inside told him he was on the third floor. One arrow pointed straight ahead to a live insect exhibit called Bug Town. A second pointed left past the elevator to the Gallery of Paleontology. Harry went left.

There was no one immediately inside the hall. Instead, confronting him was the gigantic skeleton of a bony fish embedded in a slab of Kansas chalk: *Xiphactinus*, 17 feet long, huge skull, massive jaws, a denizen of the inland sea that covered the Great Plains 80 million years ago.

Harry scoured the rest of the gallery. Empty, and eerily quiet. No Ball Cap or the guy he was tailing. No families, no kids, no visitors. Just skeletons of extinct animals that had inhabited America millions of years before humans would arrive here. The rows of exhibits hit him like the short-course on life and death he used to give at the Carnegie. Forty-foot sea monsters, mosasaurs and plesiosaurs, lying on an ancient beach in Kansas. An enormous turtle emerging from the tide, water dripping from its thick bony shell. A pterodactyl overhead, riding the thermals, a long hollow sliver of a skull, a 26-foot wing membrane stretched over arm and finger bones. On the floodplain of a river in Montana, an adult and juvenile *T. rex* feeding on the carcass of a three-horned *Triceratops*. Then, the mammals—the first horses and tapirs and rhinos and tarsiers in a Wyoming hothouse jungle. A saber-toothed tiger trapped in a tar pit in California. A lone elephantine mammoth on an Ice Age sandbar in the middle of the Kaw River.

At the rear of the gallery, in an old mahogany and glass case, Harry found the earliest inkling that *Homo sapiens* had invaded the New World: the hulking skeleton of an extinct bison, a male with massive horns. Handel T. Martin had excavated it at Twelve Mile Creek in western Kansas in 1895. Under its right scapula he'd apparently found the projectile point that a Native American had hafted from a piece of quartz 13,000 years ago, fitted to the end of a spear, and plunged full force into the bison, bringing it down in a thundering cloud of dust. It was the first evidence, preserved in stone and bone, that a tool-making killer had trekked across thousands of miles of glaciated land and water during the Ice Age and conquered the Americas.

"Excuse me, sir."

Harry sprang back, startled out of his Pleistocene reverie. It was a young woman, hands on her hips, smiling, a museum attendant in a light blue t-shirt emblazoned with a mosasaur logo. The name tag read "LORI" in large capital letters.

"I'm sorry to interrupt your visit. We'll be closing in about ten minutes and turning the lights off in the galleries. Please make your way to the exit."

Harry looked at his watch. Ten to five. "Right. Will do. By the way, did you happen to see my friend back there?" He waved at the hallway. "A guy wearing a baseball cap and a black hoodie?"

She shook her head. "No. Sorry." She turned and disappeared around the corner of the bison case.

Harry grabbed his cell phone and snapped a few pictures of the bison from the side, front and back. Martin had mounted the skeleton in this spot in 1907. Harry wondered why there wasn't a projectile point exhibited against the right shoulder blade. The label, in its original wrought iron frame, said the bison was one of five in a small herd that was trapped in a storm under a rock shelter. In the background painting, angry, dark clouds roiled across the sky, hanging low over stark, snow-covered buttes.

Suddenly, a loud shuddering clunk—the lights turned off, the exhibit hall went black. A moment later Harry felt someone shove something hard into the small of his back. The barrel of a gun. A small gun. He straightened up.

"If you're carryin', doan bother to reach for it. Not if you doan wanna vennilate your innards"

It was a strange voice. Hillbilly accent. Not female, not male. Somehow neutered. And one that abhorred consonants. Whoever it belonged to was shorter than him. The voice seemed to come from about six inches below his ears.

"Nope, not carrying," Harry stated, calmly. "And I like my innards the way they are. Listen, I know I didn't leave the museum before closing time, but isn't this a bit much?"

The voice cackled. "Haw, haw. So yer a wise guy. Listen up, wise guy. Stay wise. That means, stay out of this business. That way you'll keep yer innards. And that fine lady at KU Med? She'll keep breathin'. Ruby, right?"

25

Caterpillar

Harry stiffened. Ruby? How the hell did she figure into this? Some two-bit thug with a weird voice and a gun warning him off the Lasher case. And here, at the museum.

"Now, wise guy, git down on yer knees. Easy now ... like yer gonna pray. Y'know how t'pray, doan ya?"

Harry knelt down and rested his palms on the smooth marble floor. The barrel of the gun moved to the back of his head.

"That's good. Doan worry, I ain't gonna whack ya. Well, mebbe jes a little."

Harry felt the butt of the gun smash against the side of his skull. It sounded like the shuddering clunk in the gallery when the lights had gone out. Then the light in his head went out.

When he came to, Harry felt his head doing a painful drum beat against the marble floor. So too his ribs, but in quarter time. He was lying on his left side, his back against the bison case, his knees and elbows tucked into his chest, like a fetus. The gallery was dark. His eyes picked up the faint red glow diffusing from the exit sign at the far end of the hallway. He tried to move but couldn't. He checked his legs—a large zip tie around his ankles. Another binding his wrists. He looked at his watch: 6:37. Ironic, he thought, here he'd been, lying on the floor, just like Lasher, conked out. Whoever had cuffed him with the gun had followed up with a couple of wicked kicks to the ribs. And kept their word—they hadn't killed him.

He extended his legs against the bison case and pushed himself away, then began rolling his body from side to side, each time with greater force, each time gasping from the stab of pain in his rib cage. On the fourth roll he managed to pitch himself up onto his knees and elbows. The movement triggered a jackhammering in his skull. On the floor, his fingers felt a wet spot. Blood.

His only option was to try and worm his body down the hallway. Slowly, he slid his elbows ahead on the smooth marble slate, then his knees, his back alternately arching up and down, gaining a foot at a time. A large caterpillar, he thought, that's what he was. It took him twenty minutes to reach the exit sign at the end of the gallery. He caterpillared up the two steps, past the elevator in the entryway, pulled himself up on his knees, hit the blue handicap switch plate with his bound hands, and inched forward through the doorway onto the wet concrete walk. It was raining. He slithered out to the sidewalk on Jayhawk Boulevard, raised his head, and checked the street. A few cars passed. Their headlights didn't pick him up. If they had, he'd look like a large, humped bag of trash waiting for the garbage truck.

He heard a pair of heels click on the pavement. A woman crossing the street toward him. His savior. She stopped a foot from his head. Dress jeans, red high-heeled pumps, four-inch spikes.

"Well, well, detective," she said, with a chuckle, "creating your own slime trail, I take it?"

He recognized the voice. "Hello, Tamara."

She knelt down, fished around in her bag, pulled out a pair of curved nail scissors, and cut the zip ties around his ankles and wrists. He felt her fingers on the side of his head.

"That's nasty, Harry. A bit of blood, still oozing."

As he got up, the street began to spin. Tamara grabbed him, propped his arm around her shoulder, and staggered him over to a bench outside the Union building. Harry pointed to the parking lot across the street, beside Spooner Hall.

"See a gray minivan anywhere?"

She gave him a puzzled look, then scanned the lot.

"Uh, uh, no minivan. A couple of SUVs, a few sedans, two KU jobs, your 4Runner, my beat-up Silverado. What's this about?" She looked at him, her forehead scrunched up. "On second thought, never mind. Your eyes are flipping on and off like a pinball machine. I'm taking you down to emergency." It was an order.

Harry shook his head, then regretted it. It made the jackhammer start up again. "Wait. Give me a minute. I'll be okay. Listen, you know Duggan, the chief here?"

"Yeah, I know him."

"Okay, call him. Tell him we need to meet him in his office downtown. He's probably got stuff there to patch me up."

"Alright, tough guy," Tamara snapped, "it's your head."

She helped Harry across the street and into her Silverado and called Duggan as she eased out of the lot onto Jayhawk Boulevard and turned down 11th Street to the courthouse on Massachusetts.

"Tell him," Harry muttered, "that it's about Lasher. And Ruby. And some punk he needs to know about. You and Blevins need to know about him too."

26

Manscaped

Detective Pat Duggan had a plastic box in his office with enough bandages, gauze, tape, and antiseptic lotions to open a pharmacy.

Tamara checked the tangle of blood and hair above Harry's right ear. "I can't do anything with that mess." She turned to Duggan. "You got a razor around here?"

He nodded, rifled through a bottom desk drawer, and handed it to Tamara.

"Really?" she laughed, rolling the razor over with her fingers. Then, slowly, sensually, she wrapped her hand around the sculpted black grip. "You know what this looks like, don't you? A damn dick! Hell, it's even molded to feel like one. And look what they called it: 'Manscaped.' Not too subtle."

Duggan shrugged, his face suddenly red.

Tamara snipped the mat of congealed blood from Harry's scalp, gingerly shaved the hair around the wound, and dressed it with cotton swabs and bandages.

"There," she declared. "Now you got a white turnip growing out of the side of your head."

Harry gave her a weak smile. "Thanks."

"Okay, Przewalski," Duggan said, impatiently, "enough with the niceties. It's nine o'clock. You rassled me outta my house. I oughta be there watching the Penguins lose to the Canadiens. You said you got stuff on Lasher's murder. It better be good. But you said nothing about getting bopped on the head. Or who managed to get the drop on the famous gumshoe from Pittsburgh. Or how you happened to get chauffeured here by the one cop I've tried to steal from Abilene."

He leaned forward in his chair, furrowed his black bushy eyebrows, and tossed Tamara and Harry a suspicious look. "Wait a second ... you two aren't—"

"No!" Tamara barked, leaping up from her chair. "We aren't! Get that Manscaped stuff off your brain. I don't know if I should be pissed or just bored." She gave Duggan her death stare. "Listen, I was here for Sam Page's lecture at KU. Once upon a time I was his student. So was Ruby. After the lecture I went up to his office in Spooner. We sat around, chewed over old times. He keeps a good bourbon in his desk—not a damn porno razor."

Duggan flapped his hand at her. "Okay, okay, whatever."

"Glad we got that straight," Tamara said, still glowering at Duggan, and sat back down. She was sporting a man's white shirt and a red silk scarf to go with the denims and high heels. No necklace, no earrings, no rings on her fingers. Just long coils of black hair hanging over the shirt collar to her shoulders.

"Anyway," she continued, "I leave Spooner. It's raining, I spot this guy lying on the sidewalk across the street. Maybe he's hurt. Or homeless. Turns out to be Przewalski. He's got a lump on his head. And he's trussed up like a Thanksgiving turkey. Except the cook used zip ties, not string. He tells me to call you. And here we are."

Duggan nodded at Harry. "Okay, your turn, Przewalski. Tell me a story."

"Yeah, well, it's pretty simple. I heard about Page this afternoon from Elena Montanares. She's a faculty—"

"I know who Montanares is. Her husband committed suicide a few months back. The real estate guy, Max Dennison. We looked at her for the Lasher thing."

"She also told me about Miriam Kovitch, she's—"

Duggan groaned. "Yeah, her. We know about Kovitch too. Sued

the university a year or so back over unequal pay, blamed Lasher. She's the comedienne in the courtroom. Just not stand-up. She crawled under her table in the middle of the trial. Didn't sway the judge. She lost."

Harry nodded. "Warden told me. Anyway, Kovitch's office is in Spooner. Montanares said she could have been there that night."

"Coulda, woulda, shoulda. Tell me something I don't know, Przewalski."

"Okay ... Sam Page. According to Montanares, he and Lasher weren't anthropological pals. They—"

"I'll say," Tamara broke in. "They hated each other's guts. Even back when Ruby and I were there."

"That fits," Harry continued. "Montanares said Page had gone after Lasher in that genomics lab before, made it into a boxing arena."

Duggan grimaced. "Ha, ha, very funny. Glad to see that thick Polish skull of yours protected the wise-ass part of your brain."

"No, just the old-fashioned part, the routine part, y'know, the part that keeps ringing up motive and opportunity. Any one of these jokers could have gone down to the lab that night, found Lasher out cold on the floor, picked up that ceramic ape, and made sure he stayed cold for good. What are the chances any of their fingerprints are on that ape?"

"Really?" Duggan exclaimed, exasperated. "You holding out for the Agatha Christie scene? They all put their hands on that damn statue, then, at the count of three, smashed Lasher's head? Or, they took turns, one after the other? Next you'll tell me who went first."

Tamara chuckled. "My money is on Kovitch."

Harry held up the palms of his hands "Hey, it's what Warden hired me to do. Just raising enough dust so that Boyle can't see herself charging Nalren again."

"Yeah, okay," Duggan sniped. "You gonna tell us about that bump on your head?"

Harry reached up and fingered the bandage. "After Montanares, I'm at Page's lecture in the Union. A guy a few rows over gets up after twenty minutes and walks out. Looked like faculty—y'know, the corduroy sport jacket uniform. No sooner he's out the door, then this other guy, skinny, in a ball cap and black hoodie, immediately falls in behind him. He's tailing him. This ball cap guy looked familiar. I thought I'd seen him this morning pull into the Topeka rest area on I-70 when I was heading back from Abilene. He got out of a gray minivan. I'm saying 'he' but I'm not sure. Could be a 'she.' Didn't get a good look. Anyway, I'm suspicious of coincidence. In our business, it's underrated."

Duggan leaned back in his chair until it squeaked. "Okay, go on."

"I follow them out of the Union. Corduroy man goes into Dyche Hall. Ball Cap waits, then follows. I look for them on the third floor, the exhibit gallery off the entrance. No one's there. I'm at the bison case at the back of the hall when—"

"Wait a second," Tamara turned to Harry. "That's the bison skeleton found with the spearpoint against the shoulder blade."

"Right," Harry said, "in 1895. Then the spearpoint disappeared. Nalren told me about it. More coincidence. Could be related to Lasher's murder."

"More crap!" Duggan exclaimed. "Could also be a fairy tale, Przewalski. I'm suspicious of fairy tales. They're overrated."

Harry grinned at him. "Anyway, the gallery goes dark—it's after closing time, the museum turned the lights off. Then it becomes a B movie. Someone sticks a gun in my back, warns me off the Lasher business if I want to keep Ruby breathing in the hospital."

"What?" Tamara exclaimed. "Who is this guy?"

"I don't know. Could be Ball Cap. I didn't get a look. The voice was strange, could have been a man's or a woman's. Kind of accent you hear in the Appalachians. West Virginia, Kentucky."

"Okay," Duggan sighed, "let's say it's this Ball Cap person."

Harry nodded. "He coldcocks me from behind. So he's right-handed." Harry touched the lump on the right side of his head. "Then he does the zip-tie job on me. I make it outside, and—"

"And," Tamara mocked, "we had our hot date in the rain on Jayhawk Boulevard." She curled her lips at Duggan. "Anyway, for what it's worth, the parking lot across the street? No gray minivan."

Duggan turned to Harry. "You get a license number at the Topeka rest stop this morning?"

Harry shook his head. "No. No reason to, then."

"Doesn't matter," Duggan muttered. "Cops can't go hunting a

gray minivan just because some joe in a ball cap followed another joe in a corduroy jacket into the KU museum. The law says I need more than that."

Tamara stood up, planted her hands on Duggan's desk, leaned over, and gave him a withering look. "Don't law me. Isn't that lump on his head enough? You really need more than that?"

Duggan stayed stone faced, his jaws clenched, his temples pulsing in and out.

Harry got up, walked over to the window overlooking South Park, cranked it open, pulled his Drum tobacco and Zig-Zag papers out of his jacket, rolled a cigarette, and lit it. The smoke curled out into the dark rain. He turned to Duggan.

"Well, here's more," he said, almost offhandedly. "You might want to talk to this ball cap guy about coincidence. Like the coincidence of him trying to put two slugs into Ruby's head."

27

Skivey

Duggan held his hands up in exasperation. "Well, stone the bloody crows. That pistol whipping knocked your cranium silly, Przewalski."

Tamara looked at Harry, her eyes burrowing into his face. "What do you know that we don't?"

Harry shrugged. "Ball Cap. He's skivey."

Duggan grunted. "Stick to English. You didn't pick that up in Pittsburgh."

"Yeah, Hill District. Street talk for 'shady.'"

Tamara grinned. "Ditto on Newark streets—my old haunt."

Harry squinted at Duggan. "Lemme walk you through it, backward. Start with tonight. This guy puts a gun in my back and warns me off the Lasher case. Why me? I could have been any joe wandering around the museum gallery. How does he know me? How does he also know Ruby, know she was shot, know she's lying in a coma at KU Med, and know it's tied to Lasher?"

"Yeah, yeah," Duggan sighed, "so you think it's Ball Cap because you followed him into the museum because he was tailing some guy in a corduroy jacket. Hell, the guy who whacked you coulda been Corduroy Jacket."

"Uh-uh, he was taller."

"Crap, proves nothing."

Harry held up his hand. "Back up to this morning. Ball Cap pulls into the Topeka Rest area off I-70 East. He's behind me. What's he doing there? Yeah, he could be on his way from Colby or Hays. My money's on Abilene. He's not just stopping for a whiz. He's tailing me. Why?"

"You got me," Duggan said, sarcastically. "If we're playing twenty questions, you got sixteen to go."

"No, just a couple more. I figure he tailed me from the Abilene truck stop diner. Tamara and I were there at breakfast. He was in one of the booths."

"Wait, lemme guess, you didn't see him," Duggan said.

"No."

Duggan turned to Tamara. "You see him?"

Tamara pursed her lips. "No. But who the hell knew then to be looking for a Ball Cap? Maybe Gloria served him. Y'know, the gal that waited on us, Harry? I'll check." She pulled out a notebook and scribbled in it.

Harry nodded. "Anyway, how does he know I'm in the diner? Probably followed me over from the Holiday Inn. Or saw the 4Runner parked there."

Duggan narrowed his eyes at him, skeptical. "Get to the punch line, Przewalski."

"The punch line is that he was at Ruby's house last night. He knocked on her door, she opened it, he shot her, then hung around the area like shooters do. Probably to see if she was dead. He saw me pull up and go in under the yellow tape."

Duggan raised his eyebrows. "Okay, lemme ask again. You see Ball Cap there?"

"No, you know I didn't. If I'd have seen him at Ruby's I wouldn't have played follow the leader into the museum this afternoon. He'd be downstairs here in cuffs, and you'd be jawing with him, not us."

Harry looked at Tamara. "The gray minivan. Any chance someone in Ruby's neighborhood spotted it last night, parked or moving?"

Tamara shook her head. "We can go back and ask." Another scribble in the notebook.

Duggan sat back and ran both hands through his hair. "Your skivey business is shit, Przewalski," he growled. "The shooter is supposed to be a guy who might not be a guy. He's supposed to be Mr. Ball Cap who might not be Mr. Ball Cap. He's supposed to have been at the diner in Abilene this morning but might not have been there. And he was supposed to have been in at Ruby's house last night, but maybe not. That's the kind of yarn we called 'grumplestiltskin' in Pittsburgh. I can't do anything with that. Your favorite assistant prosecutor, Ms. Doyle, would have my balls for bookends."

He waved his hand at Tamara. "Sorry, excuse the language."

"Whatever. Heard it before."

Duggan nodded. "But I'll tell you what I can do. When Tamara gets back to Abilene, she talks to her boss, Blevins. He knows you, Przewalski. She tells him about you getting knocked on the head and seeing pink elephants. If Blevins buys it, he can call me and ask me to pick up this Ball Cap in the gray minivan. That's just being police neighborly."

28

Satchel Paige

His left hand was numb. His right hand was grabbing the lump on the right side of his head. The red numerals on the clock in the hotel room blared at him that he was awake and alive: Thursday, 7:08 AM. Then he remembered his dream. He was at the Civic Arena in downtown Pittsburgh. Duggan was beside him, twenty rows up from the ice to the right of the net. He was waving his hotdog, screaming "shoot, shoot" as Sidney Crosby, the Penguins star forward, sped over the blue line with the puck and launched a 96-mile-an-hour slapshot at the Canadiens goalie. The puck deflected off a defenseman's stick and screamed over the eight-foot Plexiglass barrier. Harry stopped it with his right temple. He felt his left arm go numb, then noticed the yellow blob of mustard on Duggan's blue shirt, then woke.

The mirror in the bathroom told Harry that Tamara's bandage job had survived the night intact. It did resemble a white turnip emerging from a mess of brown hair. Last night she'd driven him back to the Spooner parking lot, waited till he retrieved his overnight duffle bag from the 4Runner, and then dropped him at his hotel, The Oread, a block away at the north end of Jawhawk Boulevard. He blamed the dream on Duggan, who'd given him a couple of Oxycodones. "That's for the ribs," Duggan had said. "Takes away the pain. Also, makes you sleep in technicolor."

The Oread Hotel fit architect Frank Gehry's caustic verdict: "98% of what gets built today is shit." It looked like a fake stone dungeon from a 1930s B flick. Its site, though, was historic, perched on Mount Oread, a hogback ridge above the Kaw River. A sign in the room recounted that on August 1, 1854, the first settlers arrived from Massachusetts, climbed the hill, ate their first meal, and named the ridge after the Oread Institute in Worcester.

White guy history, Harry thought, recalling Duggan's quip about Magellan discovering Tierra del Fuego. What the sign didn't say was that the Kaw and Shawnee natives had settled here hundreds of years earlier. Their distant ancestors, the Ice Age Clovis people, had spread across the Great Plains after first setting foot in the Americas 13,000 years earlier. Hell, Harry mused, there were even earlier emigrants to the area, but only a paleontologist would appreciate it. The hotel had been built from thousands of blocks of Oread Limestone. Preserved in them were fossil corals, starfish, trilobites, and bivalves, remnants of an ancient shallow sea from a time 300 million years ago when Lawrence and Kansas were south of the equator, courtesy of continental drift.

At nine o'clock, Harry walked the block and a half up Jayhawk Boulevard in a crowd of students toward Spooner Hall. The night's rain had yielded the sky to a hard, crisp blue. The low sun tossed their shadows off the sidewalk onto the street. There was no gray Dodge minivan in the Spooner lot. But there was a yellow ticket under the windshield wiper of the 4Runner. He went over and grabbed it. He'd give it to Warner. The chancellor of the university must have some pull with the parking department. He leaned against the hood, rolled a Drum, lit it, and thought about Ruby in the hospital, a bullet having lacerated the side of her brain, second day in a coma.

Harry climbed the stairs to Sam Page's office on the second floor of Spooner. The light was on, the door was ajar, and Louis Armstrong was rasping *Aunt Hagar's Blues:*

She said, "Oh, tain't no use to preachin'
Oh, tain't no use to teachin'
Each modulation of syncopation
Just tells my feet to dance and I can't refuse
When I hear the melody they call the blues

Harry rapped on the window and walked in. Sam Page was in a wooden rocker at a window that overlooked the parking lot. He was engrossed in a book: *Across Atlantic Ice: The Origin Of America's Clovis Culture.* On the cover, a finely sculpted, long, slender stone spear point was silhouetted against a pitch-black background that faded down to an ice blue.

Page whipped off his silver, wire-rimmed glasses, put the book down, turned off the CD player, and looked up at Harry. "Can I help you?"

"I hope so," Harry said, fished a card out of his wallet and handed it to Page. He studied it for a moment, then motioned Harry to an armchair on the other side of a small coffee table. Page's desk was at the other end of his office. It looked like a pulped forest, stacked high with journals and papers.

"Good name ... 'Przewalski.'" Page waved the card at Harry. "And now, of course, I remember you. The Fulbright business. And now you are back. The Lasher business. By the way, we have a skeleton of your namesake horse in our osteology collection downstairs."

"Yeah, I know. Rolf, from the Topeka Zoo. Professor Montanares told me. Sooner or later we all end up in an osteology collection. Neatly curated and boxed. We call them cemeteries."

Page laughed, a sonorous rumble. "Or archeological sites." He pointed at the bandaged lump on the side of Harry's head. "That must have hurt."

"A gift," Harry said. "From someone who doesn't want me in the Lasher business. Speaking of names, Montanares told me that there's a story about your name."

"Hmmm." Page raised his eyebrows, then shrugged. "Well, it can't compete with 'Przewalski.' I'm from Cleveland. My father was a big fan of the Indians. They brought up Satchel Paige from the Negro leagues in 1948. He was forty-two then, the oldest rookie in Major League Baseball."

"Yeah," Harry remarked, "but if he'd been white, he would have been pitching in the majors twenty-five years earlier."

Page nodded. "You got it. Anyway, he went 6 and 1 with a 2.48 ERA. He helped pitch Cleveland to the World Series that year and beat the Boston Braves. So, when I was born, with a last name of 'Page,' my parents tagged me with 'Satchel.' And I got raised on his aphorisms. 'Ain't no man can avoid being born average, but there ain't no man got to be common.' Those were good words for a black kid in the ghetto. When I graduated college my father told me, 'Remember what Satchel said: Work like you don't need the money; love like you've never been hurt; dance like nobody's watching.'"

It reminded Harry of his father, Nicholas, for whom the bike was the metaphor for life. If you brake, he'd say, you'll never win. He'd wanted to name his son "Eddy," not Harry, after Eddy Merckx, the champion Belgian bike racer. Nicholas had been his domestique in the pro peloton, leading him to wins on the jackhammer cobblestones of Paris-Roubaix, up the moonscape switchbacks of Mont Ventoux, and along the twisting coast roads of Milan-San Remo. But Emilia insisted on "Harry," from the Italian "Enrico," after her grandfather. They'd settled on "Harry Edward Przewalski." Harry wondered whether being called "Eddy" would have created a different persona.

Page sighed. "The irony, of course, is that 'Satchel' wasn't Paige's real name. It was 'Leroy Robert.' As a kid he'd hang around the railroad station in Mobile and earn tips by carrying the suitcases and satchels for the passengers. Hence, the nickname. Anyway, I use 'Sam.'"

The steam radiators in the office started clanging. Page scowled at them. "It's going to be too hot in here soon. You know, one of Satchel's famous quotes is: 'I believe in training by rising gently up and down from the bench.'" As if to demonstrate, Page slowly got his 6'-6' frame out of the rocking chair, took off his tan suede sport coat, hung it on the back of the chair, opened the window, sat back in the rocker, and grinned at Harry.

"Enough small talk, Mr. Przewalski, you didn't stop in here for a primer on Satchel Paige."

"No. Montanares tells me that the evening Lasher was killed—a week ago Thursday—you were here. So was she, in her office."

"Right. I've already told the police all I know, which won't be helpful. I didn't see anything or hear anything untoward."

"Anyone else up here besides you and Montanares?"

Page thought for a moment. "Yes, Miriam Kovitch, in her office down the hall. But I imagine you already knew that from Elena."

Harry nodded. "Anyone else roaming around?"

He shook his head. "Uh, uh." Then, abruptly, he raised his hand. "Wait ... now that I think about it, Beau was supposed to meet me that evening. Here, in my office."

"Who's Beau?"

Page seemed surprised by the question. "Beau Strickland. He's director of the Natural History Museum. In Dyche Hall, over there across the street." Page waved toward Jayhawk Boulevard. "I called him, asked him to come over. I wanted to talk to him about ... uh ... an enigmatic archeological specimen."

"Let me guess. The Twelve Mile Creek projectile point. Found by Handel Martin in 1895. Lodged against the shoulder blade of a bison he was excavating—the one on display on the third floor of the museum."

Page raised his eyebrows. "My, you're well informed."

"I've talked to Nalren Warden. I've seen the bison. Nalren tells me the projectile point disappeared sometime after 1895."

"Yeah, he's one of my grad students. Bright kid. He's dug up the history of that projectile point ... its discovery ... how it went missing. He thinks he's uncovered chicanery. These are the notions that detonate in the heart of a young person."

Page paused and curled his mouth into a Cheshire-like grin. "Maybe it didn't go missing."

29

Knuckleball

Harry pulled out his Drum tobacco and Zig-Zag papers, rolled a cigarette, and motioned to the open window. "Okay if I stand there and smoke?"

Page waved at him. "You can sit right there and smoke. And blow it my way. My father smoked. I'm still drawn to the aroma of burning tobacco." He reached behind him and handed Harry a blackened, clay vessel. It looked like an ancient oil lamp, with a narrow spout near the rim for the wick and a large pour hole in the center for the oil.

"Perfect ashtray," Page said. "It's from the souk in Tunis. They mold artifacts, fire them, and pawn them off as real to tourists. As replicas, they're not bad. Some even fool the experts for a bit. You paleontologists don't have to worry about a fake fossil, a bogus T. rex. It's tough to forge petrified bones."

"True," Harry said, lighting the cigarette. "But that didn't stop the bad hoaxes. Remember Piltdown Man?"

Page nodded. "Only too well. Parts of a human skull. Some

teeth. Lower jaw of an orangutan with the teeth filed down to look more human. Everything stained brown to look old. All planted in a gravel pit in Sussex in 1912 by someone who wanted Merrie Olde England to be the cradle of human evolution."

"Like I said," Harry declared, "a bad hoax. Still, it took forty-one years to expose it."

"Hah!" Page exclaimed. "That's because good con artists know the con. They told science what it wanted to hear, and they showed science what it wanted to see. Piltdown was anthropology's perfect ancestor—half ape, half human." He hesitated, then shot Harry that Cheshire grin again. "It's ironic that the Piltdown con fits the Twelve Mile Creek projectile point."

Harry squinted hard at Page. "Okay, how do you reckon that Twelve Mile Creek was a con?"

Page held up his hands. "Talk to Nalren. He's dug up its history ... sifted its dirt, so to speak. But I will say this. With both Piltdown and Twelve Mile Creek, their original artifacts—the bones, the projectile point—did a sudden appearing act ... then a sudden disappearing act. Each had its own magic ... and magician."

"Wait, you lost me," Harry said. "The Piltdown stuff—the fake skull bones, the teeth, the orangutan jaw—aren't missing. They're still in a collection drawer in the British Museum in London."

Page laughed. "So, they are. I studied archeology there. I got to see the original specimens, all the documents, all the correspondence. The con became obvious."

"You going to let me in on it?"

Page pushed back in his rocker. "I think it was Arthur Smith Woodward. He was head of paleontology at the British Museum. He plants the Piltdown material. Then he points an amateur geologist, Charles Dawson, to the site, who finds the specimens and takes them directly to the museum. Woodward publishes on the Piltdown find. Then, he locks the bones and teeth away in a collection cabinet—but not before he makes plaster copies of the originals. And that's the only material he allowed other scientists to examine—plaster casts that don't show the file marks on the teeth, or the brown staining of the bones. Bait and switch. An old con job."

Harry stubbed out the cigarette in the fake oil lamp. "I like it. Did you publish that?"

Page chuckled. "Are you kidding? Woodward was an icon. Still is. And I was a student. I wanted a career. Maybe now's the time. I still have all my notes."

"Okay," Harry said, "back to Twelve Mile Creek. Here's my wild pitch. That 13,000-year-old flaked piece of stone. It's somehow embedded in the Lasher case."

Page shot him an admiring look. "I think that pitch might have crossed the plate. Here's a tale you likely don't know. In 2006, the Natural History Museum across the street was renovating the fifth floor. Workmen found a large wooden crate stashed behind one of the exhibits. On the top was scrawled in red paint:

Archaeological Material.
Residue of OLD Collections.
Stone artifacts and pot sherds.
Provenience unknown.
To Dead Storage.
October 21, 1948
C. S. Smith

"Who is C. S. Smith?" Harry asked.

"Obvious question," Page declared. "Carlyle S. Smith was the archeologist here from the late 1940s through the early 1980s. During that time, archeology was housed on the fifth floor over there in Dyche Hall, the Natural History Museum." Page pointed out the window to the building across Jayhawk Boulevard.

"Yeah, I know it," Harry said. He resisted the impulse to touch the bandage on his head.

"Then," Page continued, "in 1979, the curators, collections, offices and labs moved here, to Spooner, as the new Museum of Anthropology."

Harry smiled. "So, everything made it across the street—except the crate."

"Right," Page stated. "Not until the workmen found it in 2006, twenty-seven years later. They brought it here to the main archeology office. It was summertime. The archeologists, including me, were in the field at different dig sites. But Lasher was here, working in his lab. It seems he might have been the first to see the crate, open it, and check its contents."

"Wait," Harry said, holding up his hand. "Why would Smith wall up those artifacts behind a museum exhibit?"

Page shrugged "Hell if I know. Old rumor has it that he and the director then, E. Raymond Hall, a mammalogist, hated one another. Two alphas going at it. Smith from Columbia, Hall from Berkeley. Both curmudgeons. You know curmudgeons—they all think they speak the truth. Smith wants more room to house the artifacts from his archeological research sites. Hall doesn't want anthropology in his natural history museum, taking up precious space meant for his collections of fossils, stuffed mammals and birds, and pickled reptiles, amphibians, and fish." Page paused to squint at him. "It's academia, Przewalski—just two more loose gongs in the steeple."

Harry laughed. "Okay, so Smith retaliates by burying a bunch of artifacts in a wooden crate, then buries the crate in a plaster wall behind an exhibit. One of the artifacts in that crate could be the missing Twelve Mile Creek projectile point. It's 1948. Twenty-seven years later Lasher gets his hands on the crate, opens it, sorts through the artifacts, and finds the point."

Page nodded. "Very plausible."

"Good. The day Lasher was killed, the IRN protesters emptied his ultracold freezers and destroyed his indigenous DNA samples. Everyone thinks it was to stop his genomic research into Native American origins. But what if that was just a knuckleball? They also ransacked his office. Why? Could they—someone—have been searching for the Twelve Mile Creek projectile point? Did someone know he had it? Or know that he had it stashed there?"

Page's eyes twinkled at him. "That's wickedly plausible."

Harry sat back, rolled another Drum, lit it, took a long drag, and let the smoke drift toward Page. "Here's what's wickedly plausible. Someone killed him for it."

30

Beanball

Page chuckled, reached behind him, and produced a corncob pipe with an acrylic bit the color of burnt ember. He pointed it at Harry.

"Here is the lesson I teach my students—things are always left behind. People die, but clues remain. It's the basis of archeology. Or your detective business. Things get left behind: 13,000 years ago at Twelve Mile Creek; or in 1948 in a wooden box stuffed into a wall in Dyche Hall; or a week ago in Lasher's lab in the basement here in Spooner."

Harry frowned. "Yeah, trouble is, the things you're left with are old bones and stones. I got Lasher's skull oozing blood on a lab floor." Harry paused. "Speaking of blood, people tell me you and he fought. Testy enough to draw blood."

"Hah!" Page grunted. "A couple of drops. A nosebleed. Nowhere near enough for murder."

He held up his corncob pipe. "I like the reaction this pipe gets. A Black man smoking a Missouri Meerschaum. I did smoke it once. Now I just hold it between the teeth. Helps me contemplate unexpected pitches—like that deliberate beanball you just threw at me. Yes, Lasher and I fought. No, I didn't kill him. He kept insinuating he had the Twelve Mile Creek projectile point. But he wouldn't show it to me. So, yes, one day in his lab we got ... what did you call it? ... 'testy.'"

"Did Lasher tell you how he came to have it?" Harry asked.

"No. He just kept tossing out teasers. It's why I asked Strickland to come to my office last Thursday evening. When KU shut down the Anthropology Museum in 2005, they transferred the responsibility for the archeology collections back to Natural History. Strickland's the director. So, the collection is under his domain. Including the Twelve Mile Creek projectile point—if it has indeed surfaced. It should be accessible to me and anyone else. So I asked Strickland to order Lasher to produce it."

"Assuming Lasher had it," Harry added.

"Right. The word in the department was that he did. In academia, gossip is more powerful than data. No discipline is immune."

Harry grinned. "Did Strickland agree to confront Lasher? Did he go down to his lab last Thursday after you spoke to him?"

"Bah!" Page exclaimed and ran his hand over his fuzz of white hair. "Strickland never showed. Or if he did, I missed him. I was down in the sub-basement in the collections. But I didn't really expect any action. He does what he is good at—pompous blathering."

"Meaning?"

Page smirked. "He comes from southern privilege. Alabama. The name 'Beauregard' says it all. He shortens it to 'Beau.' His family had a slave plantation before the Civil War. He's an anachronism. He still thinks his white skin is upper crust. He stays clear of the administrative trenches. A few weeks ago he told me that Lasher and I should fight it out as behooves distinguished scholars at a university—'in the intellectual boxing arena.' That's verbatim. Like I said, 'pompous blathering.' Remember Foghorn Leghorn? That's him."

Page, Harry thought, could skin a persona. "So, is Strickland a distinguished scholar?"

"That's using the term loosely. He's an ornithologist. Studies flightless birds. Mostly from the butt end of a rifle. Rumor has it that he's also having an affair. But that's standard issue for the university—every second man and woman are rumored to be having an affair."

Harry let that register. He remembered Tamara saying that Ruby was helping a woman being blackmailed over an affair. "What about Lasher? Was he distinguished?"

"I'll be kind," Page said, somewhat mirthful. "He was, to use the vernacular, a gene-jockey. And he rode that horse well."

Harry chuckled, took a drag from his cigarette, and began coughing. "Okay, why would the Twelve Mile Creek projectile point be so important to Lasher? It was probably a Clovis point, like hundreds of others found on the Plains."

"Maybe not." Page held up the book he'd been reading, *Across Atlantic Ice*. "What if it wasn't a Clovis point? What if it was more like this one?"

He put his finger on the long, slender stone spear point pictured on the cover. "A Solutrean point, like the ones produced by hunter-gatherers 17,000 years ago in what is now France and Spain."

Harry sat back in his chair. "Isn't that a stretch? Montanares did tell me you're one of the few who thinks the Solutreans might have made it to the Americas across the North Atlantic."

"She's right. 'Clovis first' from Asia has been orthodoxy for a long time ... archeology's River Styx—cross it and you're banished to the academic netherworld. You're branded a heretic ... or a lunatic. I crossed it. And I've been called both. But in the rush to conclusions, Przewalski, the devil has been excluded from the details."

"Okay, give me the devil's details," Harry said.

Page nodded, chewing the end of the corncob pipe. "A scallop trawler dug up a mastodon skeleton and a Solutrean-like point off the coast of Virginia. The mastodon, and by association, the point, date to 22,000 years ago. Other Solutrean-like points have surfaced at sites along the east coast of America, thousands of years older than classic Clovis. They're only called Clovis because of geography—they're found on this continent, not Europe. It's a circular reasoning that has long bedeviled archeology."

Page jabbed the end of the pipe at Harry. "Here, I think, might be the clincher. Nalren and I just finished an AI image analysis of projectile points—their shape, their topography. Some Clovis points are not distinguishable from some Solutrean points. It's not a surprise. Not if the Solutrean stone-flaking pattern is a seemingly perfect ancestor for the Clovis technology. Some Solutrean points even have a concave base—like Clovis ones ... like the Twelve Mile Creek point."

Harry pointed at the book cover. "How would the Solutreans have gotten here?"

"Easy," Page declared. "Along the edge of the North Atlantic pack ice, likely using small boats, as Inuits do today. Imagine this: what if the peopling of the Americas happened not once, but at least twice—at either end of the continent. Two landings by two different peoples: Natives from northeast Asia invading across the North Pacific, as seemingly indicated by genomics, including Lasher's work. And Solutreans, or their kin, invading across the North Atlantic, as seemingly suggested by archeology, spreading their technology westward."

Harry mashed the cigarette butt in the oil lamp. "So, if Lasher had the Twelve Mile Creek point, he kept it under wraps just in case it could be Solutrean."

"Exactly!" Page asserted, his voice rising. "His whole career was at stake. His every publication, his every professional lecture, his every public talk had long frozen his anthropological compass. He kept it pointed to a single geographic area, northeast Asia. And to a single migration event from there by the first Americans some 13,000 years ago."

Abruptly, a loud horn began blaring, a long, low, monotonous wail. For a second Harry thought it was a tugboat on the Monongahela outside his office in Pittsburgh plowing upriver. He looked at his watch. 9:20.

"End of class period," Page announced, standing up. "Not to mix a metaphor, but if Lasher had the Twelve Mile Creek point, and if it is Solutrean, I keep seeing it stabbing him in the backside, causing him immense discomfort."

"Not as much discomfort as the whack on the head someone gave him," Harry quipped.

Page nodded. "Right. But as I tell my students, science and art are subversive acts, subversive story-telling. They're the risky search for uncomfortable truth. The archeology of the first Americans isn't meant to be comfortable."

31

Next to God

Tamara was waiting for Harry in the parking lot, leaning nonchalantly against his rented 4Runner. She looked provocative without meaning to: black slacks, a black turtleneck, black high heels, a black leather bomber jacket, large mirror-black shades, and crimson red lipstick. She could be posing for a photo shoot, Harry thought, plugging the Toyota, the Amelia Earhart number, or a neon-lit mouth that warned a kiss would be devouring. If she was wearing earrings, they were behind her drape of black ringlets. She had two bags: A black leather wedge job, one strap over her shoulder; and a large, canvas tote bag sitting on the ground.

He'd gotten her text in Sam Page's office. "Ruby's awake. Meet you by your truck."

Harry punched the KU Medical Center into the 4Runner's navigation system. It directed him to Massachusetts Street, across the Kansas River bridge to North 2nd Street and the turnpike to Kansas City. Traffic was single lane, squeezed between two rows of orange cones for the first twelve miles. The highway department seemed to be repairing I-70 from the continental crust up. Massive front-end loaders were disemboweling the earth along the shoulder, fogging the sun in black diesel fumes.

"Okay," Tamara said, "Ruby—she gets to tell us who shot her. Maybe the Ball Cap guy you fingered. Maybe someone else."

"Speaking of Ball Cap, what about Blevins?" Harry asked. "Did he get Duggan to find him and pick him up?"

"Christ, Harry!" Tamara snapped. "We only hatched that last night in Duggan's office. And I've been here, not at the station in Abilene. Anyway, it's police time, like the tortoise. Slow and steady. You oughta know that."

Harry nodded. The I-70 work zone ended at the Tonganoxie interchange. He pushed the 4Runner to 80 and hit cruise control.

Tamara pointed to the canvas tote bag. "Also, I got us lunch. I hope you can drive and chew at the same time—and think. Tell me what you learned from Sam."

Harry grinned at her. "His Solutrean peopling of the Americas across the North Atlantic. It's turned his academic dance into a tango in a minefield. Lasher planted some of the mines."

"Well, you got the thinking part down," Tamara wisecracked. "Page has paid the price for bucking, y'know, the standard out-of-Asia story."

"Yeah, it's textbook stuff—the first Americans trekked here from northeast Asia over Beringia and Alaska through an ice-free corridor 13,000 years ago."

"I'm guessing Page told you it's archeology's line in the sand," she said. "Cross it and you're excommunicated. He was. They even accused him of being racist—go figure, he, a Black man."

"How does racism figure into it?"

"How? Fucking gaslighting, that's how," Tamara spat. "They say he just wants another white guy from Europe—a Solutrean this time—to have discovered America 16,000 years before 1492. Course, there was no Europe 16,000 years ago. And those Solutreans coulda been white, taupe, khaki or purple."

Tamara bent over, unzipped the black bag, and handed Harry an orange-red drink in a glass bottle and a large rolled-up tortilla filled with hummus and roasted vegetables.

"Anyway," she continued, "it's because of Page that archeology bit us in the ass ... Ruby and me. I still remember the first words of his first lecture: 'Science thrives on uncertainty. If you're looking for certainty, go to religion.' A couple of students walked out."

"Yeah, well, science also thrives on bullshit," Harry added, biting into the tortilla. "Dinosaur bullshit. Cave art bullshit. Did Ruby tell you about Rouffignac, the cave in France?" He remembered them standing in the pitch dark at the end of the long, cold tunnel, the guide's spotlight sweeping over the black silhouettes of bison, mammoths, horses, and deer on the ceiling and walls.

"Yeah, Ruby told me," Tamara said. "Clumsy drawings. Bad fake jobs. But French archeology blessed them as authentic prehistoric art. Just goes to show—science has bullshit, but the bullshit in art is deeper. Anyway, we both got our degrees. Fat lot of good it did us. Look at me—a police tech. And look at Ruby. Went back home to Abilene to sling hash at a truck diner. Y'know, it's like Mark Twain said: schooling just interfered with our education."

Harry nodded. He uncapped the bottle and guzzled down a few mouthfuls. Acrid, raw, bitter. His face curdled.

"It's Kombucha," Tamara said, somewhat testy. "Fermented tea. Yeah, it tastes like poison, but it's healthier than that fructose crap. I got us Blood Orange flavor. Figured that would fit the Lasher case."

She pulled a brown binder from her canvas bag and waved it at Harry. "The Lasher police file. Blevins got a copy from Duggan last week. He doesn't know that I brought it here. Or that I'm gonna tell you what's in it. So, detective, you've never seen this. It could be my job."

"Got it." Harry gave her an appreciative smile. "I owe you. And for picking me off the pavement last night."

"Well, I'd to it for any vagrant," Tamara quipped. She opened the police folder. "Here's the highlights. Lasher's body was found last Friday, March 4, around 6:30 in the morning by a lab tech, a graduate student, Jennifer Finch. He was lying face down on the floor beside his desk. There was a ceramic statue of an ape, a chimpanzee, lying beside him. Had Lasher's blood on it. Finch called the campus police. She says she didn't touch Lasher orC the ape. Two cops answered the call. The floor in his office and lab area was covered with broken glass, crushed glass tubes, and a slimy liquid."

"Yeah," Harry interrupted, "human DNA extracts swimming in buffer."

"Right. The IRN emptied the -20C freezers and refrigerators in the lab. Then they trashed the adjoining cryogenic room. They opened the -80C freezers and dumped out the tubes with frozen tissues."

"But only the freezers with the tissues Lasher had collected from Canadian, Alaskan, and Russian natives."

Tamara narrowed her eyes at him. "How do you come to know that?"

"Nalren told me. Is there anything in the file about the freezers' alarm system? They're typically hooked to one. It automatically sends a signal when the temperature gets too low."

She skimmed the papers in the folder. "No, nothing here on that."

"They must have quickly dumped the tissues and closed the lids to the freezers before the temperature dropped enough to trigger the alarm."

Tamara finished her rollup, drank some Kombucha, and wiped her mouth. "Forensics confirms that the ceramic ape was the murder weapon. It had Lasher's blood, hair, and bits of scalp on it. Also, Nalren's fingerprints and those of half of the rest of KU. Clearly, the killer didn't bother to wipe it off after whacking Lasher."

"Yeah, a hit-and-run job. Hurried. Nalren also said that Lasher's desk had been ransacked."

"Right. Someone made off with Lasher's computer—at least a MacBook and a backup drive. But they left the power charger. There's a closet behind his desk. Here's the inventory. Field equipment, a bottle of whiskey, half a case of beer. Oh, here we go, a stack of porno flicks—there's our Lasher the flasher. Also, a pair of hip waders. And a Ramada Inn towel stashed into one of the waders. It has a brown stain ... dried blood ... human."

Harry turned to her, puzzled. "His blood?"

"Don't know. Doesn't say. I checked into it. In December, a sanitation guy noticed it in a dumpster for cardboard. He took it to Duggan's people. They gave it to Lasher to test the blood. He identified it as human male, someone who probably cut himself shaving at the motel. Lasher kept the towel. I told Ruby. She gave me a queer look, said it gave her an idea."

"About what?"

"She didn't elaborate."

Harry frowned. "Okay, back to where Finch found Lasher's

body. You said it was near his desk."

Tamara rifled through the report. "Right. Beside the desk. Face down."

"Nalren told me that Lasher came into the lab, saw the mess, ran over to one of the -20C freezers, slipped on the wet floor, hit his head, and conked out—on his back, face up, not face down."

Tamara closed the folder. "If Nalren's telling the truth, Lasher came to, got up, went over to his desk, and was killed there by a late visitor."

"Otherwise," Harry said, "it's messy. Your late visitor sees Lasher is alive but out cold beside the freezer, pulls him across the floor to his desk, turns him over so he's face down, grabs the ceramic ape, and finishes the job on the back of his skull."

"Uh, uh," Tamara scowled, shaking her head. "That's way too much work. Much easier to just bop him right there, on the top of the head."

She slipped the folder into her bag and stared out the window at the rolling fields of brown stubble. They rode in silence until the soft-voiced woman that inhabited the 4Runner's navigation system told Harry to turn south off I-70 at the next exit, highway 169, toward the KU Medical Center.

She turned to Harry. "Listen," she said suddenly in a hoarse whisper. "We're both thinking this, so I might as well say it. What if there's brain damage ... y'know ... what if she's reduced to a goddamn vegetable. It would kill me."

Harry knew the ache in her voice. "Yeah, I know it." He thought of his mother, Emilia, in the care facility in Pittsburgh, her brain dying in a slow, measured, cruel leisure. He wondered if bullets would have been kinder.

"Anyway, shamus," Tamara said, her tone now caustic, "you missed your chance. You blew it with Ruby. She would've been a keeper. Course, you would've had to hang your PI shingle on her porch in Abilene, our two-horse town. She's one of the horses. The other one was Eisenhower when he was a kid. Now that horse is dead and preserved in a museum."

Tamara took off her shades and pointed them at Harry. "Did you know what the ancients thought about the ruby? It was a guardian stone! If you wore one, it would shield you from poison, from the plague."

Harry grimaced. "Too bad it's not a guardian against two bullets aimed at the head."

"Well," Tamara exclaimed, "it might be. One bullet missed. The other grazed the side of her brain. Let's hope it was the crappy side."

Harry knew too much about cranial anatomy to squeeze hope from a medieval myth. He hung a left turn on West 39th Street, a right on Cambridge, and pulled into the KU Medical Center parking lot. He tossed the sandwich wrapper, napkin, and empty Kombucha bottle into the back, swiped the crumbs from his lap, and swore at the hummus stain on his jeans.

"Jesus, Harry," Tamara exclaimed, pointing to the floor of the cab and behind the seats. "You've been here for two days and look at this truck. You got cigarette butts, tobacco, matches, duct tape, pop cans, paper cups, wrappers ... it's a fucking pigsty. If I didn't know different, I'd swear you were living out of this heap. Didn't your mother hammer into you that cleanliness is next to godliness? Mine did."

"Yeah, she did, but the last thing I want is to be next to God."

Tamara chuckled. "Wait, lemme guess—you'd rather you were God, right?"

32

The Last Thing I Remember

It took twenty minutes to navigate the maze of buildings and corridors to Ruby's room in the ICU on the third floor. Harry wondered why hospital architecture didn't abide anatomical order: a brain unit at the entrance, then successive wings for the heart, stomach, liver, urogenital system, muscles, and bones.

The room was dark and windowless. Ruby was on the bed, slightly propped up, hidden behind a tangle of tubes and wires, asleep. Her face was wan, the cheeks sunken, the lips bloodless. Her head was swathed in a white bandage, like an artfully wrapped turban. A bit of her dirty-blond hair protruded down the left side of her face. Her hospital gown, light gray and loose, rumpled across a stenciling of flowers. A catheter in her left arm was hooked to an intravenous bag hanging from an IV pole behind the bed. The only light came from a vital signs monitor, blue and red sine waves flowing across the screen, its steady beep beep beep tolling mind and body beneath the skin.

The sound seared through him, this metronome keeping death at bay. Two days ago, he'd seen her on the stretcher, the white sheet pulled up to her face, the medics hovering over her head, the ambulance pulling away from her house. But, until now, something in him had choked off the fright that she could die. She could still. And she would not know the ardor, that feared intoxication, he'd left unspoken.

A tall brunette in a teal uniform quietly came into the room. Harry glanced at her badge: "Melissa, Neurosurgical ICU." Square face, serious chin, stern mouth, wary eyes, short, thick eyebrows.

"Hi," Tamara said. "We're friends of Ruby. I was notified this morning that she's no longer in a coma. I'm with the Abilene police—where Ruby was shot." She pulled out her ID badge and flashed it at her. "We get the medical updates."

Melissa slid her eyes over to Harry and raised her eyebrows, dark crescent moons ascending a night sky.

"Private detective," Tamara said. "He's helping us find the shooter."

Wordlessly, Melissa walked past them to the monitor and checked the flashing numbers: blood pressure, temperature, pulse, oxygenation.

"How is she?" Tamara asked.

"She's doing fine, considering," Melissa said, businesslike, almost brusque. Harry liked her voice. If there were mezzo-altos, she'd be one—low, sonorous, assertive, imperturbable.

Melissa motioned them out of the room into the hallway and slid the door shut behind them. "She's lucky. Very lucky. Her wound was perforating—the bullet entered and exited. It didn't stay lodged in the brain. So, the trauma was less severe."

Lucky too, Harry thought, that the bullet was small caliber, a 22 short, round nose, not hollow point. It only grazed her brain at 1000 feet per second. In Iraq he'd seen what head shots from a nine-millimeter automatic or AKG assault rifle could do. Uncontrollable pressure, swelling, bleeding, death.

"Of course," Melissa continued, "there is some damage to the brain tissue."

Tamara twisted her mouth. "I'm almost afraid to ask. How much damage?"

"Like I said," Melissa repeated, "she got lucky. The bullet went up through the tip of the right frontal lobe." She ran her finger over the right corner of her forehead. "It exited the top of the skull. So, it didn't pass through any vital brain tissues or arteries."

Harry broke in. "It missed the parietal lobes? Temporal lobes? Brainstem?"

Melissa eyed him, momentarily nonplussed at his knowledge of anatomy. "Correct." She looked up at the white bandage on his head but said nothing. Too common a sight in hospitals for comment, Harry thought.

Tamara frowned at the two of them and shook her head. "Okay, what does all that mean in people terms ... y'know ... movement, speech, sensation, memory?"

"It's early," Melissa said. "But the preliminary tests are positive. Her senses are functioning—hearing, sight, touch, smell. We don't know yet about taste. Or memory. Or space perception."

"Movement? Can she walk?"

"Don't know. But as far as we can tell she has no physical impairments to her limbs or her back. We'll get her up and moving later today."

"Speech?" Harry asked.

"Yes, speech seems fine. But it's slow. It's halting." Melissa paused, then chortled. "Is she usually ... what can I say ... brassy? Y'know ... in your face?"

"What do you mean?" Tamara asked.

"We brought her out of the coma last evening. The doctor was repeating her name real loud. She looked up at him, then around the room, then slowly mouthed the words, 'Who the fuck are you?'—excuse the language, but that's verbatim. Like I said, 'in your face'".

Melissa looked at her watch. "Go in and visit. But don't stay long. She's still on pain meds, so she'll be in and out. Please keep the lights off. Less stimulation." She pointed down the hallway to the nurses' suite. "If you need me, I'll be there."

Ruby was awake when they stepped back into the room. She wiggled a few fingers at them. "Tamara. Good ... good to see you." The words came out in a low whisper, labored, each one a ponderous step. "Harry ... shoulda ... shoulda met on my porch."

"Yeah," Harry said, "I'd've rolled us a couple of smokes. A cheap peace offering."

She raised the corner of her mouth in a weak smile. Her eyelids sagged, straining to stay open. "What's that?" She motioned to the bandage on Harry's head.

He grinned at her. "Walked into a door."

Tamara reached over and took her hand. "How do you feel, kiddo?"

Ruby turned her head toward her and winced. "Okay. The bullet ... y'know ... sometimes I think it's still flying around in there ... like it's looking for a runway."

Her eyes drifted shut. A few moments later they struggled open.

"Sorry," she whispered, "I'm ... I'm crappy company. No gigglemug here. But ..." She stopped, swallowed hard, then began again, her voice a mixture of irony and relief. "But ... I guess ... I guess there's still enough brain left to make a Ruby."

Tamara turned her face to hide the tears streaming down her cheeks.

"So ... uh ... the shooter," Ruby said, looking up at Harry.

He gave Tamara a quick questioning glance. She blinked the go-ahead.

"Ruby," Harry said, slowly, "we want to ask you what you remember about—"

She held up her palm. "Yeah ... I know. I'll ... I'll tell you what I remember." The words were strained, labored, as if clawed out of a distant void.

"I was ... I was talking to you on the phone. I remember saying I might feed you to the horses. I remember the doorbell. I remember ... I put the phone down ... and walked over to the door. I remember seeing nothing through the curtain. Someone outside ... a shadow. I remember turning the knob ... pulling the door open. That's the last thing I remember."

33

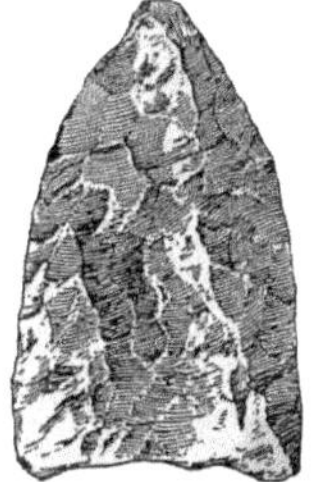

The British Baseball Bat

Harry and Tamara got back to Lawrence in the late afternoon. Before they'd left the hospital, she'd changed the dressing on his scalp with some gauze and tape she'd scrounged from Melissa.

"The bandage is smaller now. I can comb some of that long hair over it so no one sees it ... y'know the way old guys try to comb over their bald spots." She shot him a sarcastic smile.

Harry was tempted to give her a good-humored kiss, but knew that would get him another whack in the head. "My mother studied art history. Crazy things she came across. All the paintings of Julius Caesar wearing a wreath of laurels. Well, it wasn't so much Roman style as vanity. He was covering up as much of his baldness as he could. I'm not there yet."

"No, you're not. But bald can be sexy. Remember Yul Brynner ... Pharaoh ... in *The Ten Commandments*? Much sexier than Moses. Anyway, Caesar got Cleopatra. She must'a liked bald."

"She liked power. She also gave him a hair-growth potion to rub on his head: mice and horse teeth, ground up, mixed with bear grease."

Harry took the I-70 exit into North Lawrence. She told him to drop her at The Bourgeois Pig, a coffeehouse and bar on 9th Street, downtown. She was meeting a friend. He crossed the bridge over the Kaw River, ran a couple of yellows on New Hampshire Street, hung a right on 9th, and pulled up in front of a red brick building. It had a striped awning and a print of Jamie Wyeth's jumbo pig in the plate glass window. The pig wore lipstick.

Tamara pulled a thick brown accordion folder from her canvas tote bag and put it on the seat beside her. It was stuffed with papers, held in by two wide rubber bands.

"This is the Twelve Mile Creek stuff you asked about. From Ruby's house. It's Nalren's. Get a hold of him. Have him go over it with you. Blevins let me take it. I told him there might be something in there. Maybe a motive for Ruby getting shot. Who knows?"

"Thanks," Harry nodded. "I'll call him."

She grabbed her leather bag, opened the door, and stepped down on the sidewalk. As she crossed to the coffee shop, she had to deak a guy in a blue jogging suit who buzzed too close to her. For a second Harry thought it was Ball Cap. He was wearing one. Harry squealed away from the curb, and did a quick, hard right on Massachusetts Street, narrowly missing a woman on the crosswalk. The 4Runner's mirror almost clipped her chin. She hollered something after him. It started with an "F." He could fill in the rest. He scanned the sidewalk. The jogger was half way up the block on Massachusetts, weaving between shoppers. Harry caught up to him outside Sunflower Bike Shop, pulled the 4Runner alongside, rolled down the passenger window, and gave the horn a sharp blast. The jogger froze and looked around. Not Ball Cap. Too tall, too chunky. Wrong cap—Steelers black and yellow.

Nalren answered after four rings. They'd meet outside Spooner Hall. Harry took 8th Street to Indiana, hung a left, crossed Ninth, and crawled the 4Runner through the traffic to the KU campus and the Spooner lot. He expected he'd get another $100 ticket. It would join the one he'd fished from under the windshield wiper this morning.

He grabbed his package of Drum, leaned against the hood of the 4Runner, rolled a cigarette, and checked the lot. A few sedans. Three white KU pickup trucks, a silver Subaru Outback, a blue Jeep Cherokee. No gray Dodge minivan. The Jeep had a vanity plate: "BEAU-TIE." A good bet it was Beau Strickland's Jeep.

The low sun began splashing Spooner with a burnt yellow wash, turning the buff limestone blocks into a chameleon skin. The sign outside said it was built to be the university's first library. The architects had designed it as a basilica, perched at the rocky edge of Mount Oread to overlook the town and the river. It had once housed thousands of books, its tall, arched windows refracting the light of knowledge. A few of those books told a story about three ships and a discovery of the Americas. Now, Harry thought, Spooner housed a more ancient story. It was written in spearpoints, bones, and genomes, a saga of people who'd trekked to the Americas thousands of years earlier, before there were books.

Nalren rolled up on a road bike, an old steel Colnago, a 6-speed, with Campy cranks, brakes, and downtube shifters. He wondered where Nalren had picked it up. He also thought of his father, who'd want to refurbish it in his shop in Pittsburgh, make it perfect enough for Eddy Merckx to ride.

Nalren was wearing jeans, a duck-canvas jacket, and a hi-viz yellow wind vest. "That's new." He pointed to the bandage on Harry's head. "Who did that to you?"

"Yeah, fell out of bed. Y'know, strange hotels."

Nalren lifted an eyebrow. "Good detective. Shitty BS–er." He shrugged, lifted the bike, and slid the top tube onto his shoulder. "My office is downstairs. In the sub-basement."

Harry stubbed out the cigarette, and followed him down two flights of stairs, through a set of steel doors, then past rows of archeology specimen cabinets. Nalren's office was at the far end of the collection room. A large B&W photograph hung across the door: Native American men and women dressed in prison dungarees and jackets, bareheaded, stone-faced, ten crouching on one knee, nine standing behind them, posed in front of a long stucco building with dormers and windows, a guard off to the side. The sign above the photograph read:

ON THIS DAY, JANUARY 3, 1895, 19 MEMBERS OF THE HOPI TRIBE WERE IMPRISONED AT ALCATRAZ. WHY? THEY REFUSED TO ALLOW THE GOVERNMENT TO TAKE THEIR CHILDREN TO BOARDING SCHOOLS.

Nalren put the bike down and turned to Harry. "It's 1895. I find it ironic that six months later, Handel T. Martin found that projectile point against the shoulder blade of the bison at Twelve Mile Creek." Nalren paused. "Or claimed to."

His office door opened into a windowless, semi-circular alcove. Shelves with books and journals on the back wall. A 27-inch iMac on a metal desk amid a scatter of papers, note pads, pens. A lab bench along the curved wall with a Zeiss scope, artifacts in plastic trays, and a pair of calipers. A side table with an espresso machine, a bean grinder, an Illy canister, and a few espresso cups.

Something was hanging low, suspended from the ceiling. Harry had to duck under it. A blond polished piece of wood, long and flat at one end, a smooth round handle at the other.

"That's a British baseball bat," Nalren said, casually. "It's my only memento from the residential school in Saskatchewan. They used to beat us with it."

34

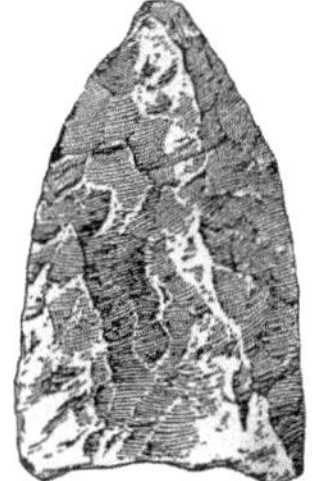

Each Hit Is A Body

Harry put the thick binder on Nalren's desk. "Twelve Mile Creek can wait. Tell me about Saskatchewan ... the residential school." He pulled out a stool from under the lab bench.

Nalren leaned his Colnago bike against the bookcase, walked over to the espresso machine, and hit a rocker button. A red light came on.

"Not much to tell. They tell me I was born at Fond de Lac. But they're not sure. It's on the eastern side of Lake Athabasca, way up in northern Saskatchewan, near the Northwest Territories. They took me when I was four or five. They dropped me off 500 miles south, in Punnichy, Saskatchewan, at the Gordon Residential School there, north of Regina. I don't remember the trip. I spent five years at Gordon. With the others. They shut it down in 1996."

He spoke in a monotone, his voice flat, detached, as if he were reciting an obituary. "I don't remember the village. I don't remember the lake. I don't remember my mother or my father. Or whether I had brothers or sisters."

He pointed to the espresso machine. "You want a coffee?"

Harry nodded. His last brew was two mornings ago in his south side Pittsburgh walkup, up the hill from West Carson Street. He'd watched the Bodum Vacuum do its volcano act, poured himself a cup, gone out on the landing, lit a Drum, and looked at the defunct steel mill eroding to dust below on the banks of the Monongahela River. The color of the coffee matched the rusted metal. He'd chucked it, grabbed his bag, tossed it into his yellow Corolla hatchback, and drove to the airport for the flight to Kansas City.

Nalren grabbed some beans from the Illy canister, weighed them, and tossed them into the grinder. The high-pitched whir lasted for ten seconds. He worked like a skilled barista: dosed the grounds into the portafilter basket, leveled, tamped, locked it into the group head, and hit the brew button for 30 seconds. He divided the double shot into two small cups and handed one to Harry.

"Nice," Harry said. "Tastes like cocoa and brown sugar. Where'd you learn to do that?"

"My adopted mother, the second one."

"What do you mean?"

"When the school closed, a couple in Regina adopted me. Dorothy and Walter Hoffman. Good people. They were childless. I was nine or ten."

Nalren took a sip of his coffee. "They were killed that winter, less than a year later. Car slid off the road in a blizzard, hit a telephone pole. I saw them go through the windshield. I was in the back. They'd buckled me in."

"Sorry," Harry said, quietly.

Nalren shrugged. "Like they say, it is what it is. Dorothy's maiden name was Warden. Her younger sister took me in. Margaret. She's my second adopted mother. She took me to Fairbanks, then Anchorage, then here when she became the chancellor. I got to hang around archeology labs at three universities. It stuck."

"The reports ... of 751 graves."

"Yeah, that's three times more than what they found at the Kamloops Residential School in British Columbia last month. They're using ground-penetrating radar. First they only checked the Gordon school grounds. But the elders kept telling them that bodies had been buried further out. They've now scanned about eleven acres around the school. The radar technology has a 10-15 percent error rate. That means at least 600 kids buried out there. No mass graves. Each hit is a body."

"Is there any documentation?"

"Not much. Some had headstones. But a priest in the 60s got pissed off at one of the elders, took a bulldozer, knocked down the gravestones, and hired people to haul them away. When a kid died at Gordon, the family usually was told they'd run away or disappeared. Bodies weren't shipped back to the village. Distances were too long, transportation costs too high. So, the dead kids were sent back only when it was cheaper than burying them on the school grounds."

Harry grimaced. "Your mother told me there's a Canadian commission investigating the residential schools."

"Yeah. They were out there, holding hearings, taking evidence. They think as many as ten thousand died at all the schools. Disease, malnutrition, beatings, suicide. Some kids tried to escape. A few made it. Most didn't. There was a boy at Gordon who took off during an outing near a lake. It was winter. He never turned up, either at home, or elsewhere, or dead. We think he froze."

He shrugged. "At Gordon they taught who Sir John A. MacDonald was, the first prime minister of Canada. They didn't teach us that he'd started the residential schools. Or that he'd ordered agents to starve the Indians into submission."

Nalren pointed to the wooden bat hanging from the ceiling. "Anyway, it's not just the bodies. It's also the minds. They'd beat us at Gordon if we spoke our language. Or if we sang the songs we remembered being sung to us. When I was up there last week, I spoke to one of the elders. He's a witness, giving testimony to the commission, reliving his memories, his stories. The Gordon school had taught him a lesson, he said. There's never been a time in human history when the world has not lived in horrendous evil."

He turned to the espresso machine, pulled two more shots, and gave one to Harry.

"The elder told them about William Starr, the Gordon school administrator from the 60s into the 80s. Starr raped the boys every day for twenty years. Openly. He'd done it before at schools in Alberta and New Brunswick. The church just relocated him from place to place, then to Gordon. He described being called to Starr's office in the evening, just before bedtime, ostensibly to watch TV. Starr pushed him onto the couch, pulled his pajama bottoms down, and began to rape him, shoving a rag in his mouth to stifle the screams of pain. He bled for a week and could barely walk. Years later, he said, he finally overcame the shame and told his mother. She'd been to a different residential school. He said she'd held him tight, then whispered that she too had been raped again and again by the priests at her school. She was lucky, she said. She did not conceive. But the priests fathered many infants with the other girls. Some of the girls committed suicide. Some died in childbirth. The babies that were born were taken away, killed, then thrown into furnaces."

Nalren shook his head. "People now find this shocking ... unbelievable. We don't. We've always known. The residential schools thought they could bury history. But everything that's buried is eventually dug up. Page drummed that into us. Whether it's ten bison and a projectile point at Twelve Mile Creek. Or the 751 graves at Gordon school. The ground is soaked with native blood."

35

Now A Secret

Harry motioned to the Twelve Mile Creek binder on Nalren's desk. "Your major prof, Page. He says that Lasher was obsessed with that projectile point. Tell me there's something in that file that might finger Lasher's killer?" And Ruby's shooter, Harry thought.

Nalren shook his head, skeptical. "I don't know. Murdered over an arrowhead?"

"Suppose Lasher had the projectile point? Suppose someone wanted it bad enough to kill him?"

Nalren raised his hands. "That would be crazy. It's a fraud! The arrowhead was a plant."

"Wait. The guy who found it, Handel T. Martin, was a paleontologist collecting for the KU museum. You're saying he salted the site?"

"Absolutely!" Nalren turned to the binder, pulled out a bunch of papers, and held it up. "Here's the evidence. It's circumstantial. But it's evidence. And there's enough to convict."

Harry nodded. "Circumstantial works. Show me."

"Okay. There are three big lies. Lie number one occurs at Twelve Mile Creek that summer day in 1895—no one witnessed Martin find the projectile point."

"Didn't he have an assistant at the dig site?"

"Yes. His name was Thomas Overton."

"So he must have seen it."

"No, he didn't!" Nalren declared. He handed Harry a newspaper article, *Kansas City Star*, August 30, 1902. "Here's Martin's own words, recounting the moment of discovery."

> One day about noon and after Overton had gone to dinner, on raising carefully the shoulder blade of a large bull bison, I found a perfectly shaped arrow-head embedded in the clay and pressing into the bone.

"So," Nalren continued, "Overton was away when Martin found the point. Overton never saw it in situ."

Harry frowned. "You think Martin took a flint arrowhead from his pocket, planted it, and exclaimed 'eureka'!"

"Right."

"But it could be legit," Harry countered. "Witness or no witness, Martin could have found it the way he said he did."

Nalren shook his head. "Except for big lie number two. The projectile point disappears—and Martin covers that up for thirty years. Thirty years! Until he gets a letter on September 11, 1925. It's from Barnum Brown at the American Museum of Natural History, in New York."

"Mr. *T. rex* himself," Harry quipped.

"Right. Brown says he'd come through the KU Museum a few weeks earlier. Martin was out of town. Brown went down to the third floor, to the Twelve Mile Creek bison on display. He sees the projectile point hanging against the right shoulder blade. He's astonished! He writes that Martin it's 'the spitting image' of Clovis arrow heads being uncovered in New Mexico. He asks Martin to send him the point or a cast for comparison as soon as possible. Here's what Martin tells him."

> September 14, 1925
>
> My Dear Mr. Brown. About the arrow point. Now a secret! The one you saw while I was away was not the original. It was Stolen at a science club lecture at Dr. Wil-

> liston's house here years ago by a woman who was crazy for old relics. He passed around a tray with some of the bison bones and the arrow point. When the talk was done it was gone. Sellards was at the meeting. We talked it over several times. He told me of a woman who he felt sure SNITCHED it for her own collection. Her name was Apitz, Mary Apitz. She was always at the science meetings. Now, I expect you will think this is a drawn out rigmarole but this is the only way I could tell you the facts. I had to place an arrow point of some sort closely resembling the original in the case with the bison skeleton. It is for the public to look at, not to gull any scientist.'

Nalren grinned at Harry. "Lies, lies, lies. The projectile point was never stolen. The group that met that evening was the Old and New Club, the who's who of Lawrence and KU. I have a list of the members and the monthly lectures. Williston talked about 'The Antiquity of Man' on January 21, 1899, four and a half years after the discovery of the projectile point. Martin wasn't there—he wasn't a member. Neither was Mrs. Apitz—the Old and New Club was men only. No women were allowed at club meetings, except for the wife of the host, in this case, Annie Williston."

"Lemme guess," Harry interrupted. "Sellards was there because he was Williston's student then."

"Right. Annie Williston wrote two letters a week to her mother in Connecticut about everything that went on in the town, the museum, and the university. You'd think if some woman had stolen the Twelve Mile Creek projectile point during a science club meeting at Annie's home she would have written about that to her mother. But she didn't. Her letters are archived at the Connecticut Historical Society in Storrs. I've read them. Nothing about a projectile point, stolen or otherwise."

Harry rubbed the three-day stubble on his face. "You're saying Martin concocted the Apitz story to keep Brown from seeing the projectile point."

"Exactly. By 1925 there was no one left at the museum to contradict him—they'd left or died. Martin knew about Mary Apitz. Might even have met her. She was an avid amateur scientist. Hung around the museum. Won every county science fair. Co-authored a paper with KU Chancellor Snow on a Kansas salamander. She had a natural history collection in her house. Also archeological artifacts— she sold them to Baker University in Baldwin City, south of here. I've looked through that collection. No Twelve Mile Creek projectile point."

Nalren brewed two more espressos and handed one to Harry. "By the way, you'll like this. Mary Apitz was a witness in a sensational murder trial here—a doctor accused of poisoning his patient. He was having an affair with the patient's wife. Apitz covered the trial for the local newspaper under her maiden name, Mary Fanning—the first woman reporter west of the Mississippi."

Nalren paused, then shot Harry an impish, almost conspiratorial look. "It's a cold case. The doctor got off. Maybe you should tackle it."

Nalren's first words of lighthearted banter, Harry thought.

"Anyway," Nalren continued, "I found a picture of Mary Apitz on Ancestry. Posted by her great-granddaughter in Topeka."

He brought up a black-and-white image on his computer: a narrow face, hair severely pinned back, lips pursed in revolt, eyes fierce, focused, pinning an insect.

"No thief, no theft." Nalren declared. "What clinches it is big lie number three."

36

The Red Man Has Made The Least Progress

Harry sipped his espresso. "Okay, what's the third big lie?"

"Skip ahead twenty years," Naren said. "It's 1945. Martin's dead. The head paleontologist at the KU museum is Claude Hibbard. He gets a letter. It's from none other than Edwin Sellards—the same Sellards who Martin claimed had witnessed the theft of the projectile point at Williston's house back in 1899 and pinned it on Mrs. Apitz. Sellards is now the director the Texas Memorial Museum. Here, read it."

November 13, 1945.

Dear Mr. Hibbard.

The year I entered the University of Kansas, 1895, was also the year in which Martin found the bison with the projectile point under the scapula. Martin told me of the loss of the point. I am writing a compendium on early man in the Americas and want to refer to Martin's find. What can you tell me about the lost point? Was it lost before Williston left Kansas in 1902?

Nalren raised his arms, his voice indignant. "If Sellards was there, why is he now clueless about the arrowhead? Why is he asking Hibbard what happened to it? Welcome to big lie number three."

Harry plunked down the coffee cup. "Okay, forget espresso. I need a stiff drink. I'm beginning to think Page is right. We had Piltdown. Now we have Twelve Mile Creek. The whole business is fishy. If the projectile point that Brown saw on exhibit with the bison in 1925 was not the original, but a substitute, where the hell did Martin get the substitute?"

"Who knows?" Nalren exclaimed. "As a matter of fact, when Martin retired, he asked Hibbard to remove this so-called substitute point from the bison case and destroy it. Hibbard complied. Williston and others published articles on the Twelve Mile Creek discovery. No one mentions a lost point. Then there's a glass negative of a photograph."

Nalren handed Harry a black-and-white print of a blade-like projectile point, part of the base broken off, with shadowed hints of knapped bumps and depressions. "It's too fuzzy for a definite cultural ID. But archeologists see what they want to see—a Clovis point with the characteristic sculpted flute along the shaft, where a hunter would have attached it to the end of a spear."

Harry smirked. "You gotta squint hard to see that. Squint just as hard, Page told me, and you could see a Solutrean point from Spain or France."

"Right. In the box with the negative was a handwritten note from Martin."

> To whom it may concern. Don't ever let this negative get away from KU. This is the only picture of the original arrow head found with the Bison skeleton.

"How do we know this too isn't one of his lies—like everything else?" Nalren folded his arms across his chest. "In the end, we're left with nothing. No original point. No substitute point. A blurred photo. No evidence of anything except deceit. All we have is a story."

A sudden clap of thunder sounded outside, muted by the thick limestone walls. The lights in the office flickered and died. Nalren switched off the power strip for his computer, grabbed a Coleman lantern in the corner, pumped it, and lit the mantles. It reminded Harry of evenings in the Wind River Basin, the canvas mess tent, the steady hiss of the warm yellow light, reassuring, safe, a radiant speck marooned under the cold, dark vault of the universe.

Harry leaned back in his chair. "Finish the story."

"Martin grew up in England. He was an amateur collector, fossils and artifacts from all over Europe, including, almost certainly, Solutrean points. He knew Solutreans used them to hunt mammoths and aurochs. Martin emigrates to Kansas. The KU museum hires him to collect fossils. But he wants a permanent position there as a paleontologist. At Twelve Mile Creek he finds ten bison: six adults, three juveniles, and one fetus, unborn, preserved inside the mother. He recognizes the perfect opportunity: plant the killing weapon, for fame, prestige, and a job. And history is created—a Clovis projectile point from Twelve Mile Creek. Except, it's probably a Solutrean point from what now is Europe."

Harry winced. "If so, Martin has to keep it from being examined too closely. The quartz core is likely different from the core of a Kansas Clovis point. Any geologist would have spotted that."

"Exactly. So, Martin makes sure that no one ever sees the point firsthand. He puts it behind glass in a sealed exhibit case resting against the shoulder blade of the bison. He thinks he gotten away with it. Until Barnum Brown shows up twenty years later, wants to see it. Martin makes up the Mrs. Apitz story. It's now become museum legend, repeated in journal articles and dissertations."

The lights in the office ticked on. Nalren cut the gas for the lantern, stood up, and checked his watch. "Gotta go."

Harry nodded. "Nice rehearsal for a dissertation defense."

"Working on it."

"Did Lasher ask you about the projectile point? About it possibly being Solutrean, not Clovis."

"He did. He fought with me about it."

"Anyone else?"

Nalren thought for a moment. "Yes, Strickland ... Dr. Strickland, director of the museum. He called me to his office. He wanted to know if Lasher could have found it after all these years. I told him it's possible."

"How so?"

"Martin hides the projectile point in his house. After he dies, his kids find it and bring it to the museum to the head archeologist then, Carlisle Smith. He tosses it into—"

"A wooden box," Harry interrupted. "And gets the box plastered behind a new exhibit on the fifth floor of Dyche Hall. Page told me about it. By luck, Lasher gets to open the box twenty-seven years later, sifts through it, finds the point, and squirrels it away."

"Because it looks Solutrean," Nalren added. "And that would mean the first peopling of America could have happened at least twice, on the Pacific side from Asia, and on the Atlantic side from Europe."

Harry pointed to the stack of papers. "Ruby ... Dr. Pettecek ... helped you dig all this up?"

Nalren nodded. "She ... and Professor Page."

"So, the day of the IRN protest, she was supposed to meet Lasher. Was she going to confront him? Tell him that the projectile point, if he had it, was Solutrean?"

Nalren shrugged. "I don't know. Maybe. She didn't say. Ask her."

Harry didn't tell him she was lying in a bed at KU Med hooked to a forest of wires, her mind meandering in and out, a ghost adrift in the machine. "I will."

Nalren riffled through the papers and pulled out a yellowed newspaper article. "She also dug this up." He handed it to Harry. *The Chanute Daily Tribune*, Chanute, Kansas, May 29, 1909.

> Chancellor Strong of the University of Kansas was the commencement speaker at the Chanute H. S. Graduation. He told of the bison skeleton found by a University scientist. In its shoulder bone was imbedded a flint arrow head such as the Indians used when the white man came to this country. "That bison had been buried thousands of years," Chancellor Strong said. "But that arrow head shows that the red man of that age used the same weapons that the Indians of more modern times used. The red men belong to one of the oldest of races, and to one which has made the least progress.

"Christ," Harry muttered.

Outside it was drizzling. Half the lights on Jayhawk Boulevard were out. Nalren put on his yellow hi-viz vest and got on his Colnago.

"Forget that," Harry said. "Too dark, too wet. I'll give you a lift."

"OK," Nalren said.

They put the bike in the back of the 4Runner. Harry exited the Spooner lot onto Jayhawk Boulevard and turned to Nalren. "I bet Pettecek told you to put that 'red men' quote in the dissertation."

"You win the bet. She did. She said it would be archeological irony. Me, one of those red men, 'which has made the least progress,' exposing that damn projectile point."

Harry slowed in front of the long, tan limestone building. "Strong Hall. It's named for that guy, the former chancellor. The current chancellor is your mother. She runs this university from this building. What does she think?"

Nalren chuckled. "She doesn't know. I haven't told her yet."

37

March Tryst Four

"You have your clothes on."

"Very observant. Congratulations. What does that tell you?"

"Easy. You're waiting for me to unbutton your blouse ... unhook your bra."

"No. I'm waiting for you to tell me about your goddamn gambling debt ... the loan shark guy ... the hundred grand. Money first, sex second. That's how the business works."

"Very funny. I don't know. I haven't seen the guy since Wednesday. Or his Dodge Caravan following me."

"Yeah, but the day is long. Did you check outside?"

"I did. I drove around the block. No minivan."

"I thought he wanted half by Friday, fifty grand. That's today."

"I know."

"Well, at least we switched motels. Maybe he won't bust down the door in the next hour. But if he does, do you have the fifty grand? Or any part of it?"

"I managed to get ten grand."

"Oh, yeah? How?"

"Uh ... it's complicated."

"Lemme guess. You told Betsy. You got some of her savings."

"No."

"Okay, do we have to play twenty fucking questions for you to tell me how you got hold of ten complicated grand?"

"Uh ... KU Endowment funds. Cash advance."

"Really? Cash advance? Advance for what?"

"Never mind. It's better you don't know. You'll have ... what do they call it ... deniability."

"Screw 'deniability.' When they can't get the fifty grand out of your hide, they'll come after mine."

"Okay, okay. It was an advance for field work. In Africa. An upcoming expedition to Botswana. In the market stalls it's cash only for supplies. Same for bribes to get permits, gas, whatever. Even if you could use a credit card, it would be hacked the same day."

"Maybe I've missed something. If the ten grand is for the field work, how does that help you pay off the loan sharks?"

"I got it worked out. No need to get into the weeds."

"Weeds? They'll bury you in the fucking weeds if you stiff them. What do you mean you 'got it worked out'?"

"It's better if you don't know. Trust me."

"Trust you? How the hell can I trust you? A gambling addiction you never told me about. Loan sharks you never told me about. Because of you I could be in deep shit with these guys. And with George. Y'know, I thought I cared, but now I'm just pissed off. Tell me about the goddamn cash."

"Okay, okay. Cool it. The cash advance was actually for twenty grand. Ten grand will go to the field work. The other ten is for the loan sharks ... uh ... to buy more time, y'know, a good faith installment."

"How are you going to account for that ten grand to KU Endowment—the ten grand that wasn't spent in Botswana?"

"Uh ...we'll submit chits for twenty grand. You can't get official receipts for the expedition stuff. So we keep an expense log."

"An expense log with double the expenses?"

"Right."

"Christ, that's fraud. You get caught, they'll put the cuffs on at KU and take them off at Leavenworth."

"I won't get caught. We've ... we've done it before."

"Really? Who's 'we'?"

"A couple of the expedition leaders."

"And you trust them to keep their lips zipped?"

"Yeah, they have as much to lose as I do. Y'know, it's like nuclear war—mutually assured destruction. It's what keeps the peace."

Pause.

"You're smirking! You're really proud of yourself. But, face it, you're a crook!"

"I'll pay it back."

"Oh yeah? With what? Your big fat salary?"

"Naw. My mama is selling the spread in Alabama. Everything. The big house, the stables, the horses, the land."

"The slaves too? No, I guess you sold them long ago."

"Very funny. Listen, did you ever get a hold of that woman in Abilene. What's her name. The one who had an idea about Lasher, about the blackmail, about him knowing you were ... uh ... having an affair."

"Ruby. I've tried to call her several times. But I can't reach her. I don't think she has a cell phone. Maybe she's traveling."

"Keep trying. By the way, that detective Warden hired. Przewalski. He's coming to see me this afternoon. For the life of me I don't know why."

"Maybe someone saw you in Spooner that evening."

"Naw, the cops would have asked me about it. I seem to remember Ruby being involved with him in the Fulbright business. Maybe she's talked to him about Lasher. About you and me."

"Maybe. I don't know. She did help him. It was in the papers. He's okay. I met him then. Back to the loan shark guy. What makes you think that ten grand will buy you more time? They want their pound of flesh—actually half a pound, not a tenth of a pound."

"Pound of flesh?"

"You never read Shakespeare in Alabama? The *Merchant of Venice*? The Jew ... Shylock?"

"Uh ... no. Only *Hamlet*. But, come to think of it, the loan shark guy could be Jewish. He kind of looked it."

"What?"

"He looked Jewish. And it's what they do. Lend money."

"Oh, yeah? So, what do Jews look like? You saw a lot of them in Alabama?"

"Well ... you can tell, y'know ... the nose. Look at Kovitch in anthropology."

Pause.

"Do I look Jewish?"

"Ha ha, not a chance. Not with your clothes on or off."

"Really? Well, asshole, it so happens I am, with my clothes on—or off."

"I'll be damned. You never said. Angela is not a Jewish name."

Pause.

"I'm bringing up this painting on my iPhone. Isn't Google wonderful. Here, look at it. It's by a Dutch artist, Pieter Claesz. He painted it in 1625. It's a simple still life. A table in a room. On the table there's a lit candle, a pocket watch lying open, a red-and-white flower with a long green stem, and a human skull bathed in the candle's yellow light."

"Uh ... I guess ... okay."

"You understand what Claesz is saying here?"

"Um ... I don't know. But I know you'll tell me. Maybe he got tired of painting bowls of fruit."

"He's tired, all right. So am I. He's saying that all things must pass. The watch is telling you that time has slipped away. The flower will soon wilt. The flame on the candle is down to its last bit of wax and will soon go out. The room will grow dark. And the skull spells death."

"Okay. So?"

"So, asshole, you've just been kissed off with a great work of art."

38

A Fish Choking On Air

Harry took the elevator in Dyche Hall to the sixth floor of the museum and turned right into the administrative wing. There was no one at the front desk. But he didn't need directions. There was a large oak nameplate on the office door at the end of the hall. It announced in a fancy, italic font: "Beauregard Strickland, Director." The door was ajar. Harry rapped on it and walked in.

Strickland was sitting behind his desk, a piece of Danish modern shaped like a kidney bean. Another, smaller kidney-bean table extended back from the end of the desk to form a snug, L-shaped enclosure. The desk was bare except for a silver 27-inch iMac, white keyboard, and a KU coffee mug. No papers. On a side shelf, mesh-wire file racks held neat vertical echelons of manilla folders. A row of windows behind the desk looked out onto Jayhawk Boulevard.

He'd seen him before, Harry thought. Then it registered. Strickland was the guy in the tan corduroy jacket in Alderson Auditorium who had stepped out of Page's distinguished professor lecture on Wednesday. He was the guy who Ball Cap had slipped behind and followed out of the Kansas Union and into Dyche Hall. Why was Ball Cap tailing the director of the natural history museum?

Strickland stood up and shook his hand. “Good to meet you, Mr. Przewalski. Interesting, being named after a horse.”

Harry gave him the benefit of the doubt—ignorance rather than insult.

Strickland pointed to Harry’s head. ”The bandage ... looks like that hurt,” but he didn’t wait for a response. “Your reputation precedes you. The Fulbright affair. It was all over campus.”

Harry nodded. He noticed the corduroy jacket hanging on the back of the desk chair. It went with his blue shirt, yellow tie, and tan slacks. The light from the windows behind him framed his face. Tanned skin—a sunlamp, Harry guessed—brownish black hair, brush cut, a bald spot on top, a widow’s peak in front, blue eyes, puffy cheeks. Mid-fifties.

“Let’s ... uh ... let’s sit over there.” Strickland motioned to a small conference area at the far end of the office: three black leather sofa chairs, a glass coffee table, also bean-shaped. The windows provided a view of Mississippi Street, the Spencer Museum of Art, and, beyond it, the football stadium.

“What can I do for you?” Strickland folded his hands in his lap and smiled at him. Forced, almost pained, Harry thought. He seemed nervous, like a perp at a police interrogation. Harry decided to pitch a few softballs for starters.

“You can help me with the Lasher murder.”

“Yes, I know Chancellor Warden hired you. But ... uh ... I’m not ... I’m not sure how I can be of help.” Another pained smile.

”Well, Professor Page tells me that he called you last Thursday evening—the evening Lasher was killed. He asked you to come over to his office across the street.” Harry pointed toward Spooner Hall. “He wanted to talk to you about the Twelve Mile Creek projectile point. You know, the one discovered in 1895, then lost, then, as rumor has it, subsequently found by Lasher. Did you go over to Spooner?”

Strickland nodded. “As it happens, I did. But Page wasn’t in his office. So, I left. Page was probably down there ... in the collection ... 1.2 million artifacts ... all those arrowheads and potsherds. Most of it’s from salvage mitigation during federal road construction. I joke with Page that in Kansas the Corps of Engineers produced more archeology than engineering.”

Harry resisted the temptation to ask him how many birds in the ornithological collection were salvaged roadkill. "Did you tell the police ... Detective Duggan ... you were in Spooner around the time Lasher was killed?"

Strickland shrank back. "You don't know that," he blurted. "Anyway, uh ... no, I have not spoken to the police. Or them to me. I didn't think it was important. Like I said, I went up to Page's office, his door was open, but he wasn't there. I waited for a few minutes, thinking he might be down in the collections or in the washroom. Then I left."

"Did you see anyone else in Spooner?"

Strickland leaned back and crossed his legs. "No, I didn't. Or hear anything—which I assume will be your next question. But I did notice that Professor Montanares was there—at least the door to her office was open. Same with Miriam Kovitch."

Harry nodded. That jibed with what Page had said. "Did you go down to Lasher's office in the basement? Chat with him?"

Strickland narrowed his eyes. "No, I had no reason to. As a matter of fact, I don't think I've ever gone down there. I'm an ornithologist. I study the evolution of flightless birds. He studied indigenous people's genomes. Opposite ends of the biological world."

"Perhaps," Harry said, "but not the museum administrative world."

Strickland smiled. "I remember now. You come from academe. Carnegie Museum. University of Pittsburgh. I asked our paleontologist here. He said ... uh ... you never finished your degree."

Harry heard the jab of superiority. "No, I didn't. I got tired, y'know, like your flightless birds ... got tired of flying."

Strickland looked at him, seemingly dumbfounded.

"So, Lasher's office being ransacked, his frozen tissues dumped—what if all that was just a feint, a distraction? What if they were searching for the Twelve Mile Creek point—where Lasher might have squirreled it away? Page asked you to make Lasher cough it up, so he could study it."

"I know nothing about that artifact." Strickland said, indignant. He uncrossed his legs and leaned forward. "I only know what's in the published archeological literature. It was found, lost—likely stolen—and never seen again. Page has discussed that rumor with me, that Lasher had it. But I felt it was not my calling to mediate their dispute. And I did not intercede. They could settle it themselves, as distinguished faculty should."

"Which brings me to Page's distinguished professor lecture on Wednesday afternoon," Harry said. "Tell me about this skinny guy in a ball cap. He followed you when you left Page's lecture, out of Alderson Auditorium, out of the Kansas Union, up the street, and into this building."

Strickland blanched, his lips suddenly quivering. "What ... how did you ... I don't know what you're talking about." He stood up. "I think you should leave."

"I think you should sit back down." A soft command. "The chancellor might be interested in why some hood is tailing the director of the natural history museum. That it might involve Lasher's murder. Detective Duggan would also be interested."

"He has nothing to do with Lasher's murd—"

Harry nodded. "Okay, tell me what he does have to do with. He was tailing you on foot. I'm betting he's tailing you on the road. He drives a gray minivan."

Strickland sat down. He clasped his hands in his lap to stop them from trembling. His mouth opened and he tried to speak but strangled on the words. Abruptly his body doubled forward in the sofa chair. He began shaking, sweat beading on his forehead, breathing in short, hoarse gasps, like a fish choking on air.

Harry stood up and grasped him tightly by the shoulders. "Look at me, Strickland, you're having a panic attack. Breathe ... breathe slowly ... deeply ... breathe in ... breathe out ... in ... out." Harry remembered the trench in the desert, shaking, being held, the bullets screaming overhead.

It took a couple of minutes for Strickland to recover. He pulled out a handkerchief from his trousers, wiped the sweat from his brow, and leaned back in the chair. The armpits on his blue shirt were blotched.

"Christ. Tell me, how did you find out about him ... the guy in the ball cap following me?"

"I get paid to find out things," Harry said. "What's he got on you? What does he want?"

Strickland bowed his head. "I need a drink."

He got up, walked over to a low cabinet beside his desk, pulled out a dark red glass bottle, unscrewed the cap, poured some into his coffee mug, and took a generous swig. "Want some?" He held the bottle out to Harry. The label said "Dettling Bourbon, Alabama style. Small batch. Six grain."

Harry shook his head.

Strickland put the bottle and mug on the glass coffee table, sat down, and sighed deeply. "He's been following me for a while. I don't know his name."

"Where else has he tailed you?"

Strickland hesitated. "Uh ... all around. To my house. To work. To ..." A red blotch appeared on his throat. "To the store."

"Anywhere else?"

"Uh ... no."

He was a lousy liar, Harry thought. "Was he waiting for you outside the museum last Thursday? When you went over to Spooner to see Page?"

Strickland looked startled, his lips stretched tight. "Uh ... if he was, I didn't see him. He approached me the morning of Page's lecture. In the Spooner parking lot. He's a collector for a loan shark outfit in Kansas City." Strickland turned away, the red blotch growing on his neck. "I'm ...," he began to stammer, "I'm into them for a lot of money ... uh ... gambling. They ... they want half today."

"How much?"

"Fifty grand."

"You have it?"

"No. Just ten grand to buy time."

"You won't buy time. With these guys all you buy is bodily injury."

Strickland shuddered. "What should I do?"

"Go to the cops. Loan sharking is a crime. Tell them everything you know. Then make yourself scarce. Scarce enough that they can't find you until the cops find him. Take a sabbatical. Make it up—make up an ornithology meeting in South Africa. Or New Zealand. Lots of flightless birds there."

Strickland downed the rest of the bourbon. The skin on his face was back to being tanned.

"One more thing," Harry said. "The woman you're seeing, is he also following her?"

Strickland controlled his face as best he could. "Where did you hear that? What woman?"

No sense telling him that he'd heard the rumor from Page. "Universities are medieval villages. People know everything. And they gossip about everything they know. Affairs. Blackmail. Was Lasher blackmailing you?"

"No, absolutely not!" Strickland said, adamantly. "There's no affair and there's no blackmail." He looked at his watch. "I have another meeting. Thank you for the advice on the gambling debt. I'll handle it."

He got up, walked over to his desk, grabbed his corduroy jacket, and ushered Harry out of his office.

Yeah, Harry thought, a lousy liar.

39

A Burnt-Out Chassis

The steam whistle sounded across campus as Harry walked out of the museum. He looked at his watch: 3:20. Students poured out of the buildings, thronging the sidewalks along Jayhawk Boulevard. Across the street in the Spooner lot, a tow truck was hoisting up the back end of the 4Runner. Harry went over to the dark blue car sitting nearby, engine idling, window down, guy smoking a cigarette, a "KU Parking" decal on the door.

"That's my rental," Harry told him.

The guy looked at Harry and smirked. "Congratulations. You got three tickets in three days. You can get your rental back at the pound." He handed Harry an invoice. "After you pay the fine: $322.54."

Harry pursed his lips. "Call the chancellor's office."

"What?"

"Call the chancellor's office. Tell them it's Harry Przewalski." He handed the guy a card and pointed to his name. "The chancellor okayed my parking here without a permit."

The guy looked at him askance. "Yeah, right. I've heard lots of stories, buddy, but that takes the cake. Tell you what. You got a check on you? Make it out to KU Parking for $322.54, give it to me, get in the car, and I'll give you a lift to the pound."

"Trust me," Harry said in his best, reserved authoritative voice. "You want to check with the chancellor's office before that 4Runner get's towed."

The guy looked at him, a tinge of doubt creeping across his face. He grabbed his mobile phone, punched in a number, waited, spoke to someone at the other end, waited some more, said "Uh huh" a couple of times, hung up, and gave Harry a quizzical look.

"You got it. Must be nice to have that kind of pull," he muttered, then motioned to the tow truck operator, and drove off.

Harry rolled a Drum, lit it, and watched the 4Runner get lowered down and the cables unhooked. His phone started buzzing in his pocket. The call wasn't from his father in Pittsburgh. It was a number in Abilene, Kansas.

"Talk to me," Harry answered.

"Hey, glad I got you. It's Tamara. We just got a call from Duggan office. I'm not telling you this, but they found Ball Cap's van. At least they think it's his minivan. A Dodge Caravan. They—"

"Where is it? Where is he?"

"Hold on and don't interrupt. I'm doing you a goddamn favor. They thought they spotted it last evening, parked at one of the campground sites at Clinton Lake. Apparently he had been holed up out there, living out of the minivan. They didn't run the license plate until this morning. Don't ask me why. Probably not their highest priority. Anyway, the plate was stolen from an SUV in Kansas City, Missouri. By the time they went back to the campground today, the minivan was gone. He must have seen the patrol car last night. They found it where he ditched it, in East Lawrence, in a trash field behind the train station, near a makeshift homeless camp. He'd torched the van. They're checking for prints, but the odds aren't good. Don't go out there."

Harry took a last drag on the cigarette and stubbed it out. "Okay. There won't be much to see. Just a burnt-out chassis. Anyway, if I show up they'll figure out you called me. Duggan will be on Blevins' ass, and he'll be on yours."

"Glad to hear you can still detect. Learned anything since yesterday?"

"Ball Cap is hustling for a loan shark outfit in Kansas City."

"I'll be damned. You know who he's squeezing?"

"I do. It's the director of the KU Natural History Museum, Beauregard Strickland. He's into them for a hundred grand. Gambling debts. They wanted half today. But Ball Cap hasn't shown up yet to collect. He's probably out there getting a new set of wheels. Strickland's lucked out. Sounds like the cops bought him another day or two."

"Wait a second,"Tamara exclaimed. "I don't get it. Strickland is the guy you saw Ball Cap follow into the museum on Wednesday afternoon, right?"

"Yeah."

"And then this Ball Cap guy cold-cocks you at the bison exhibit. After warning you about the Lasher case ... and Ruby at KU Med."

"Right again."

"Don't give me this 'right again,' Przewalski," Tamara fumed. "What's the goddamn connection to Strickland and his gambling debt?"

"Don't know yet. Remember Ruby told you about a woman friend and Lasher and sexual blackmail. It might also involve Strickland."

"Coincidence?"

"You don't believe that. We're not in the coincidence business. Strickland's tied to the Lasher murder. He doesn't know it. Or he's hiding it."

"There's —" A siren in the background drowned her out. Harry heard Tamara yelling something at someone. The siren stopped.

"Those fuckers,"Tamara swore. "It's the guys bugging me. I'm in the lot with the cruisers. They see me talking on the phone, they put the screamer on. Listen, you wanna hear coincidence? I did a quick check on Lasher. Turns out he and Kovitch were in grad school at Stony Brook in New York at the same time. Y'know Kovitch—she sued him a year ago and lost. Guess what. Turns out she filed charges against him back then too. Assault. Rape. But the charges were dropped. Don't know why. You talked to her yet?"

"No. When did she file the charges?"

"1985. Somehow, they both ended up in the anthro department at KU. Fucking fate. Maybe she finally got her revenge."

40

A Dose Of Derangement

Miriam Kovitch's office was at the end of the hallway on the second floor of Spooner. It was the size of an outhouse on the prairie, albeit one with vinyl flooring. No window. A desk the size of a card table. A banged-up metal file cabinet, pale green, one drawer, shoved under the desk. There was a yellow folding chair for visitors, but there wasn't enough room to sit in the office.

"Just leave the door open," she instructed Harry, as if she were reciting a manual. "Put the chair a bit into the hallway ... the rear legs on the other side of the sill. It's our new definition of 'private.' Fortunately, we're alone now. Sam and Elena are gone."

Harry glanced down the hall. Their offices were dark, the doors shut. Kovitch rose to shake his hand. Harry recognized the sweater she was wearing, the same gray color, the same Shaker Rib cardigan that his mother, Emilia, had once painstakingly knitted for herself. It suited Kovitch's thin face, pensive, slightly melancholic. Her hair was cropped short, almost mannish, wisps of gray failing to hide amid the black.

"I'm going to guess you are a knitter," Harry said, pointing to the cardigan.

Kovitch eyed him, oddly. "Very good, Mr. Przewalski." A tinge of sarcasm. "You've now earned the detective moniker. I am an avid knitter. And I did knit this Reading Cardigan. Appropriately, I have read many books in it. The yarn is called Brooklyn Tweed. I once met the designer, Jerod Flood. That's likely much more than you cared to learn. Or why you are here. Lasher's murder."

Harry settled carefully into the yellow chair. "Right. You and he have a history. When you were both at Stony Brook."

Her eyes flashed a controlled bitterness. "Hah, I see you've done your homework. Yes, a sordid history. Lasher raped me there in 1985. I paid the consequences. Now ... now it is a private matter ... a painful matter, best left at the bottom of the well. The water down there has long been poisoned ... undrinkable ... unthinkable."

"Poisoned enough for murder thirty years later?" Harry asked, quietly.

She winced, as if wounded. "I'll be honest. The answer is yes ... more than enough. But motive alone is insufficient. It's a dormant venom. To kill, you need to add a dose of derangement, of frenzy."

Harry nodded. "True. Any frenzy last Thursday evening when Lasher got bopped? You were here."

Kovitch shot him a wry grin. "Yes, I was here. In this cubby-hole. With the door open. But, sorry, no frenzy. I'm afraid I was too far into a bottle of good Malbec. I put a cushion right here," she pointed to a spot on the desk,"I laid my head on it and drifted into a different life."

She looked at her watch. "Speaking of which, it's close enough to five o'clock, the witching hour for wine."

She bent down under the desk, screeched open the metal file cabinet, and emerged with a bottle, a couple of wine glasses, and a huge, silver corkscrew.

Harry recognized it. "A Campagnolo wine opener. My father has one in his bike shop in Pittsburgh. Made from bicycle components—brake levers, a rear sprocket, a wheel hub."

"Yes," she said, uncorking the bottle. "It cost me $300. When I'm on my death bed I won't say I should have bought a cheaper corkscrew. It's aesthetic and functional. Rare for a work of art."

She sniffed the cork, nodded approval, and poured two generous glasses. "It's a Luca Old Vine Malbec, from Argentina. I'm assuming that you will drink with me. Assure me that I'm not being presumptuous. You do drink with suspected killers?"

"Yeah, it's expected etiquette," Harry deadpanned.

"Good!" She lifted her glass. "Here's to people like Lasher meeting their deserved end. Notice I did not say 'just end.' There is no such thing as justice. It's a human invention. And, like all things human, it makes mistakes. Lasher was a mistake."

Harry took a long sip of the wine. "A dead mistake."

"The death was too gentle. Do you know Greek mythology, Mr. Przewalski?"

"A smattering. Only through the art it generated. My mother was an art historian."

"Perfect. There is a story about a giant, Tityus, who used his overpowering strength to rape Leto, the goddess of motherhood. His punishment? He was stripped naked and tied to a rock in an open meadow, where a vulture plucked out his liver—each day, again and again. That's the punishment I wanted Lasher to suffer."

She took a healthy swallow of the Malbec, pulled a tissue from a box on her desk, and dabbed her lips. "You want to know why?"

Harry shook his head. "No. Not necessary."

"Too late. It's a brief brutal story. The rape lasted twenty seconds. That's one of the lessons of life. The most horrific acts are done in seconds. A terrorist decapitating a prisoner. A classroom of students executed with an AK-47. A guard at Auschwitz locking the door of the gas chamber."

She leaned forward and folded her hands on the desk. "Twenty seconds. A hot summer evening in my tiny apartment. He'd walked me home from campus. He said he needed to use the bathroom. I showed him where it was. It's crazy what you remember and what you don't. When he came out of the bathroom, his fly was unzipped. He grabbed me, threw me down on the sofa, and before I knew it my shorts and panties were off, a few thrusts, a grunt, and he got up. It was so quick he must have had practice. Then he sneered at me, said if I reported it no one at the university would believe me. He was right. It was the '80s. Women had the right to vote. But not the right to be believed."

She finished the wine and poured herself another glass.

"It's bizarre, then," Harry commented, "that you both ended up here, at KU."

"Hah!" she exclaimed, raising her voice. "More like diabolical. God playing Mephistopheles. I was hired first. Seven years later they hired Lasher—while I was away on sabbatical in Germany! I had no input!" She waved her hand, dismissively. "It wouldn't have mattered. He was brought in as a full professor. Endowed. None of the letters of recommendation mentioned woman-hater."

Kovitch was no longer sipping the Malbec, but gulping it. Harry noticed a slight tremor in her left hand. "Anyway," she continued," what happened at Stony Brook thirty years ago remained unspoken. Until last year."

"When you sued Lasher and the university. Warden told me."

"Right," she declared. "Here, drink up." She filled his glass. "It will make me feel you're commiserating. Lasher was chair. He gave me a minuscule annual pay raise. I protested. He laughed at me ... said I didn't even deserve that. He called me a lousy teacher, a lousy researcher, a lousy colleague."

She paused and downed more wine. "Then he resurrected the rape. I remember his exact words: 'Remember Stony Brook? The worst fuck I've ever had. You're a prune in the classroom, a prune in your studies, and a prune in bed.'"

Kovitch grabbed the wine bottle by the neck, as if to smash it across someone's skull. "You know, Harry—can I call you Harry? It's easier than Przewalski, although less intriguing."

Harry nodded. "Sure." The wine, he noticed, had put a faint blush on her face and a gentle slur in her words.

"Well, Harry, when provoked I can be given to hysterics. We were in his office. Had there been a bottle on his desk I would have clubbed him with it. I should have used the ceramic ape, just didn't think of it. Someone else did last Thursday. Instead, I sued him, the university, everyone. You probably read about the trial in the papers."

"I heard about it," Harry acknowledged.

"No doubt. I was hung out like the proverbial laundry, except the washing occurred in public. And I engaged in hysterics. The newspapers made me out to be batty. I lost, I appealed, I lost again. Now I'm up for dismissal."

Kovitch held up the bottle of wine, the tremor in her hand now pronounced. "More?"

Harry shook his head.

She emptied the rest of the bottle into her glass. "I'll become the second faculty member in the history of KU to be fired. The first was a law professor. He made blow jobs a requirement for the Juris Doctor degree for his female students."

She swallowed the wine, plunked the glass on the desk, tried to stand up, wobbled, and sat back down. "Time for the cushion, Harry." She moved the wine glass aside, reached behind her, produced a small, plain tan pillow, and laid it on the desk.

Harry noticed the wine stains from previous evening booze-ups. He rose, folded the yellow chair, and leaned it against the door.

"So, last Thursday evening, you managed to keep the dose of derangement at bay. You didn't go down to Lasher's office, grab the ape, and whack him on the head. If we check your shoes we won't find bits of glass, and traces of human tissue and DNA buffer."

Kovitch gave him a tippled smile. "Hah! I said I would be honest. Of course I did—go down there. Stumble is more like it—after the bottle of wine."

"Do you remember the time?"

"No, sorry. I would have checked my watch if I knew I'd be questioned in a murder investigation."

"Did you go down there to kill him?"

"Hah," she laughed. "Maybe. Who knows. But we can't rewind that tape. The bastard was on the floor by his desk. That ceramic ape was beside him, eyeing him, grinning at the caprice of history. Sometimes there is justice."

She paused, as if savoring the memory of the moment. "Then, I came back up here, put my head on this pillow, and slipped away into an avenged life—but not one that I had avenged."

41

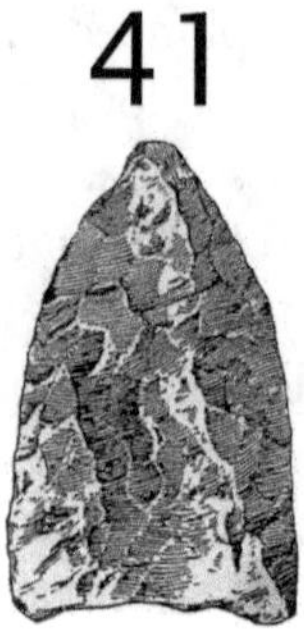

Accursed

On Saturday morning a fog descended to the ground, shrouding the earth, flattening the contours of the land behind a gray mist. I-70 East to Kansas City was back to two lanes through the construction zone. But a jackknifed semi-trailer at the I-435 interchange jammed up traffic for an hour. Tamara told Harry that there was no update on Ball Cap, either his whereabouts or fingerprints from his torched minivan. Harry briefed her on Kovitch being brined in Argentinian Malbec.

"You believe her?" Tamara asked. "That she didn't kill him."

"I would like to," Harry muttered.

He got her to find an FM jazz station. It was playing oldies: Miles Davis, blowing a smoky, muted horn through *Kind of Blue*, improvising scales and tone. The year was 1958, the DJ said, with "Cannonball" Adderley on alto sax, John Coltrane on tenor, Bill Evans on piano, Paul Chambers on bass, and Jimmy Cobb on drums. One take, no rehearsal.

It was past ten o'clock when they got to Ruby's room on the third floor of the KU Medical Center. The sliding door was open, the lights were on, and Ruby was sitting in bed, propped up, paging through *The Kansas City Star*. Most of the wires and tubes were gone. Not the vital signs monitor, which kept beeping her body rhythms in the background. Her hair was in a loose ponytail, with long tufts hanging down below the bandage around her head. She put the newspaper down and waved at them.

"Hey there," Ruby said, smiling, her gray eyes alert, spirited, mirthful. "Nice morning surprise." Her cheeks sported a bit of blush, her lips a light shade of pink.

"You look great, kiddo," Tamara said. "Love that color!" She slipped off her bomber jacket and hung it on the back of a chair.

"Yeah," Ruby acknowledged, pointing to a large red cosmetic stick lying on the bedside table. "I'm embarrassed. I never use this stuff. It's called 'Palladio–I'm Blushing.' Can you believe it? One of the nurses brought it in. Gotta say, it does wonders for the near-death post-coma look, don't you think?"

Tamara laughed. "Soon you'll lose that hospital gown. Those damn things look like coffin-wear. Anyway, hell of an improvement since Thursday."

Ruby chuckled. "Yeah, I musta looked like crap. I think they combed my hair with a scalpel." She reached up and gingerly touched the right side of the bandage. "I am lots better. But, gotta say, it felt as if my head had been trepanned ... like the ancients did. Chisel a hole in the skull, let the devils out. Trouble is, it also let the remembering out ... y'know ... the shooting. It's just blank. The doc says it's trauma to the hippocampus."

Ruby held up a piece of paper with a sketch of a brain. "He showed it to me on the X-ray. It's a goddamn piece of nothing, this hippocampus. Sits in the middle of the brain, kinda looks like a seahorse. He said it stores episodes, incidents. Well, my seahorse ain't storing much—at least not the shooting. Or what happened afterward."

"No worries," Tamara said. "It'll come back to you when it's ready ... when you're ready."

"Speaking of which, the doc hinted that they might toss me out of here on Tuesday. Maybe even Monday. I'm gonna need a ride."

She looked expectantly at Tamara and Harry.

"I'll be here," Harry said. "Maybe we'll have nailed the bastard who shot you by then."

Tamara broke in. "We have, as we say, 'a person of interest.'"

"Oh yeah? Care to tell me who the fucker his? Do I know him? Or her?"

Tamara shook her head. "Nah. Anyway, Blevins is on it. We're on it." She nodded at Harry.

"Right, of course. How is ol' Buster?"

"He's pissed, pissed as hell. At the shooter." Tamara turned and playfully jabbed Harry with her elbow. "And at our prize detective, here."

"Oh yeah?" Ruby rasped, and started coughing. She reached over and grabbed the large hospital water mug from the table, a clear, 32-ounce plastic job with a blue lid and large straw. She sucked down a few mouthfuls.

"Well," Tamara said, waving her hand, "you know Buster. He likes his bourbon. And he likes you—a lot. The other day he and I went back to your place, moseyed around inside, sat down on the porch. He took out the bourbon and laid into it. He got sloppy. He said you and Harry are accursed. Every time Harry shows up you end up in the hospital with a banged-up head. Last year, you got bopped at the diner. Two days ago, you got shot on your own doorstep. He likes Harry. Said he likes jawing with him. But, he'd like to have him banished from these parts. From you! 'For your goddamn own good!' is what he said."

Tamara raised her eyebrows at Harry, then at Ruby. "Okay, I think now's a good time for me to get outta here for a bit." She grabbed her bag, waved her fingers at them, and slipped out of the room.

Ruby reached up and began fingering a tassel of hair below the bandage. "Yeah, Buster might be right. Maybe ... maybe we are accursed, Harry. You with me, me with you. Or we with ourselves. Sometimes I think ol' Dostoevsky got it right ... y'know ... that 'you were destined for me, perhaps as a punishment.' Maybe the bullet has cured us of that. Me anyway. Maybe it went through that place where fate stows itself away. I've been looking for that place in books. Never found it."

She took another sip of water from the mug. "What do you think, Harry?"

He shook his head. "People want the universe to be listening, but it's indifferent. I'm fine with random ... with the contingencies of history. I don't plumb them for meaning. Or for good or evil. Maybe I should, but I don't hold with fate ... or destiny. Cheap euphemisms for 'chance.' Or worse, 'God's will.'

"Or the devil," Ruby muttered. "Y'know that's what they hammered into us in church in North Branch: 'The devil hides behind the cross.' Maybe you can blame us on him. Maybe he's been hiding behind us."

Behind me, Harry thought. He saw Nicole and the 50-gallon drum in the barn north of Pittsburgh. He got up, leaned over the bed, took Ruby's face in his hands, and softly kissed her on the lips, lingering long enough to harken intimacy.

She blushed as he pulled away. "I should kick your ass for doing that, Harry." Ruby whispered.

"Yeah, probably," Harry said. He shoved his hands into the front pockets of his jeans, and hunched his shoulders, as if a cold wind had suddenly sliced through his body. "There's something I didn't get to say ... when I called you from the road. Before you were shot."

Ruby raised her eyebrows. "Okay, you're giving me trepidation. Say it now. It better be good."

Harry nodded. "I know I went missing this past year. There's a Slavic Yiddish word my father would use, *farblondjhet*. It means being lost—but worse ... disoriented ... befuddled ... emotionally marooned." Harry paused, then shrugged. "I was getting *farblondjhet*, lost in my head ... and afraid of not knowing how to get back."

Ruby leaned forward. "Damn you, Harry, you're getting soppy on me," she rasped. "That's unlike you. Quit it ... taking advantage of a vulnerable woman with half a brain. But," she added with a shy smile, "you need to kiss me again."

He did.

The door to the room slid open and Tamara strode in with a bouquet of flowers, a riot of reds, blues, and yellows erupting into the air. "These are from me," she announced. "Harry can get his own."

Ruby laughed. "Thanks, Tam."

Harry pulled his chair closer to Ruby's bed. "Listen. When we were here on Thursday you said you remember going over to the front door. You remember seeing the shadow of a person on the other side of the curtain. Tall? Short? Skinny? Fat?"

Ruby creased her forehead, then shrugged. "I don't know, Harry. I can tell you this, though—it wasn't Joe Palooka. Or the Sandman. The guy who put me to sleep was a real fucker, not folklore. He used bullets, not magic sand. And no dreams."

She closed her eyes for a long moment. "Maybe short ... yeah ... short. Maybe skinny."

42

Enough Coincidence For A Conviction

"Okay, good," Harry said. "Any other details? Male? Female?"

Ruby shook her head. "Sorry, it's a blank ... a blur." She closed her eyes again. "A skinny blur ... a shortish blur."

"Got it. So, think back a week. The day of the IRN protest. When Lasher bought it. You told Tamara and Nalren you were going to see him."

"Hey," Ruby said, raising her hands in protest. "I'm laid up here. What's this with the third degree?"

"No, no," Harry said, gently, patting her shoulder. "We're just trying to nail down the timing. Duggan says Lasher died around 8:30-9:30 in the evening, give or take. Nalren says Lasher came in around 7:30, ran over to one of the upright freezers, slipped on the gunk, hit his head, and conked out. I talked to Miriam Kovitch yesterday. She had it in for Lasher. Something made her go down to his lab that evening from her office. She doesn't know the time. She was looped on wine."

"Yeah, I know about her. Social anthropologist. She sued Lasher.

He made her life shit at the university ... then at the trial. Maybe she's the one who killed him. I wouldn't blame her."

"Maybe." Harry leaned back in his chair and stretched out his legs under the bed. "She said he was already dead, on the floor by his desk, that ceramic ape beside his head. So, there's a window of an hour or so, maybe two. Lasher is lying near the freezer. He comes to, gets up, and goes over to his desk. Someone comes in, argues with him, picks up the ape, and finishes the job."

Ruby narrowed her eyes, indignant. "Well, fuck you, Harry. You think that was me?"

Tamara cleared her throat. "Well, gang, there goes romance."

Harry waited for a moment and looked at Ruby. "You know me better than that," he said, quietly, his voice tinged with disappointment. "No, I don't think it was you. You're not wired that way. I just want to know whether you saw Lasher. And if you did, when."

Ruby bowed her head, then looked up at Harry, her face rueful. "Sorry. Didn't mean the 'fuck you.' Truth is, Christ, I'm embarrassed ... I'm ashamed. I don't remember a goddamn thing." Her voice rose. "I'm also goddamn pissed about it, not remembering shit."

She began coughing, reached for the mug, and sucked in a mouthful through the straw. "Okay, you called me from the road. That I remember. The doorbell—that I remember. The blurred figure. That I sorta remember. The IRN protest? I seem to remember walking with them. But it's hazy. Then the brain goes dead. Nothing about going into Spooner. Or talking to Lasher. Or, hell, driving back to Abilene that night. Christ, I must have been on autopilot. The doc tells me it's the trauma—the brain's been shocked. It's 'taking a vacation' is the way he put it ... flew off somewhere to a goddamn beach. I told him I hope it wasn't a one-way ticket."

She turned to Tamara. "What the hell was I going to talk to Lasher about, anyway?"

"Twelve Mile Creek," Tamara said, "the projectile point. You were gonna take the file with you—Nalren's research. Y'know, that it was likely Solutrean, maybe tied to a fraud." Tamara raised her eyebrows. "Y'know, I called you that night. After you got back."

Ruby frowned, pursing her lips. "No."

"Well, you said you were too bushed to have a drink. You said Lasher had been an asshole."

"Ha!" Ruby exclaimed. "There you go, detective. I musta seen Lasher. The 'asshole' part nails it."

"Okay," Harry said. "Do you remember anything about that friend of yours being blackmailed by Lasher. Some sexual affair. She asked for your help. Tamara mentioned it."

Ruby's face brightened. "Yeah, now that I remember. Angela, an old classmate in anthro. She's having this dalliance with a guy. Somehow Lasher found out, told her he'd keep it quiet if she put out. She said he was ... well ... pornographic. Not a surprise—Lasher the fucking flasher. Anyway, she was desperate. She and her guy even talked about offing him."

"Kill the blackmailer," Harry said. "Wouldn't be the first time. Did she tell who the guy is?"

"No. And I didn't ask. I figured she'd volunteer it if she wanted to."

"My hunch it's Strickland, the director of the Natural History Museum. You know him?"

"By name only. Why him?"

"Page intimated to me that Strickland's fooling around. Two KU folks two-timing at the same time—that's enough coincidence for a conviction. Odds are it's with one another."

"Angela is not at KU. She's director of the Salina Art Museum. You met her."

Harry remembered. The Fulbright business. Angela Phillips. Tall, trim, fortyish, black hair, close-cropped. A colonial house overlooking the Smoky Hill River. Drove a red Audi. Married to George, a guy with a trigger temper.

"How did Lasher finger her for the affair?" Harry pressed.

"I have a hunch. No, better than that ... a wicked suspicion. But I haven't told her yet. She hasn't called me. Hell, I can't be reached—no mobile phone. And I can't reach her. She probably doesn't know that I'm in here with a brain on the lam. Does anyone out there know I've been shot?"

"No," Tamara said. "We've kept it under wraps. A few know: Duggan, Blevins, Harry, me, a few cops, that's it." She turned to Harry. "Did you tell Nalren?"

"Uh uh." Harry raised his eyebrows at Ruby. "Tell me about the wicked suspicion?"

"It's up your alley, Harry—crazy odds, crazy coincidence. In December, Angela and her guy met at the Ramada Inn on Old Highway 40. It was their first time. She ... she shared some delicate details. She was having her period. They made love on a bath towel. She was embarrassed to leave it in the motel. The guy told her he'd toss it in a dumpster. Two months later, in February, Lasher hit her with the blackmail."

"The towel," Harry muttered, "the one the cops found in the closet in Lasher's office. Stuffed into a wading boot."

Ruby shot him a conspiratorial smile. "Yeah, Tamara told me about it. What are the odds that this towel ends up with Lasher? They're good—if God *is* wicked. The sanitation guys see the towel. It's got a suspicious red stain. They take it to the cops. The cops take it to Lasher. Tell us who the blood is from. Pig? Dog? Human? Lasher ID's the blood as human male. I say Lasher lied."

Suddenly, Tamara smacked her head. "Christ, I don't deserve to be a cop. Lasher's genomic anthro seminar. He asked every student for a cheek swab. Every year. For his comparative DNA database, he said, to measure against Native American genomes. Like naive, fucking idiots, we gave it to him."

Harry swore at himself, silently. He remembered Tamara mentioning the mouth swabs. It was at breakfast at the Abilene Truck Stop the morning after Ruby had been shot.

"Lemme guess," he muttered, "Angela was a student in Lasher's class. He had her DNA profile."

"Congratulations, detective," Ruby declared. "He had all of our DNA profiles. He puts the blood on the towel through the sequencer. Bingo. He gets a match. Angela. So, he wonders, what the fuck is her blood doing on a Ramada Inn towel? Answer: she's screwing someone there. And it ain't her husband."

Tamara bowed her head, then looked at Ruby. "God, that fucker, *is* wicked. Blevins isn't gonna believe this." She looked at Harry. "What about Duggan?"

Harry pushed his chair back and stood up. "I'll tell him. Also about Lasher's laptop. The killer walked off with it. Not a coincidence. They knew it had the DNA database."

43

The Cold-Water Trial

It was late afternoon when Harry crossed the Kansas River bridge into downtown Lawrence and dropped Tamara at her car near The Bourgeois Pig. The Saturday evening revelry had begun on Massachusetts Street. Students strutting in high heels, hose, and miniskirts despite the 40-degree chill, some hanging on the arm of a beau, some flaunting the pheromone of not being attached.

Harry headed south toward the County Courthouse, hoping Duggan would be there. He passed a bank, a pizza shop, and a bar with the doors open, a live band strumming out the decibels of love found and lost. Harry thought the name of the band was apt: Flash Floods. Fevers washing in and out.

The courthouse was a historic site. The sign in front said that the elaborate minarets and six-story clock tower dated to 1903. The light from the low-angled sun was teasing a faint bluish tinge from the stone, the veined ghost of an ancient sea. Harry ran his fingers along the rough-faced surface of the limestone blocks. He felt the slight rugosities, the petrified shells of ancient single-celled animals, foraminifera, compressed over 300 million years into this chalky, alabaster rock. The building was historic, Harry thought, only because geology had foretold architecture.

Harry took the stairs two at a time and met Duggan walking out of his office.

"Christ, you need to work on your timing, Przewalski." Duggan glanced at his watch. "It's 4:30 on a Saturday afternoon. Don't you have a life?"

Harry shook his head. "Not much, these days. That's why I came to see you."

"Hah, hah. I hear your Ms. Pettecek is recovering nicely. The docs at KU Med might let her out on Tuesday."

"I know. I've just come from there. I'm gonna be picking her up ... be her chauffeur."

Duggan smirked. "I hope that's all you'll be. Anytime you get around her she gets hurt."

"You sound like Blevins ... both of you ... mother hens."

"Yeah, Blevins and I've been talking."

Harry motioned to Duggan's office. The door was open. "Can we do this in there?"

Duggan glowered at him, then shrugged. "I guess." He ushered Harry in, took off his jacket, and tossed it on his desk.

"Y'know," he said, "the wife is preparing a nice pasta dish. Garlic. Olive oil. I'd invite you but there won't be enough to go around. Goddamn Mediterranean diet—she's weighing out the portions."

"No worries, I just ate," Harry lied.

Duggan patted his stomach. "I'll need the carbs for tomorrow morning's Chug Ride from Sunflower Bike Shop. 9:30. Gravel. Should be mid-forties, no rain, not much wind. You should come. I'm sure the shop will lend you a bike."

Harry went over to the window overlooking South Park, cranked it open, dug his tobacco and papers out of his jacket, rolled a Drum, and flicked the Zippo a couple of times. Sparks, but no flame. Out of fluid.

"I've probably smoked too many of these to keep up. I'll see. You got a light?"

Duggan pulled open the top desk drawer and tossed him a couple of matchbooks. "How's the noggin?" He pointed to the bit of bandage on the side of Harry's head.

"Better than Ms. Pettecek's," Harry quipped. "She doesn't remember much. Starting with who shot her."

"Yeah, 'maybe skinny, maybe short.' Like I said, Blevins and me been talking. Tamara keeps him in the know. Could be that ball cap guy you're fixated on. Could be a million other guys."

"Yeah, well, Vegas has upped the odds on Ball Cap. You know why he's here? He's a juice collector for a KC loan shark outfit. He's been tailing one of your finest citizens up on the hill, busting his nuts for a gambling debt. A hundred grand."

"Who would that be?"

"Beauregard Strickland, Director of the Natural History Museum. He was supposed to pay half yesterday, but Ball Cap never showed." Harry didn't tell Duggan he knew about Ball Cap torching his minivan.

Duggan buried his fingers in his black hair, a dense field of spikes that angled up from his head, and began scratching his scalp. "I don't think we talked to Strickland."

Harry took a long drag on the cigarette and blew the smoke toward the gazebo squatting in the middle of South Park. "No, he said you didn't. But he was there, in Spooner, the evening Lasher bought it. Page, the archeologist, had called him to come over, to talk to Lasher about that Twelve Mile Creek projectile point."

"Crap," Duggan said, rubbing his face. "Przewalski, I know you. You see a donkey, you want to load it up. With a bunch of crimeys. Now you're telling me to add Strickland to Page, Montanares, Kovitch, and Nalren. Like I said last time you were here, this ain't a goddamn Agatha Christie novel, y'know, *Murder on the Orient Express*." He raised his hands, his face incredulous. "What? All five are down there, grab the ceramic ape, whack him, then sing a quick chorus of Kumbaya?"

Harry crushed the cigarette butt on the sill, tossed it out, cranked the window shut, and sat down facing Duggan. "Very funny."

Duggan frowned at him. "Anyway, remember what they taught us in detective school—motive. If Strickland was gonna kill anyone, it would be Ball Cap, not Lasher." Duggan narrowed his eyes. "Is there something else I should know, Przewalski?"

"Yeah, motive. Strickland is fooling around on the side with a woman from Salina. Lasher found out."

"How?"

"Remember the towel in Lasher's closet? You guys gave it to him last December—to test the blood. It started there." Harry told him about Lasher's seminar class, the student cheek swabs, the DNA database, and the hit on the woman's sequence when he tested the dried blood.

"Crivvens!" Duggan exclaimed. "Okay, Lasher was a distinguished prof. Even he could deduce how her blood got on a Ramada Inn towel." He scowled. "I'm being sarcastic."

"I got that. Lasher began to blackmail her."

"What did he want? Money?"

"They called him 'Herbert the pervert.' Think genitalia."

Duggan rubbed his face. "Popular guy, that Lasher. With Strickland, and now the woman, we got six of'em who didn't cry at his funeral."

He opened a desk drawer, pulled out a bottle of Scotch and two shot glasses, and filled them with a flaxen yellow liquid. "Get busy, Przewalski," he growled, "seven more and we have ol' Agatha beat."

The Scotch was Kilchoman, the distillery on Machir Bay, Islay. Harry pulled out the Drum and papers, rolled another cigarette, lit it, and cranked the window open. The Scotch was seductive, smooth-tongued, a smoky mead steeped in peat.

Duggan raised his glass. "*Slàinte*!" He took a long sip and leaned back in his chair. "The chief is on my ass over Lasher. Boyle walks in here every second day spitting battery acid. She walks out leaving my pants around my ankles. It's an old Scottish saying."

He took another lick of Scotch and grabbed a pad of paper and a pen. "The woman in Salina—what's her name? Where does she hang out? We'll bring her in. Find out if she was here for the IRN demonstration. We'll bring Strickland in too. I know where he is."

Harry held up his hand. "Whoa. Let me talk to her. Or Tamara. Off the record. I met her during the Fulbright case. Never mentioned her because she ended up not being involved. Same here. She might have nothing to do with Lasher's murder. No sense in making a private affair public, either for her or him. Y'know, there's a husband, a wife, and a life to live after Lasher is history."

Duggan opened his eyes wide. "Przewalski, I never took you for a fairy-tale tender heart."

"No worries. My father raised me on Polish fairy tales. Dark, sinister woods, evil creatures, loud shrieks, horrible acts. Makes Grimm's tales seem like reading the phone book."

Duggan tossed down the rest of the Scotch. "One drink and I'm getting soft in the head, like you. You got till Monday to clear the woman."

Harry flicked the ashes out the window. "Thanks. What about Ball Cap?"

"I wondered when you were gonna get around to him. We rousted him a few days ago. He was camped in that jalopy minivan out at Clinton Lake, about seven miles west of here. He took off before we could grab him. Torched the jalopy. Couldn't lift anything from it. No fingerprints, nothing. He knew what he was doing. Makes sense if he's a loan shark leg-breaker. Anyway, we've put the word out. Nothing yet. He'll surface in KC, or Topeka, or back here. With another set of wheels, probably a hot piece from Arkansas. Strickland's hundred grand is a pretty good lure. Hope the hospitals are stocked up on splints and plaster casts."

Harry winced. "Yeah, I told him to go to ground on another continent."

Duggan looked at his watch. "Jeez, it's six. When I get home it's gonna be goddamn pasta la vista." He got up, put on his jacket, and pointed to the door. "Put out the fag, Przewalski, and shut the goddamn window."

On the stairs, Duggan grabbed Harry by the shoulder. "Listen. I owe you for digging up the blackmail. But I'm not telling you this. We're trying to get the shoes that three of 'em wore that night: Page, Montanares, Kovitch. We'll test 'em. Now we gotta add Strickland's and the woman's to the pile. You got a prediction?"

Harry shrugged. "Yeah, I'm going with Yogi Berra: 'Prediction is tough, especially about the future.' I've learned to expect the unexpected. Kovitch's soles will have splinters of glass and traces of indigenous DNA. For what it's worth, she was a hundred sheets to the wind when she told me. And another hundred when she went down there. She said Lasher was already a goner."

"First law of police work," Duggan said. "The lie comes first. Then liquor lubricates the truth."

Harry chuckled. "Too bad you guys can't use the ancient

cold-water trial. They took a suspect, tied a long rope under his arms, and threw him into the river. If he sank, he was innocent, and they'd quickly haul him up. If he floated, he was guilty—the water had rejected him because of his iniquity."

"Damn," Duggan quipped, "save us a lot of court time. Anyway, I'm betting on Strickland and his paramour. Blackmail is powerful iniquity. The rest of 'em? I'm praying to a God I don't believe in that they weren't all down there. Fucking Christie."

Outside, it was dark. Harry walked down Massachusetts past a bagel shop and a US Army recruiting center. The lights were off, the blinds down. They were on and up when he'd volunteered, when he'd fled to a desert war in a long fit of madness. He'd called his parents from basic training at Fort Riley. Nicholas had answered, cursed, and handed the phone to Emilia. She'd begged him to return. He'd not been in Kansas before, in the reverence of tall grasses sweeping over an endless earth. He'd not divined that later, in a truck stop cafe a few miles down the road, he'd meet Ruby.

A drizzle began falling on the neon-lit sidewalk, turning it into a pointillist canvas. Near a corner, in the shadow of the eave of a cafe, a young woman with a cello was bowing a tune to the passersby. It sounded to Harry like the hushed wails of *Paris Blues*. He wondered whether Seurat had risen during the night storms and painted the drops of rain being dyed as they hit the pavement. It was then, in that moment, that it consumed him, the ache of not having Ruby there. He crossed the street and walked the ten blocks to the hotel.

44

I Promise To Confess

Harry showed up at Sunflower Bike Shop at 9:30 Sunday morning in blue jeans, hiking boots, and a Levi jacket. Riders in their cycling kits crowded the sidewalk, chatting, eating donuts, packing energy for the Chug Ride. Duggan came over. Harry didn't recognize him in his black knickers, yellow Castelli jacket, black helmet, and sunglasses.

"Steelers colors," Harry remarked.

"Yeah," Duggan said. "Sentimental." He looked Harry up and down. "Doesn't look like you're riding."

"No. Heading to Salina. The woman Lasher was blackmailing."

Duggan nodded. "Swipe her shoes while you're at it. Tell her she'll be saving a Lawrence cop a lot of paperwork." He sounded half serious.

The group rolled east down 8th Street. Duggan had said they were headed to Eudora. Harry thought of them passing the Stonehenge fence, then the Jewish cemetery, the stratigraphy of stories in the soil below—the immigrants in the 1800s and, 13,000 years deeper, the indigenous Americans that came before them.

The bike shop had a mini cafe. Harry got a double espresso and a couple of chocolate muffins. The large screen TV above the bar was broadcasting a pro bike race live from Italy, the Strade Bianche, 200 kilometers on the narrow white dirt roads of Tuscany, San Gimignano to Sienna, finishing in the Piazza del Campo.

It was two and a half hours into the race. A lead group of eleven riders had a three-minute gap, enough time for the white dust to settle before the chasing peloton arrived. Harry thought of his father in the bunch, 175 riders jammed side-by-side, flying at 55 kilometers an hour.

Suddenly, a crash taking down half of the peloton in a hurtling mass of bike frames and bodies. Harry shuddered. As a kid, he'd seen the film of Paris-Roubaix, the brutal cobblestones, the crash that had ended his father's career. Ever since, he couldn't watch a bike race without seeing his father hit the ground and not move.

Harry left with forty kilometers to go in the race. He hit I-70 at the West Lawrence interchange, set the 4Runner's cruise control to seventy-five, and began scanning the radio for something jazzy or classical. Seven stations. Four were pounding out rock; three, Bible-Belt warnings of woe. He finally found a station playing Bach and Mozart and Handel, cello, flute, and harpsichord harmonics.

He called Angela Phillips. He'd gotten her number from Tamara, who said she had access to such things. Angela remembered him. He told her he was headed to Salina. She tried to maintain composure, hiding behind a nervous laughter. Perhaps George, her husband, was within earshot. Harry could almost see knots in her body unwind when he said he wanted to meet her at a bar, quiet, dark, where people who knew her would be unlikely to go on a Sunday morning.

"Your car has GPS?"

"Yeah."

"Punch in 'The Confessional.' It's across from a church, by an old railroad siding. I'll be waiting inside." She paused, then said in a low, deliberate whisper, "I promise to confess."

45

The Confessional

Traffic was light. Past the turnoff to Alma, the first stretch of Flint Hills rolled away to the south, the grasses not yet tall enough to flow over the rise and fall of the terrain. On one hillside, a lone stone house stood mute, long abandoned. It reminded Harry of the badlands, relinquished to the winds blowing through, unapposed, histories now buried in the crevices. Above the open roof, the clouds in the sky were teasing the sun, allowing it to poke through, igniting the henbit in the plowed fields into a purple fire.

It was one o'clock when he took the North Ohio Street exit from I-70. The lady with the British accent on the 4Runner's GPS instructed him to head south for four and a half miles, then turn right onto East North Street for a couple of blocks.

He spotted the church at the corner of York Street, the steeple cracked, the red brick eroding. An old, faded banner, half on the ground, was still readable: St. Mary's Catholic. An iron bar and chain lock barricaded the door. Prayer, Harry thought, had not staved off the departure of the faithful and ecclesiastical extinction. Two blocks further west, a water tower and a grain elevator were still feeding the multitude. A row of low sheet-metal buildings abutted the street: a welding shop, a wholesale electric company, a

Culligan water supply store.

From the outside, The Confessional could have passed for another industrial sheet-metal shop. Harry pulled the 4Runner into the lot, crunching the gravel as he slowly eased forward to park beside the red Audi. There was a dent in the metal siding where a car had kissed the side of the building. Two pickups were parked nearby, both Fords, one white, one blue, both bearing the bruised, rusted scars of farm work. A railroad siding ran behind the bar. It looked abandoned. The sign for the bar hung over the door. It was the color of a pale amber beer, with white lettering in all caps. Weathering had gnawed away the letters at either end of the sign, until it now beckoned patrons to CONFESS. Harry wondered whether this too was part of God's plan, the bar pinch-hitting for the church.

Inside, it was pitch dark. Harry waited until he could see in the dim light suffusing the bar. Angela had chosen well. He spotted her at a table in the corner, her back to the wall. She gave him a faint wave with her fingers. Two guys were at the counter drinking bottled beer, jawing with a woman behind the bar. Harry put them with the two pickup trucks. He went over to the table, pulled a chair back, and sat down opposite Angela.

"Hi," she said, an affected smile.

She'd let her black hair grow out to just above her shoulders, a long bob hanging down on the left, and side-swept bangs that angled across the right half of her face. It suited her. She was wearing a black leather jacket over what looked like a dark turtleneck sweater. Her hands were folded on the table: no rings, no bracelets.

"Thanks for meeting me," Harry said. "Sorry for the short notice." He looked around the bar. "You know this place?"

"Yes. I know it well. I escape here when I need a refuge from the museum. It's on the wrong side of town, the proverbial wrong side of the tracks. But it does have Wi-Fi. And it's dead quiet."

Harry looked around. Metal walls, no windows, black paint, old beer and liquor signs, nothing fancy: Pabst, Bud, Coors, Bacardi, Smirnoff, Jim Beam, Johnnie Walker Black. No neon. No jukebox. No big screen TV.

"Listen," she said, brushing the bangs from over her eye and forehead. "I don't have too much time. It's Sunday. You've met George. Lucky there's an NBA game on the tube."

"I understand. What did you tell him?"

"Had to do something at the museum."

"Did you tell Strickland you were meeting me?"

She sneered. "Absolutely not! I dumped him on Friday. I've made two big mistakes in life. Beau was one of them."

"What was the second? Killing Lasher?"

"NO!" she blurted out. "I said on the phone that I would confess—everything. I am. I didn't kill Lasher. I admit I wanted to. I thought about it, even planned it. I wanted to shoot the bastard between the legs, where it hurts before you die."

Someone behind Harry muttered, "Damn!"

Harry jerked around, scraping the legs of the chair against the floor. It was the woman from behind the bar. She'd come over with two plastic menus. "Take it easy, there. I hear lots of interesting stuff in this place. Gotta say, though, that's a winner. And I wouldn't have bet it would have come from you, Angela. Anyway, no worries, my dear. Like my mother would say, deaf in one ear, blind in the other. But, hey, if you did kill him, I know he deserved it. Fucking men."

Angela put her hands over her face, shook her head, then looked up at the woman. "Thanks, Alex. I owe you." Angela motioned to Harry. "That's Harry Przewalski, a private detective. He's ... he's investigating a murder in Lawrence, a professor I once took classes from. Harry is one of the good guys."

"Good to meet you, Mr. Good Guy." She plunked down the menus, turned, and walked back to the counter. She was a large woman, medium height, fifties, in black dungarees and a tight charcoal tank top that revealed muscled arms, a taut stomach, and an attitude. Printed across the back was "Don't Fuck With Me."

"She's really a sweetheart," Angela said. "But she doesn't take guff from anyone."

"I gathered."

"She comes from back east. Somehow ended up out here. She bought the bar. It used to be called The Dive. She renamed it The Confessional because of St. Mary's over there. She noticed that parishioners would arrive early for services—early enough to walk across the street and down a beer or two before mass. Then they'd come back after the sermon. Here, check out the menu."

Harry looked at it, and grinned. The bar food had three sections: *Pre-Prayer* for the appetizers—onion rings, chicken nuggets; *Prayer* for the entrees; and *Absolution* for the desserts.

"Cute. Go ahead and get an absolution. I happen to believe you."

Angela bowed her head, then whisked the long bangs from over her eyes, the relief spilling across her face. Slowly, she reached out, took hold of his hands, and squeezed them for a long moment.

Alex appeared. "That's touching. Literally and figuratively. Now, you guys going to touch any food?"

Angela blushed. "Yes, sorry. Apple pie and some of that whipped cream."

Harry ordered a couple of servings of bacon. Alex picked up the menus and left.

"Do you know how Lasher learned about my ... my affair?" Her face reddened.

Harry told her—the towel, the blood, the sequencing, the hit on her DNA profile in Lasher's database. "Ruby figured it. I should have."

Angela stared at him, dumbfounded. "I'll be damned. Now I know the meaning of 'twist of fate.' But that's not a twist, it's monstrous! Lucky we're not in that church across the street. I'd be on my knees acknowledging 'divine punishment.'"

Harry shook his head. "Just bad luck—it's jinxed a lot of history. Tell me, you were at the IRN protest a week ago Thursday."

"I was. I have a courtesy desk in the Spencer Museum of Art at KU. I know the director. I succeeded her here at the Salina museum."

"Did you go into Spooner? Down to Lasher's lab with the rest of them?"

"No. I went back to the Spencer."

Alex brought the food and a couple of tumblers of Scotch. "Enjoy. On the house."

Harry chewed a strip of bacon and chased it with a sip of the Scotch. It wasn't Black Label and there wasn't an ad for it on any of the walls. Maybe Talisker, or Laphroaig.

"What about Strickland," Harry continued. "Did he kill Lasher over the blackmail?"

Angela dug into the apple pie and wiped her mouth. "Beau? I'd like to think he would have been capable of it. But he's not. Anyway, he swore he didn't. And I think I could read him well enough to know whether he was lying. Although he hid other things from me."

"Lemme guess. His gambling debt. The loan shark guy with the ball cap in the beat-up Dodge minivan."

Angela shuddered. "I figured you would know. Yes, that. Also ... never mind. I dumped him. Like I said, he was one of my two mistakes."

"But Strickland went into Spooner that evening, to see the archeologist there."

"Yes, I know. He told me. Sam Page."

"Right. Did he notice the loan shark guy follow him into Spooner?"

She shook her head. "No. If he did, he didn't say. And he was paranoid about this guy, thought he was following him everywhere. He would have told me. He said he might have heard the front doors close as he was heading up to the second floor. Probably one of the IRN protesters leaving the building."

"Okay. You should know that the cops put the panic to the loan shark guy. He isn't around now, but he'll be back for that hundred grand Strickland owes him. I advised Strickland to take his wife on an expedition. Same goes for you. Convince George to go snorkeling off one of those islands that's going under water."

Angela shoved her pie aside. "Just lost my appetite. You mean the Maldives? Tuvalu?"

"Yeah, those'll work."

Harry finished the bacon, tossed back the rest of the Scotch, went up to the bar, and dropped thirty dollars on the counter. "She's a good lady," he said to Alex, "just wandered down the wrong alley one day."

"Don't we all," Alex grumbled, then flashed him a thumbs-up.

In the parking lot, Angela stopped Harry before he got into the 4Runner. "Dare I hope that the cops will keep me out of the headlines?"

"Yeah, I don't deal in hope. Five people know about you and Lasher: Strickland, Ruby, a detective in Lawrence, a cop in Abilene, and me. If Strickland whacked Lasher, you'll be a star witness for the prosecution. If he didn't, you're free of him, us, and this business.

But you can do the cop in Lawrence a favor."

"What's that?"

"The shoes you were wearing during the IRN protest march. Box them up. Send them to Detective Duggan at the Douglas County Courthouse."

"Is this a joke? I don't get it."

"He'll get the soles tested for genomic chemicals that were swimming around Lasher's body." Harry paused, then raised the corner of his mouth into an amiable smile. "It'll prove your confession—you weren't there."

Angela brushed the hair back from her face. "I'll go one better. The shoes are under my desk at the Spencer. I'll hand deliver them."

Abruptly, she leaned forward, put her fingers on his cheek, bussed his other cheek, whispered, "Thank you," got into the Audi, backed out of the lot, and drove off.

46

The Ideal Cerebrum

Harry headed east on I-70 back to Lawrence. The clock on the dashboard of the 4Runner showed 3:07. Impulsively, at Abilene, he took the North Buckeye Avenue exit, headed south on the strip for a couple of miles past drive-ins, motels, and churches, turned right on 5th Street to Broadway Avenue, and pulled into a parking slot in front of the police department. Maybe Blevins or Tamara would be in the building. The receptionist at the desk checked the log-in register. They weren't.

He got into the 4Runner and drove to the house with the big wrap-around porch and the yellow police tape strung across the door. It was only four blocks from the police station. The cops must have just missed Ruby's shooter driving off.

Harry stepped onto the porch, grabbed the pink cushion in the metal lounge chair, poked as much of the stuffing as he could back through the open seam, and sat down. He pulled out the Drum and Zig-Zag papers, rolled a cigarette, and used one of Duggan's matchbooks to light it. The first drag, he knew, would be exquisite, the last, acrid. Much like ardor, he thought, hunger deflating to habit. He kicked himself, silently. Sitting on Ruby's porch was making him maudlin. She'd called it soppy yesterday at the hospital.

Up the street, toward Eisenhower Park, a group of kids were playing tag in Mud Creek. Down the street it was quiet, a few cars parked on either side: a black Ford Escape, a silver Kia Sportage, a red Mazda CX3. He couldn't make out the tags. If Ball Cap was hanging around Ruby's place in Abilene, it wasn't evident.

He stubbed out the cigarette, went over to the door, and tried to turn the big brass knob. Locked. At the edge of the porch, he sat down on the steps, steering clear of the spell of the lounge chair. A couple walked by, arm-in-arm, in their sixties, coming from Eisenhower Park. They scrutinized him—a burglar casing the place? He smiled at them. Ruby's neighbors, he realized, when they crossed the street, turned at the Kia Sportage, and went up the walkway and into their house.

Harry rolled another Drum, swearing to quit after the second drag. He felt his iPhone vibrate in his pocket. He fished it out and looked at the number—913 area code, Kansas City. He took the call.

"Hey there, detective," Ruby said, her voice laced with elation. "I'm on the hospital phone. At the nurses' desk. Melissa let me use it for a minute. She's timing me. They're letting me outta here tomorrow afternoon. Four-thirty, they say. Pending one more brain scan. I told Melissa to submit it to the MENSA Bulletin ... for their cover, y'know, the archetype of the ideal cerebrum. Okay, my minute is up."

47

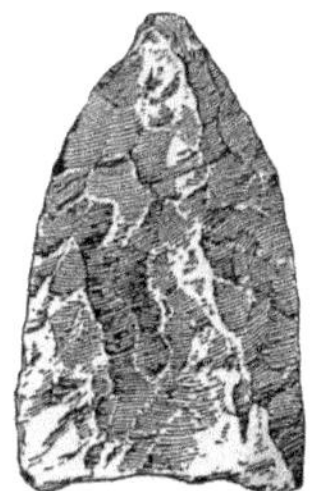

I Been Waitin' For Ya

At 4:15 on Monday afternoon, Harry took the elevator to the third floor at KU Med. He walked down one hallway, then another, past the nurses' station, and into Ruby's room. The bed was empty, the sheets and cushions in a pile, the monitor silent. A stab of fright.

"Hey, you're a sight for eyes tired of this room, that bed, that fucking beeping machine, and the steady in and out of uniforms."

Ruby was sitting in a chair in the corner, dressed, hair combed over the strip of bandage, jeans, sweater, running shoes, broad smile. He went over to her and ran his finger over her lips.

"Hey, quit that. The doc tells me to keep the brain from getting too excited. I told him not to worry. I'll start reading Ayn Rand's *Atlas Shrugged*. I got a copy at home."

Harry laughed. Melissa came into the room with a wheelchair.

"Okay, Ruby, paperwork is done. Ready to go? Got all your stuff?"

"Yeah. But do you really have to wheel me outta here in that contraption? I'm not a damn cripple—no offense to cripples. But save the chair for someone who needs it."

Melissa eyed her with a tired patience. "It's the rules. Lawyers.

Insurance. As soon as you're out the door you can bunny hop to whatever transportation you got."

Ruby eased herself into the wheelchair and sat stoically, her bag of belongings in her lap, until Harry pulled the 4Runner up to the hospital exit and helped her into the front seat. He took Rainbow Boulevard north to 7th Street, crossed the Kansas River, and merged onto I-70 toward Lawrence, Topeka, and Abilene.

The jazz station was playing Keith Jarrett at Carnegie Hall, his modern fugues on the piano, haunting timbres of love and loss. They drove west in silence under an overcast sky, Ruby staring straight ahead, once reaching over and rubbing the back of her fingers against his cheek.

An hour later the golden dome of the capitol building in Topeka rose in the distance. Harry asked her if she wanted food. Ruby shook her head. South of Manhattan, she kept gazing at the land as if she were trekking across unknown terrain, the rolling grass of the Konza Prairie, the small herds of bison grazing on the hills.

Abruptly, she said, her voice quiet, contemplative. "You must have talked to Page ... his idea about Solutreans. Them crossing the North Atlantic to the east coast."

Harry glanced at her, wondering whether the bison had resurrected an archeological ghost in her past. "I did. Why?"

She shrugged. "Just reverie ... being bedeviled. I tuned in to the news channel this morning in the hospital. Researchers at Texas A&M found spear points at a site they've been working for years near Austin. The points look identical to Solutrean ones. They're perfect pre-Clovis ancestors—concave base, like Clovis, but no fluting. Here is the kicker. They're from below the Clovis stratum. They're 15,500 years old—2500 years before Clovis, 1500 years after Solutrean."

The sun went down. They pulled into Abilene in the dark. The clock in the 4Runner read 8:16. Harry eased down 5th Street and parked adjacent to Ruby's walkway. Two of the three SUVs had moved a few yards up closer to the corner. The Kia had stayed put in front of the house with the elderly couple.

Harry held Ruby's arm as she stepped onto the porch. He ripped away the three strips of yellow police tape, took her key, unlocked the door, and followed her inside. A bit of light from the streetlamp filtered through the curtain on the door into the entryway. Ruby flipped the wall switch. Nothing. Harry felt a sudden gnawing of unease. She went into the living room, fumbled for the switch on the standing lamp, and clicked it. A warm yellow light suffused the room.

Harry looked around. Not much had changed since he'd been here a year ago. A worn gray velveteen couch and two sofa chairs around a low table; a frayed Persian rug; a couple of armoires, the doors open, stuffed with books and mammal skulls; a big conch shell on the table.

A sudden noise. Then a voice. "I been waitin' for ya."

48

Who'd You Send To The Morgue?

Ruby gasped. Harry swiveled around. A woman pointing a gun at them. Short. Skinny. She motioned them to the couch, waving a small pistol. She was wearing a camo outfit, a brown and grey pattern: pants, shirt, high-collar hooded jacket, army boots. The jacket was unzipped, the hood down. Straight amber hair to the neckline, bangs to below the eyebrows. Thin face, bony, sallow skin, almost colorless.

"Sit yerself down," she said. "Take a load off."

Harry had heard the voice before. Odd hillbilly accent, a high-pitched drawl. Then he placed it. Ball Cap poking a pistol into his back at the museum. He took Ruby's hand and squeezed it, reassuringly. They sat down on the couch. Ball Cap moved around the table and eased into one of the couch chairs.

"Cute wig," Harry said. "Walmart?"

"Har har," Ball Cap chuckled. "I fergot yer a wise guy. Yeah, it works."

"You can lose it. Put the ball cap back on. It's good to see a familiar face."

Ball Cap snickered, dug around on the inside of his jacket, came out with his KC Royals cap, plucked the wig off his head, and put the cap on. In the instant his head was bare, Harry noticed the mottled, sickly skin, like algal patches on a lagoon. He also noticed that Ball Cap had somehow lost his eyebrows, or never had any.

"It's you!" Ruby exclaimed. "You're the one who ... who—"

"Yeah, it's me. Back again." Ball Cap winked at her and waved the pistol at Harry. "Are ya carryin'?"

"No."

"Okey, let's prove it. Empty them pockets."

Harry dug out his wallet, loose change, pouch of Drum tobacco, Zig-Zag papers, Zippo lighter, and two matchbooks, and tossed them on the table.

Ball Cap picked up the Zippo. "Nice." He flicked it a few times. No flame. "Haven't held one of these in a while. You woan be needin' it. I'll spring for the fluid."

He slipped it into the front pocket of his camo pants and waggled the pistol at Harry again. "Now, take yer duds off."

Harry squinted at him. "Didn't know this was going to be a peep show."

"Har har. Very funny. Take yer clothes off. Jus to make sure you're not packin' anythin' against yer skin. So, strip time, wise guy."

Harry took off his Levi jacket, pulled the turtleneck over his head, and tossed both on the table. He slipped off his sneakers, socks and jeans, and left them lying on the floor.

"And the underwear. Like I said, y'cain't be sure. Hell, I bet you could hide one of these little jobs in those briefs." He wiggled the pistol. "But I couldn't. I'm a boxer guy, y'know, let 'em dangle free, like the dice I got hangin' from the mirror in the SUV."

He motioned to Harry with the pistol. "Don't be shy. Let's see what you got hidden there." He grinned at Ruby. "I'm sure the lady's seen it all. Jus show us it's meat, not metal. Har har."

Harry glanced at Ruby and winked. Her face was ashen, her right hand clenched over the arm rest. He dropped his underwear.

"Good. Now turn around. Nothin' taped to your backside? Good. Okey, you can get the duds back on. Slow, easy, jus like you jus done laid that lady and are gettin' goin'."

Harry stayed stone-faced. He put on his clothes, sat down, then pointed to the wallet, coins, and tobacco stuff on the table.

"Nah, jus leave 'em there," Ball Cap said. "You woan be needin' 'em either."

"In that case, I'm going to have a smoke. Last rites."

Ball Cap nodded.

Harry took his time. He grabbed the pouch of Drum, papers, and one of the matchbooks off the table. He took a pinch of tobacco, rolled the cigarette, tore off a red-tipped match, struck it against the gritty black strip, cupped his hand around the flame, and lit the smoke.

"Yeah," Harry said, coolly, "you're right. You shoot me, I won't need this stuff. But neither will you. The cops are all over your face. Two murders here, and you'll be real popular on the wanted posters—with that wig or a ball cap."

"Three."

"Three what?"

"Murders."

Harry narrowed his eyes at him. "Oh yeah? Who did you send to the morgue? Strickland?"

Ball Cap looked over at Ruby. "You gonna tell 'em?"

49

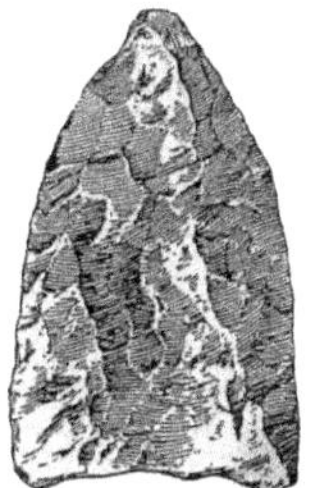

How Many Whacks?

Ruby opened her mouth, closed it, then quietly rasped, "It's Lasher." She turned to Harry, her face forlorn, rueful, despairing.

Harry sat back, pursed his lips, silently rewriting the history he thought he knew. "Memory come back?"

She shook her head. "It ... it never left. I had to pretend. Sorry, Harry. Be ... be merciful. I made a deal. I kept it."

Ball Cap flipped the gun at Harry. "Yeah, she made a deal—with me. Seems you ain't as smart as you think. Cuz you never figured any of this out."

Harry took a last drag on the cigarette, reached over to the conch on the table, and stubbed it out. "I'll tell you what I did figure. You're tailing Strickland. You want to collect the hundred grand he owes the loan sharks."

Ball Cap raised his forehead where his eyebrows were supposed to be. "You know about that?"

"Yeah. He was supposed to deliver fifty grand last Friday, but you got rousted at that campground and torched the minivan. So you went out and boosted yourself that Ford Escape—the one sitting down the block. I bet it doesn't have Kansas plates."

"You win that bet. Texas. Amarillo."

"Go back ten days ... Thursday, March 3 ... the day of the protest march. You're waiting for Strickland outside the museum. Around 8:30 or so, you see him come out of the building. He crosses the street and goes into Spooner. You follow him. By the time you're in the entryway, you've lost him. You don't know which way he went. Maybe up the stairs to the second floor. Maybe down to the basement. You guess wrong. You go downstairs to Lasher's office and lab. And Ruby is there."

Ball Cap smirked at him. "Yeah, you got the drift."

Ruby began rocking, her hands clasped on her knees. "Yes, Harry, I was there." Her voice had become unmoored, anguished. "I wanted to talk to Lasher about Twelve Mile Creek, the projectile point, show him Nalren's work. But he didn't give me a chance. I went over to his desk. The floor was wet, gooey. He was sitting there, face all red, angry. It looked like he had a bit of blood on his head. He yelled at me. He said 'What the fuck do you want? Did you put the chancellor's kid up to this ... what's his name ... Nalren? I came in here, I saw them—him and his white broad.'"

Ruby licked her lips. "I said, 'No. I just came to tell you what Nalren dug up about that projectile point, the one Martin found at Twelve Mile Creek. If you have it, he'd like to see it.' Lasher said, 'Oh yeah? He, and Page and the rest of the world. Whether I got it or not is no one's business. Fuck 'em. What did the kid find?' I said, 'It could be a Solutrean point—'"

Ruby stopped rocking and sat up. "Lasher never let me finish the sentence—'a Solutrean point brought over by Martin from Europe.' He just flew into a rage, came out of his chair, grabbed me by the throat, and started to choke me. He was shouting 'Fuck you and that goddamn Indian kid you're probably fucking.' We fell to the floor ... into the muck. He had his elbow on my windpipe, pressing down, I couldn't breathe, I couldn't scream. I started to black out. And then, suddenly, it stopped."

Ruby looked at Ball Cap.

Harry nodded at him. "You walked in, you saw a lady in distress, you grabbed that ceramic ape, and you let Lasher have it. How many whacks?"

"Two," Ball Cap said. "Then I rolled him off her."

"You had gloves on?"

"Always. Even in summer. Never know when you have to go into a meat locker. Har har. So, no fingerprints. I say to myself, 'We're good here.' But I never been in a situation like this—not workin' for the bail bondsman in KC, or the loan shark outfit."

Ball Cap flicked the gun at Ruby. "The lady here props a deal. I saved her life; so she'll stay zipped about who did the savin'—about the whole business. She says, 'Let's get outta here. No one's seen us so far. No one's heard anythin'. We were never here.'"

Ball Cap paused to scratch the side of his head. "I think it over. We can't play straight with the cops, y'know, tell 'em I'm the hero. I'm wanted in too many places. Hero here, in the slammer in Missouri. So we shake on the deal. The lady here knows that building. She leads us out through the sub-basement, a back exit onto a side street. She takes off, I take off."

Harry glanced quickly at Ruby. "You took Lasher's laptop."

She blinked, then said in a hushed tone, "Yes, I did. The DNA database ... all our genetic profiles. It's gone now."

Harry turned to Ball Cap. "Trouble is," he said, not hiding his contempt, "five days into the deal you reneged. Maybe she'll talk, you thought. Maybe someone saw her go into Spooner and down to Lasher's lab. What if the cops have a go at her. You'd be cooked."

"You goddamn fucker!" Ruby spat. "You're the bastard who shot me?"

"Naturally," Ball Cap said. "Takin' care of myself."

"Whatever," Harry cracked. "You drove over here, went up to the doorbell, pushed it, she opened the door, you fired two slugs at her head. With that." Harry pointed to the pistol.

"Yeah," Ball Cap said, admiringly, holding it up. "It's an NAA-22S—North American Arms, 22-caliber short, made in Provo, Utah, five-shot capacity. Cost me 225 smackers."

"Congratulations," Harry quipped. "One bullet missed. The other went up, nicked the forebrain. If that were a nine-millimeter, she wouldn't be here. Neither would we. Thanks for using the toy pistol. I like this lady a lot."

Ball Cap straightened up in the sofa chair. "It ain't a toy," he said, indignant, as if he'd been insulted. "Which you're gonna discover in a couple minutes."

"Aim good, or it'll be messy."

Ball Cap aimed the pistol at Harry's head. "Har har, wise guy. See me worry."

Harry tossed Ruby a defeated look, then shrugged. "I'm going to roll another smoke. And one for the lady."

"Why not. Like you said, last rites."

Harry shifted forward on the couch, got the tobacco pouch, Zig-Zag papers, and matchbook from the table, and rolled the cigarette. He tore out a match, struck the red tip till it flamed, cupped his hands, and, in one swift motion, ignited the remaining 27 matches into a ball of fire and hurled it at Ball Cap's head.

Ball Cap jerked his hand up to protect his face. It was the instinct Harry had counted on. He leapt across the table, smashing his shoulder full force into Ball Cap's skinny chest. He heard ribs crack. Ball Cap squeezed off one shot before Harry grabbed his wrist, levered it across his knee, then snapped it hard.

Ball Cap screamed. Harry grabbed the gun and shoved it against his temple. He felt Ball Cap's body go rigid.

"If ... if ya gotta do somethin'," Ball Cap stammered, "why doan ya smack me across the head. Like I did ya at the museum."

It wouldn't be neat, Harry thought, shooting him, splattering brains everywhere, dumping the body. He eased his finger off the trigger, got up, and left Ball Cap prone on the sofa chair. The ribs and wrist were enough.

He pointed to the ceiling. "I told you to aim good, or it would be messy. You made a mess up there."

At the end of the couch, Ruby sat frozen, inert, a manikin in shock. Harry went over to her, held out his hand, pulled her up, and kissed her on the mouth. "It's over. Get us something to drink. Liquor."

She started out of the room, then turned. "Harry, you're not ... tell me you're not going to kill him."

Harry stared intently at Ball Cap. "Three glasses, But it could-be two. Depends on the new deal."

50

The New Deal

Ruby returned with three tumblers and a bottle of Wild Turkey. Her cheeks had regained some of the blush she'd put on at the hospital, the hollows slowly losing their sickly pale shadow.

Ball Cap groaned, holding his wrist as he leaned forward, grabbed the bourbon with his left hand, and took a serious gulp.

Harry swished the bourbon in the tumbler and took a sip. "Listen up," he said to Ball Cap, "here's what's going to happen."

"Fuck you. You bust my wrist. You bust my ribs. I can barely suck in air. You can't tell me shit. Dare ya to put one in me."

Harry shook his head in disappointment. "Careful. You don't want to die over a lousy bluff. Think about it. We toss your body in the town dump. They find it, this dead weirdo with a red wig, with fingerprints that the cops use to close a couple of open cases."

Harry picked up the cigarette he'd dropped when he'd jumped Ball Cap, got the other pack of matches, lit the smoke, and took a drag. "We can also let you crawl out that door and into the pen. The Abilene Police Department is four blocks down the road. I give Sheriff Blevins this pistol. It convicts you of attempted murder—Ruby. They got the bullet that missed. It'll match this piece."

Ball Cap pointed at Ruby with his left arm. "Not so fast. I'll trade with 'em. Me for the lady. I tell 'em she killed that guy, Lasher. I tell 'em I was there, saw it all. He was sittin' at his desk, peaceful like. They started fightin' about somethin', then she picked up that ape and put a dent in his skull. I tell 'em the lady said she'd pay me to keep the trap zipped."

Harry chuckled. "Nice try. You worked for a bail bondsman. You know the meaning of corroborating evidence. There's nothing that pins Lasher on Ruby. Besides, the cops would believe a tin-pot weasel over you. They're looking for you in how many states?"

Ball Cap didn't think for very long. "Four."

"Okay, good we got that straight. Like I said, here's what's going to happen. We're going to load you up with pain pills. We're going to walk you out to your Ford Escape. And you're going to drive off to wherever you hole up."

Ball Cap downed his bourbon, then winced when he bent over, put the glass on the table, and motioned to Ruby for a refill. She poured him another shot.

"Okay, wise guy," he said, "what are ya offerin'? What's my cut on this deal?" He took a quick swig, then wiped his lips on his sleeve.

Harry narrowed his eyes at Ball Cap. "Here's your cut. You get to take off. You get to stay out of the slammer. And you get to never see us again. Or we, you. If you're smart, you'll steer clear of Strickland, of Lawrence. The cops there will smell you at the county line. If you're smarter still, you'll burn the shoes that you wore in that lab. They're full of fine glass and chemical buffer."

Harry stubbed out the cigarette. "Ruby will get permanent amnesia about you whacking Lasher that night. She's good at it. She's been practicing." He looked at her. She gave him a wounded smile.

"Oh yeah?" Ball Cap waved the glass toward Ruby, spilling some of the bourbon on his camo pants. "Why should I trust her?"

Harry pointed the pistol at him. "You have no choice. And this time you won't renege on the deal. See this little gun? It's her kill-switch. When the banks open tomorrow, we're going to put it in a safe deposit box. There will be two notes in the barrel. One will ID this little banger. It'll tell the cops to test it against the slug that missed Ruby and buried itself in the back wall of the entryway. Like I said, the Abilene police have that slug. The other note will ID the shooter—you."

Ball Cap stared at the bourbon, then downed it. "Who gets the key to the bank box?"

"Good question," Harry said. "Shows you're thinking. A person who will use it if you ever come within shooting distance of this place or Ruby. If you do, the cops will get you. If they don't, I will. And I'll use a nine-millimeter."

Ball Cap again raised the eyebrows he didn't have and looked back and forth at them. "I'm missin' somethin' here. So, who's gonna go down for the murder of this guy, Lasher?"

Harry poured himself more bourbon, drank a lick, and said, nonchalantly, "Nobody. Three days ago someone told me about justice, that it's a human invention. That, like all things human, it makes mistakes. Lasher is going to be a mistake."

Ball Cap stared at Harry, then at Ruby, shrugged, took off his cap, and put on his wig. Ruby went to the kitchen, returned with a bottle of Ibuprophen, and slipped it into the pocket of his camo jacket. Harry walked him out the door, eased him down the porch steps, helped him across the street, and buckled him into the black Ford Escape.

"You did the right thing," Harry said, "saving her life." He paused, then said, pointedly, "It just bought you yours."

He watched Ball Cap roll slowly down the street toward North Buckeye Avenue. He fished the phone out of his pocket and dialed Margaret Warden. She answered after four rings. He told her the case was done. Nalren was free of the Lasher business. And not to ask any questions, because there were no right answers.

Then he called Duggan. Angela was clean, he told him. She'll be bringing her shoes in.

Ruby was waiting on the porch with the Wild Turkey. "Roll yourself a cigarette, Harry. And one for me. Tamara gets the key, right?"

"Right."

They sat on the stoop, drank the bourbon, and smoked until a sliver of moon came out from behind a cloud and lit its acre of sky.

She got up and took his hand. "This body wants a bed, Harry. And I need you to hold me in it."

Author's Note

Novels begin with the disclaimer that "this is a work of fiction ... any resemblance to actual events, locales, organizations, or persons, living or dead, is entirely coincidental." This is true only in part for *Native Blood.*

In 1895, Handel T. Martin and his assistant, Thomas Overton, working for the University of Kansas Natural History Museum, excavated a herd of ten fossil bison from a sandstone layer, approximately 13,000 years old, along Twelve Mile Creek, Logan County, Kansas. Martin reported finding a flint projectile point under the shoulder blade of one of the large male bison. A single illustration of the point was subsequently published in numerous scientific and newspaper articles—now it also graces the beginning of each chapter of *Native Blood.* The skeleton of the male bison, prepared by Martin for display, is on exhibit on the third floor of the museum in Dyche Hall on the KU campus.

The correspondence between Martin, Barnum Brown, E. H. Sellards, and Claude W. Hibbard relating to the Twelve Mile Creek projectile point and its mysterious disappearance is archived and quoted verbatim.

Also factual are: Mary Fanning Apitz, an amateur collector in Lawrence of archeological artifacts, fossils, and other scientific specimens; Carlisle Smith, a KU archeologist; E. R. Hall, a KU mammalogist and former director of the KU Natural History Museum; and the discovery of boxes of archeological artifacts that Smith had secreted behind a museum exhibit in 1948.

Finally, the Indian Residential Schools were a monstrous reality; their horrific history and effects are still being investigated by Canada's Truth and Reconciliation Commission and other bodies.

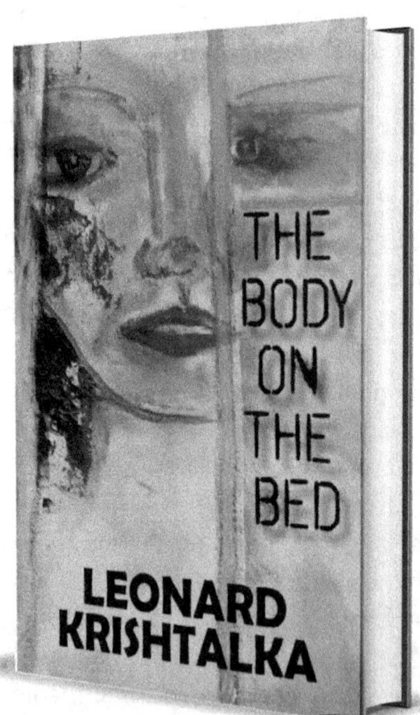
THE
BODY
ON
THE
BED
LEONARD
KRISHTALKA

Enjoy an Excerpt from

The Body on the Bed

by Leonard Krishtalka

Chapter 1

In the long-shadowed light of early morning, a man in a harness buggy rolled past her window. He slowed at the Ruthman house next door, glanced nervously over his shoulder, then continued on. She recognized him—Dr. John Medlicott, the Ruthmans' physician. He'd come past the Ruthman house often, but never at seven in the morning.

An hour later, she heard a loud commotion from inside the Ruthman home. It sounded like Belmont, Isaac Ruthman's fourteen-year-old stepson. She heard him shout "Father! Father!" Suddenly, he came around the side of the house and began pounding frantically on his father's bedroom window. It was slightly ajar. He tried to raise it, but couldn't. He disappeared behind the house, returned with an ax, wedged the handle under the window, and managed to pry it up just enough to stick his hand in.

Why, she wondered, was Belmont trying to get in through the window? Had Isaac locked himself in his bedroom? Was he ill, unable to get up?

She watched Belmont move the curtain aside, then grope between the slats of the headboard that rested against the window. The white satin pillow caught the low, clear morning sun from the east. He pressed his face against the window pane then shrank back, turned, and dashed down the street.

Isaac must have been stricken, she thought. He'd seemed well yesterday evening. She'd spoken to him outside when he'd returned from work.

A few minutes later Medlicott's buggy pulled up to Ruthman's house. Belmont was with him. She quickly draped a sweater over her shoulders against the morning chill and went out to her front yard. The doctor looked pale. His hands trembled as he hitched the horse's reins to the post. Belmont ran up to the window, yanked the ax out, and handed it to Medlicott. He smashed the glass in the bedroom's adjacent window and climbed in over the sill. Belmont followed.

She heard muffled conversation through the open window. Abruptly, Belmont came tearing out of the front door of the house and raced past her up the street. Dr. Medlicott must be tending to Mr. Ruthman, she surmised. He's probably sent Belmont to fetch medicine, or another doctor.

She crossed the yard to Ruthman's front door. It was open. She found Medlicott in Ruthman's bedroom, leaning against a wooden dresser, reading a pamphlet. She could see the title in large block letters: MANHOOD! An Essay on the Cause and Cure of Premature Decline in Men. Startled, Medlicott jerked around and hastily put it back on the dresser.

Isaac Ruthman was stretched out on the bed, his body covered with a sheet, his face with a towel. She noticed the pillow, lying near the side of the headboard, stained with blood and spittle. There were shards of glass on the floor below the window from the broken pane.

"Is he dead?" she asked, lifting the towel. She didn't need to hear Medlicott's response. Ruthman's face looked like a leaf in winter. She wondered where the color drains to at the end, this ruddiness of life sapped from skin and veins.

"Yes, he's dead,"Medlicott said, placing his fingers on the side of Ruthman's throat. "But he's warm yet. Who are you?"

"Mary Fanning. I live in the next house. You might know me by my married name, Mary Apitz. I know you, Dr. Medlicott. I've seen you visit here often."

He blinked, seemingly taken aback. "I see … yes … Mr. Ruthman was my patient. Also Mrs. Ruthman. I've sent the son … em … Belmont to the county courthouse." He motioned north toward

Henry Street. "The authorities should be here any moment."

"Yes, he ran past me. But I'm bewildered." She pointed to Isaac's body. "He seemed healthy yesterday evening. How did he die?"

Medlicott stepped away from the bed and shoved his hands into his pockets. "I honestly don't know."

She hesitated. "Do you think it could be suicide?"

Medlicott stiffened. "Why would you suggest that?"

"Why … you had to break in here through that window. Belmont must have found the bedroom door locked. I assume Isaac locked himself in here last night. Why … why else would he do that?"

Medlicott shrugged. "I don't know. The coroner will determine the cause of death."

She looked around the room. Four windows, two facing east, two north. A high-backed French bed. A plain nightstand. A chest of drawers. The most expensive piece of furniture was an upright piano in the corner. Last night, before retiring, Ruthman had folded his coat, vest, trousers, and shirt neatly on top of the piano. A last rite before suicide.

They stood in awkward silence waiting for the authorities. Medlicott kept checking his pocket watch. The dead, she thought, imposed this uncomfortable quietude, whether here in Ruthman's bedroom or in a funeral parlor, forcing us to stare at our own mortality—so feared, so private, so certain. And yet so uncertain. That we will pass, we know, but where to, we don't. It is how death begets belief. Faith assures us there is an afterlife when reason whispers there is not.

John Hutchings, the Douglas County Attorney, arrived first, on foot. He had a full head of short red hair. In the light it looked as if it had sprouted in patches. His cheeks and forehead were peppered with freckles that age had not matured away. He introduced himself, mumbled that the others were right behind, and checked the body on the bed.

"He's dead?" Hutchings glanced questioningly at Medlicott.

"Yes."

Three other men came into the bedroom. Mary recognized them. Andrew Carnes, the County Marshal, sporting a large, silver five-pointed badge on the front of his jacket. Charles Chadwick, judge and County Coroner. She'd attended his speeches in Lawrence in favor of women's suffrage. And Andrew Sharman, whose reporting in the *Lawrence Daily Journal* she thought was more recitation than journalism. Buggies pulled up outside the house. Dr. William Saunders and two other town physicians, Samuel Morse and Alonzo Fuller, hurried in, each carrying a leather medical bag.

Judge Chadwick yanked the sheet from the body. Ruthman's right hand was folded across his chest over his night shirt. His left hand still grasped the whiskers of his mustache. Saunders bent over Ruthman's face, then pointed to the froth around his lips and the blood and spittle on the pillow. He turned to Chadwick, motioning toward Mary with a quizzical, almost sheepish, expression.

"Judge, we … er … we need to remove his underclothes. Perhaps the lady should … er … be excused from the room." Saunders' round face turned red. He was short, slim, and had a stubble of yellow-blond hair that looked to Mary like a cropped hay field.

The other men stared at Mary, who was leaning against the piano in the corner. She folded her arms and flashed a defiant smile. "Gentlemen, I am Mary Apitz, married to Frederick Apitz. I've conceived two sons. And, although my name is also Mary, I assure you those conceptions were not immaculate. I know the nude male body. No part of Mr. Ruthman will be a surprise or seem indelicate. Please proceed."

Judge Chadwick nodded at her with a hint of admiration, then flicked his hand toward the bed. Saunders and Morse stripped the long night shirt from Ruthman's body.

"His skin is warm," Saunders remarked, "especially around the heart … almost lifelike to the touch. He appears to be dead, but strangely still animate. As if his eyes ought to open and his chest heave."

Hutchings, the County Attorney, ordered the doctors to try to resuscitate Ruthman. They applied heated bricks and hot water to his chest, then attempted to shock the heart to life with a galvanic battery. But Ruthman's eyes remained shut and his chest still.

"Judge," Saunders finally declared, "Mr. Ruthman is undoubtedly dead." He covered the corpse with the bed sheet. The shroud, Mary thought, that final, wordless verdict.

Heavy footsteps sounded on the wooden porch. A policeman in a blue uniform ushered six stern-looking men through the doorway.

"Good," Chadwick grunted, motioning to the policeman. "Dr. Medlicott, this is Deputy Marshal Jim Wright. He will take you to another room in this house where you will enjoy his company. And Jim, escort the good lady … Mrs. Apitz outside to the porch.

Mary planted herself outside Ruthman's broken window, determined to witness the proceedings. Chadwick shook hands with each of the six men, asked them to raise their right hands, and swore them in as the coroner's jury. "For the record," he stated, "the inquest into the cause of death of Isaac Miles Ruthman is now in session."

Marshal Carnes and Hutchings began a methodical search of Ruthman's bedroom. In the drawer of his nightstand Hutchings discovered two boxes of medicinal powder. Carnes rummaged through Ruthman's clothes on top of the piano. Between the vest and the coat he found a memorandum book. Carnes adjusted his spectacles and paged through it.

"Ho!" He held up the memorandum book, triumphantly. "The last entry. It's a letter. Ruthman wrote it last night. To his wife."

Darling, the Doctor—I mean Dr. Medlicott—gave me a quinine powder Wednesday night April 26th. The effects are these: I have a terrible sensation of a rush of blood to the head, and my skin burns and itches. I am becoming numb and blind. I can scarcely hold my pencil and cannot keep my mind steady. Perspiration stands out all over my body, and I feel terribly. The clock has just struck eleven, and I took the medicine about 10:30 pm. I write this so that if I never see you again you may have my body examined, and see what the trouble is. Good-bye, and ever remember my last thoughts were of you. I cannot see to write more. God bless you, and may we meet in heaven.

Your loving hubbie, I. M. Ruthman.

Acknowledgments

The following people, institutions, and sources were invaluable in writing *Native Blood*:

The Canadian Broadcasting Corporation and their exposure and coverage of the record of Residential Schools across Canada.

The Briscoe Center for American History, University of Texas at Austin, for E. H. Sellards correspondence.

The American Museum of Natural History, New York, NY for Barnum Brown correspondence.

The Connecticut Historical Society, Storrs, for access to the letters of Annie Williston.

Kansas State Historical Society, Topeka, KS for access to newspaper archives, specifically, *The Kansas City Star*, *The Chanute Daily Tribune*, *Lawrence Journal-World*.

At The University Kansas, Lawrence: the Natural History Museum, for the Twelve Mile Creek bison exhibit and photographs; the Spencer Research Library, for newspaper articles, dissertations, and correspondence involving the Twelve Mile Creek projectile point, Handel T. Martin, Thomas Overton, Samuel Williston, and Claude Hibbard; and Watson Library, for access to professional journals.

Fossil and Flies: The Life of a Compleat Scientist, Samuel Wendell Williston (1851-1918). Elizabeth Noble Shor, University of Oklahoma Press, Norman, 1971.

Thirty Years Later: The Long-term Effect of Boarding Schools on Alaska Natives and Their Communities. Diane Hirshberg, Suzanne Sharp, University of Alaska Anchorage, 2005.

Federal Indian Boarding School Initiative Investigative Report. Bryan Newland, U.S. Department of the Interior, Bureau of Indian Affairs, 2022.

Reports: Truth and Reconciliation Commission of Canada, 2015. https://nctr.ca/records/reports/#trc-reports

Mission and Justice Relationships: Gordon's School - Punnichy, SK. Anglican Church of Canada, 2008. http://www.anglican.ca/relationships/histories/gordons-school-punnichy.

Molly Krishtalka, for providing references and insight to reports on the Indian Residential School investigations in Canada.

Carl Gallagher, for his research on Annie Williston's letters archived at The Connecticut Historical Society.

John Hoopes and Michael Crawford, Department of Anthropology, and Jordan Yochim, School of Business, The University of Kansas, Lawrence, for discussions of anthropology departmental history, Clovis archeology, and the genomics of the peopling of the Americas.

Jack Horner, for the AI Clovis/Solutrean Projectile Point Image Classifier, analyses, and discussions.

Carol Shankel, for research into the Twelve Mile Creek projectile point; the Old and New Club of Lawrence; Mary Fanning Apitz; and the correspondence of H. T. Martin, S. Williston, B. Brown, C. Hibbard, and E. H. Sellards.

Jerry Masinton, Martha Masinton, and the Write-On group for honing the words and the story; Martha Masinton for tenacious copyediting; and Maureen Carroll for book design and production.

About the Author

Leonard Krishtalka has enjoyed two parallel careers: professional paleontologist and author/novelist. As a paleontologist he has led and worked on expeditions throughout the fossil-rich badlands of western Canada and the US, Patagonia, Europe, China, Kenya, and Ethiopia, excavating and studying the past life and cultures of the planet. He has held academic positions at the Carnegie Museum of Natural History, Pittsburgh, the University of Pittsburgh, the National Science Foundation, Washington, DC, and The University of Kansas, Lawrence.

As a novelist, Krishtalka uses the mystery genre to explore the human condition buried beneath the science of petrified shards, skin, and bones.

He is the author of the award-winning Harry Przewalski series: *The Bone Field*, *Death Spoke*, *The Camel Driver*, and the forthcoming *Native Blood.* His fifth novel, *The Body on the Bed*, is historical fiction that investigates a murder and sensational trial in 1871 amid the social upheaval of post-Civil War Lawrence, Kansas.

Krishtalka is also an op-ed contributor to the *Lawrence Journal-World*, a past columnist for *Carnegie Magazine*, and author of the acclaimed book, *Dinosaur Plots.*

www.ingramcontent.com/pod-product-compliance
Lightning Source LLC
Chambersburg PA
CBHW070349200726
48294CB00003B/815

9781960462176